A Clean Sweep

A Clean Sweep

David Berlinski

St. Martin's Press
New York

Library of Congress Cataloging-in-Publication Data

Berlinski. David.
   A clean sweep / David Berlinski
      p. cm.
   "A Thomas Dunne book."
   ISBN 0-312-08744-6
   I. Title.
  PS3552.E72494C54   1993
  813'.54—dc20   92-36534
                                                     CIP

First Edition: January 1993

10 9 8 7 6 5 4 3 2 1

For Claire and Mischa

I am very grateful to Arthur Cody, who encouraged me to write for the sheer pleasure of writing.

Contents

A Clean Sweep

I might as well get it all out on the table: I do not like Blacks, Hispanics, Mexicans, Chicanos, Chicanas, Orientals, Chinese, Filipinos, tough Israelis, hell, anyone from the Third World, American Indians, Eskimos, Gays, Lesbians, the Gay Olympics, body builders, men who wear their hair in pony tails, women over thirty, women in sweatpants, women with long necks and short hair, happy hours, radio talk shows, boom boxes, country music, vanity license plates, people who love to dance, men who wear tooled cowboy boots, or the word 'gal.'

I don't care what happens to the rain forests. I really don't.

Debt of Honor

I crossed the Bay Bridge in the direction of Berkeley. The sky above the yellow-brown hills was low, flat and smoky. I could see the cleanliness of the gray San Francisco light disappear in my rearview mirror. I got off the freeway by a cluster of Taco Bells and Burger Kings and drove toward those yellow-brown hills, stopping at every light, of course. I turned at Ashby. The fast-food outlets now had names like The Upstart Crow or The Wife of Bath. They sold espresso instead of coffee and croissants or the sort of grim bran muffins absolutely guaranteed to raise intestinal hell.

A voice on my answering machine had suggested that I come to the office of Councilman Lawrence Williams. The matter was—the voice cleared its throat decorously—private and confidential. I knew the councilman only by reputation. He was generally referred to with an upward eye roll as Mad Bad LeRoy. He was an effulgent Marxist; in his election campaign, he had endeavored to portray himself as a man of substance. He was very fat.

I parked illegally in front of a fire hydrant and walked toward the Martin Luther King Memorial Building. In San Francisco, it is cold and damp in the summer; Berkeley lies on the trailing edge of the fog and the place shimmers like tinfoil in August. I was sweating by the time I reached Encina. I loosened my tie and wiped my forehead with my index finger and thought cool thoughts.

The office was full. There was a hugely pregnant teenager taking up two chairs all by herself, her plump posterior spreading across the metal seats; and a dignified middle-aged woman with sharp mean eyes, carrying herself, even while seated, with an air of uncorrected injustice; and a young, muscular hoodlum in a Day-Glo shirt, the thing pulled tight across his shoulders, who sat stock-still on his chair, radiating heat and energy into the air, his face expressionless. He was listening to a Sony Walkman. His face was turned upward slightly. He was waiting for a message.

I stood for a moment by the door and then walked over to the secretary. She wore a SMASH RACISM! button on her blouse; she was chewing gum voluptuously. She gave the impression that if she were unable to smash racism any substitute would do.

"I've got an appointment," I said, placing my card on the desk.

She looked down at the card and then up again. "Take a number, take a seat," she said, pointing with her head to a wire

2

rack on which a succession of cardboard numbers had been strung.

"You've got it backwards. I don't want to see him. He wants to see me."

She lifted her onyx and ebony head and looked into my eyes.

"Don't try and figure it out," I said. "You'll get a nosebleed."

She slid my card across the cool metal table and snapped it downward at the table's edge, her third finger tapping indignantly at its center. A moment for meditation passed. She reached for the telephone.

"Someone says you want to see him," she said.

A rumbling and musical baritone asked who it was. I could hear his voice through the office wall.

"Some asshole," said the secretary.

"Aren't they all?" said the voice, chuckling. The both of them said something simultaneously. I couldn't catch the rest. She swivelled, that secretary, on her secretary's chair so that she was facing her typewriter. "He'll see you now," she said, inclining her head toward the door.

If the three zombies in the room minded the fact that I had bumped them from the line, they did not let on.

Mad Bad LeRoy got up from his desk chair like a slow Malibu wave when I entered his office. He hung over his desk, one splay-fingered hand braced on the desk top, and held out his other hand. He was dressed in a white shirt with French cuffs, his initials embroidered at the wrists, and gray trousers, which he wore with red silk suspenders. He was short and had short arms.

"I'm glad you could come," he said gravely, holding my hand in his own.

There was a little green metal chair in front of his desk, and an old-fashioned sofa—red plush, wooden sides, wooden claws—alongside the wall. The blinds in his office were drawn to the window casements so that the sun streamed onto the carpet in dusty slits. From another office far away I could hear the sound of an air-conditioning unit.

3

Mad Bad LeRoy looked searchingly into my eyes, released my hand, and then sank back into his chair. "Sit," he said. He meant the chair. I sat on the sofa.

"What can I do for the revolution, Councilman?" I asked. I was pretty jaunty.

Mad Bad LeRoy placed his hands ceremoniously behind his neck.

"Not much, I'm sure," he said with a certain sour malice.

He stared straight off into space as if to marshal his thoughts. The frisky little devils were way ahead of him.

"I've been told that you are a victim of circumstances," he finally said, nodding his massive head comprehensively.

"Imagine that."

"No need to be defensive. I haven't asked you here for legal advice."

"I'm so relieved," I said. "How'd you come by my name?"

"One of your wives," said Mad Bad LeRoy, smiling now.

"I don't get my very best references from that quarter."

"One seldom does."

Mad Bad LeRoy looked as if he were making up his mind. It was evidently hard going.

"Well, good," he said. "Does the name Roger Ellerbee mean anything to you?"

"Not a thing. Does he eat red meat?"

Mad Bad LeRoy looked at me: The amusement had vanished from his eyes.

I said *ah*.

"He owns a company on the Peninsula. A prosperous individual. Even well-off. You would think that a man in his position would be able to pay his debts."

"But I would be wrong?"

"He owes me two hundred and fifty thousand dollars."

"A quid pro quo?"

"He got the quid. I'm waiting for the quo."

"You don't think the check is in the mail?"

4

"It would appear not," said Mad Bad LeRoy. "Mr. Ellerbee no longer returns my calls. I can't seem to—how shall I put this?—attract his attention."

"You have an unusual problem," I said, "for a dedicated Marxist."

Mad Bad LeRoy looked at me balefully.

"Not to worry. I've always regarded bribery as a debt of honor."

Mad Bad LeRoy kept his brown popped guppy eyes on my face.

"So have I," he said.

"You want I should collect the money?"

Mad Bad LeRoy placed a broad index finger to the crease beside his nose and nodded.

"A dunning letter is not the sort of thing you had in mind?"

Mad Bad LeRoy rotated in his chair so that he was now facing directly forward.

"I don't think a dunning letter would quite do the trick," he said. He placed both his massive brown hands on the table, the palms down. "Perhaps something more vigorous might be in order."

"How vigorous is vigorous?"

"A hint here, a hint there. A word to the wise."

"You don't want to drop these hints yourself?"

"That would be extortion," said Mad Bad LeRoy smoothly. "A terrible thing."

I thought the matter over for a moment.

"Comes to messages, I generally charge by the word," I said. "This message is apt to have a lot of words."

"Five thousand dollars," said Mad Bad LeRoy. "You may charge by the word, but I pay by the paragraph."

"Councilman," I said, "do you really think I would risk a great deal of unpleasantness for five thousand dollars?"

"I was hoping you would," Mad Bad LeRoy said smoothly, still looking directly ahead, facing the door.

"I don't run those kinds of risks," I said. "Not for that kind of money."

"You *do* run those kinds of risks, though," Mad Bad LeRoy said imperturbably. "That is surely the essential point. What would you consider adequate remuneration?"

I leaned back on the couch. I badly wanted a cigarette; I was afraid to smoke.

"I'll take ten percent of recovery," I said, "*if* there is a recovery. If not, you don't owe me anything."

Mad Bad LeRoy leaned his enormous head backward just slightly and smiled, his white teeth showing.

"Done," he said.

The zombies were still waiting outside when I left. They hadn't even moved.

Roger Doesn't Have Any Friends

On Telegraph Avenue the Bloods were selling jewelry and tie-dyed tee shirts and coarse woolen sweaters that looked like the sheep were still in them somewhere. The beggars were out in full force in the weak warm sunlight, shuffling down the street on blackened caked bare feet or weaving around pointlessly or squatting on the stoops next to the pile of crap that they were forever dragging from one place to another. There was graffiti on the walls, even on the sidewalk; every lamppost had some sort of imbecile announcement: If someone somewhere wasn't outraged about something, someone else was especially eager to hear what Bhat Vat Fat or the enlightened Sufi Master had to say or had big plans to communicate with the Goddess or worship the Mother and wanted everyone else to know about them.

Great place, Berkeley.

I drove back across the Bay Bridge, the slanting sunshine filtering through the salt air. Chris on KPFA was explaining that Gee it was just so terrible what we were doing in the Third World that she could hardly stand living with herself. Gee I hoped she wouldn't have to do it much longer. I could see the fog forming above the bay. Driving back into San Francisco from Berkeley is like taking a cool shower after heavy exercise.

That year I rented a second-floor walk-up on Greenwich Street, on the western slope of Telegraph Hill. I paid nine hundred dollars a month for two rooms with high ceilings and beautiful windows, the kind with ripples in the glass. I could see the bay and the Golden Gate Bridge and the tawny Marin Hills from my living room. On the slope behind the house there was one of those wild uncultivated little gardens that you still find in San Francisco—blackberry vines, straggling pink and ivory flowers, a stubby tree growing in defiant isolation, the lonely smell of sage. My bedroom window faced the concrete wall of the building next door.

Two Dutch sisters lived on the second floor in the apartment that faced the street; they were in their eighties and smoked continually. The hallway around their door reeked of perfumed Indonesian cigarettes.

My landlord lived on the first floor. He was a Cantonese with a high forehead and a somber round moon face; everyone called him The Chairman. He spoke only a few words of English. An Italian restaurant named La Cucina had come into his possession under complex and questionable circumstances; there were pictures of Palermo on the wall and checkered tablecloths with Chianti stains on the tables. On taking over the management of the place, he told the Vietnamese cook to reduce portions severely. Everyone was charmed. He made a few other judicious improvements. No one noticed. The restaurant received a favorable review in *The Chronicle* and flourished. It was The Chairman's destiny to be rich. He reduced his emotional life in consequence to a simple sane system. He was prepared to offer his friendship in exchange for money.

I trudged up the steps. The hallway had that smell of eucalyptus that many wooden buildings have in San Francisco. The Chairman had stacked four letters by my door. I leaned against the splintery jamb, and loosened my tie, and looked over the mail. There was an invitation to join a new health club called The Spa on Sutter. The glossy brochure had some great-looking bimbo on the cover. She was wearing Spandex and making love to the seat of an exercise bicycle. There were two bills from Pacific Bell, one marked *urgent*, and a letter from my second wife's attorney asking me when I was going to address my fiscal responsibilities. The letter was written more in sadness than in anger. I could tell.

I took a leak, washed my hands, splashed some cologne on my face, and held up the skin on my temples to see how much better I'd look without the bags under my eyes. The toilet took a long time to flush, the gurgles going and finally gone.

Yesterday's towels and underwear were still on the floor. The windows in the living room were still closed. The dust that had settled on my glass-and-chrome coffee table was still there. Live alone and the only thing that changes is your face.

Most of the day had gone to the place where most of the days go. The fog had started to thicken over the bay, white now mixed with gray. I raised the living-room window up a crack. The wild sweet smell of the sea came into the room.

I don't much like looking for people. You spend weeks looking for a thirteen-year-old runaway named Rhoda only to discover that the elusive silhouette you've been following belongs to a thirty-four-year-old cashier from Grand Union named Wanda.

Wanda is not generally too thrilled about being followed. That trustworthy husband you've been assigned to track down turns up in the Castro living with a gay lover named Milton; when the door opens, Milton tries to sock you; the husband calls out: "What is it, precious? Is something wrong?"

I had the red *Guide to Bay Area Business* on my desk. Ellerbee was listed in a section entitled "Movers and Shakers." His firm was named LRB. Ellerbee was the CEO; somebody named J. Madford Wunderman was listed as the Senior Vice-President. Whatever it was that LRB was making, they hadn't made any of them yet. As far as I could tell from the Guide, they hadn't made a dime either.

I called Leo Rubble at the *San Francisco Independent*. He was a reporter with a red potato nose, the last of the great alcoholics. He covered local business. He chuckled obscurely when I mentioned LRB. Someone else I knew said that Ellerbee had graduated from Yale and belonged to a secret society in which bones were passed around at midnight in a crypt. The editor of a computer journal thought little of Ellerbee's technical competence: "Nah," he said, "he's just up front, the real talent they keep in the basement, throw in some raw meat and vitamins every night, clear out when there's a full moon." A stockbroker clucked his tongue in a peculiar way and said that Ellerbee was one very shrewd cookie; he clucked his tongue again and said that LRB was the sort of thing he'd put his mother into if he put his mother into anything.

I called Leo Rubble back and he gave me a little fact, a factoid. He said there was a rumor going around that Roger Ellerbee was talking to the Japanese.

"Not about sushi?"

"Not about sushi," he said.

The next morning was cold, wet and foggy, the kind of cold wet fog that makes your thighs ache and that generally comes in late summer. The foghorns were ha*rummp*ing out in the bay, a few little ones and then the monster, which sounded every thirty seconds with a deep throbbing moan.

I got the newspaper from behind the front door and shuffled back into the kitchen and put some ground coffee into the red and black Italian espresso machine that stood dutifully on the kitchen counter. I had managed to salvage the thing from one of my marriages. I remembered tiptoeing late at night from my house in Belvedere with the machine under my arm, the moist flapping sound of my wife's snores following me down the gravel road and to my car.

There was a donut somewhere at the bottom of the refrigerator; I fished it out from the vegetable bin and smeared some cherry jelly on top of the icing. The jelly was made with honey, not sugar. Some mummified farmer in Sonoma was very proud. It said so on the label.

I sat at the formica breakfast bar in my underwear and sipped coffee and ate my donut and read *The Chronicle*. The usual crap. There wasn't enough water. State Assemblyman Dorkface had been caught with a ten-year-old hooker. It had snowed in Truckee. Our sainted mayor had slipped on a banana peel. A group of queers were outraged by something and were going to hold their breath until it went away.

I finished up in the kitchen, washed the dishes, gave the counter a once over, and went back to the bedroom to collect the dishevelled clothes on the floor and make the bed. I was the soul of tidiness. I moved my bowels, showered, shaved carefully, trimming the hair from my ears and nose, and got into clean clothes.

It was only eight-thirty in the morning; the downstairs buzzer rang just as I was sitting down at my desk.

I padded over to the door in my stockinged feet and shouted something down; someone shouted something right back up. I left the door ajar and padded downstairs.

There was a manila envelope propped up against the copper

shield at the bottom of the front door. My name was typed on a white tag; below the tag it said "private and confidential."

I looked at the envelope briefly: It was the sort of thing attorneys use. I padded back upstairs and closed my apartment door quietly behind me.

I slit open the envelope at my desk. Inside was a very professionally done glossy photograph of a middle-aged man being straddled by a voluptuous young woman. The man was dressed in a leather restraining harness; he had a leather hood over his head and an apple in his mouth. The woman was dressed in leather knee boots and a latex corset. The photograph was printed on unusually heavy lustrous photographic paper. A note had been paper-clipped to the top corner. It said "leverage." Mad Bad LeRoy had signed his initials.

I studied the photograph for a while. It wasn't the sort of thing a man might care to mount on the walls of his den. On the other hand, I didn't see that Roger Ellerbee's love life had much to do with his debts.

I called LeRoy at his office; there was no one there, of course, but I left a message on his voice mail. I said that I didn't do darkroom work. I trusted Mad Bad LeRoy to know what I meant. I was feeling pretty virtuous.

I put the photograph back in its envelope and walked over to my living-room window. The fog hadn't started to break up yet. It hung in the air, wet and heavy and cold. I couldn't even see the bay. It was the kind of morning when you'd like warm cereal and eggs and coffee with cream for breakfast; it was the kind of morning when you'd play soft guitar music on the stereo; it was the kind of morning when you'd like somebody to say: "Honey, let's go back to bed."

After a while, I thought I might as well try calling Roger Ellerbee.

"LRB," said a young fruity voice, "can you hold?"

"No," I said. It didn't do any good. It never does.

In a minute, Fruitjuice came back on the line.

11

"May I help you?"

"Roger Ellerbee, please."

"Mr. Ellerbee is out of the office."

"All right," I said, "let me speak to J. Madford Wunderman."
A stab in the dark.

"Who should I say is calling?"

"Henry Kissinger," I said. "Tell him it's about the Sudan."

"I'll ring now," tinkled Fruitjuice.

In a moment, a resonant deep organ voice boomed: "George,
you son of a bitch, is that you?"

"No," I said, "and it isn't Henry Kissinger either."

There was nothing but silence on the line. But J. Madford
Wunderman didn't hang up.

"I don't think I want to talk to you," he finally said.

'Tell me where I can find Roger Ellerbee. You won't have to."

"Why do you want to know?"

"You wouldn't understand," I said, "it's a Black Thing."

"Try me."

"I'm calling for a friend."

There was a long pause; I could hear J. Madford Wunderman
breathing stertorously.

"Roger doesn't have any friends," he said.

There was a click and that empty sound you get when someone hangs up on you. I thought of calling back but I knew it
wouldn't do any good.

Swimming with Sharks

Atherton looks the way old scotch is supposed to taste but never does. The houses are very big and set back behind brick or stone walls. The streets are lined with stately deciduous trees. The only people walking around are the Japanese gardeners; they wear hip boots and carry rolled hoses over their shoulders. At night, the police cruise slowly down the streets, stopping every now and then to peer at the big houses, a gabble of static floating out of their cars from the radio. It used to be an old money kind of place in the days when money was old.

Montecito was just off Atherton Avenue, but I parked on Atherton anyway, and walked over one block. The Peninsula is generally warmer than the city, but someone long ago had planted elms on Montecito; it was leafy and cool on the street in the way that only large shaggy shade trees can make a street leafy and cool.

Ellerbee's house was the smallest one on the block; it was sandwiched between two monsters. It was big enough to be imposing anyway. There was a brick wall around the property and an iron gate in front. A large brass plate on the brick wall next to the gate said "Arcadia" in florid italic letters.

The house was one of those fake English tudor jobs, with an enormous steeply sloping slate roof, and wooden shutters on all the windows, and a huge red door facing out to a flagstone patio. The lawn was scrappy-looking, with a lot of dead leaves lying about.

The gate was locked. There was a telephone in a white wooden box mounted on the brick wall. You were supposed to punch in a code to get in. At the bottom of the telephone it said: 'Tradesmen ring 0.' I was a tradesman. Yes indeedy. I rang 0 and waited. After a long time someone answered and said *yaüs* in a voice with a heavy Spanish accent.

"Mr. Ellerbee there?"

"He no here," said the voice, "He . . ." Another woman's voice cut in abruptly. It was cool and calm and clipped and collected.

"May *I* help you?"

"I'd like to talk to Roger Ellerbee," I said.

"This is *Mrs.* Ellerbee. In reference to what, may I ask?"

"Money," I said. Time paused in the bright sunlight. There was a click on the telephone and the lock on the gate opened. Money has a key all its own.

It was no more than twenty yards from the gate to the big red door, but the stone walkway had been designed to give the impression that it was longer. The large stones were irregular so that you had to pick your steps and the walkway itself curved like the letter S.

When I got to the fieldstone patio the front door opened and a good-looking sunny blonde woman stepped out and closed the door behind her.

"I'm Lauren Ellerbee," she said, extending her hand.

"Asherfeld," I said. Her hand was dry and soft and warm. I took a moment to take a better look. She was dressed in a black leotard and those white fish-head tights that everyone was wearing that year; she had a red sweatshirt draped over her shoulders, the sleeves knotted around her throat. She was trim and curvy and sparkled in the sunlight; her eyes were very blue, with whites the pure color of very fine bone china.

"Roger's not home now," she said, still holding on to my hand, "is there something I can help you with?" She smiled hopefully, showing me a set of large, shapely white teeth.

"Roger's not here, he's not there, he's not anywhere," I said.

A look of pain filled her eyes.

"Maybe you'd better come in," she said, turning to the door, but just then the door swung open further. A young man stepped

14

out to the patio, blinked at the bright sun for a moment, and then tried to scowl at me. He wasn't much good at scowling.

"Problem, babe?" he asked.

Lauren Ellerbee took him by the elbow and brought him outside.

"Bobo," she said, "this is Mr. Asherfeld. He's here to see Roger."

"Pleased to meet you," Bobo said, and extended his hand. He didn't look pleased to see me at all.

"Mr. Asherfeld, I have an idea. Would you like some coffee? We can take it on the terrace in the back."

I said that that would be just wonderful. Lauren Ellerbee turned and said: "Bobo, be a dear and tell Conchita to make us some coffee and some of those little biscuits and jam, you know, the ones you like so much."

Bobo looked doubtful but he turned back into the house. Lauren Ellerbee touched my elbow lightly and inclined her head.

"We can walk around to the back. It is such a beautiful day."

"Beautiful," I said.

The terrace in the back looked over a lawn that ran from the house to the back brick wall. Someone had taken a lot of care with the flower beds beside the house; there were azaleas in bloom.

We sat in those horribly uncomfortable wrought iron chairs with white pads that people in California think make them look as if they were living in Connecticut. I looked out over the lawn and let the sunlight warm my face.

Bobo came out from the house, nodded to Lauren Ellerbee, and sat down in a slouched sort of way that suggested he had cut too many classes in charm school. He was a big, rangy, powerful kid, no more than twenty-three or so, with sloping shoulders and bunched pectoral muscles. He looked like he might lift weights. He might just have been stupid.

"Why don't you join us?" I said after he had sat down.

The maid, Conchita, waddled out with coffee and biscuits on

15

a tray. She was short and very fat and looked miserable in her black maid's uniform. Her upper lip was covered with perspiration.

"I put eet here, all right?" she asked. She meant the glass and iron table.

"That's fine, Conchita," said Lauren Ellerbee. She went through the usual one-lump-cream-just-black? business and I said no-lumps-just-black and she poured the coffee. We all sat for a moment in the warm sun. A fat robin flew onto the lawn from the madrone that threw shade over the back of the house and began hopping industriously. The biscuits were those dry English numbers that taste like chalk; Bobo helped himself to a couple and slathered enough jam on them to launch a diabetic coma. Lauren Ellerbee shrugged off her sweatshirt, showing me her buttery shoulders. "Like sweets, do you?" I said to Bobo. He couldn't answer: His mouth was too full.

"Now what's this all about, Mr. Asherfeld," Lauren Ellerbee asked with a brisk let's-clear-this-up intonation to her cheery voice.

I nodded toward Bobo.

"This is something we might discuss in private," I said.

Bobo looked up and allowed a cloud to pass over his face; Lauren Ellerbee gave a tinkling laugh.

"Bobo is my support system," she said. "I would be lost without him."

That cloud lifted from Bobo's face.

"Now you said something about money. Is it an inheritance? I know, a lucky lottery number."

She was pretending to be girlish. It was like watching a retriever pretend to be a lap dog.

I nodded slowly, and stroked my cheeks with my thumb and forefinger. I knew she wasn't telling me the truth. I didn't know if she was lying.

"Your husband is a difficult man to find, Mrs. Ellerbee," I said. "And I need to find him."

16

"Why?" asked Bobo. At least he had finished what he was chewing.

"I've been asked to settle an outstanding account. It's in arrears."

"Mr. Asherfeld," Lauren Ellerbee said with a verbal flounce, "do you mean to say you've wasted a perfectly beautiful Saturday morning just to present a bill? Couldn't this have waited? How terribly tacky." She gestured toward the house and then the grounds. "I mean do we look like the sort of people who don't pay our bills?" Her voice had risen.

"I don't know," I said. Lauren Ellerbee blushed furiously. She had wonderful coloring. Bobo leaned forward on his chair and gripped the arms so that I could see his forearms tighten.

"Now wait a minute," he said.

Lauren Ellerbee made a show of catching her composure and let a stream of air through her shapely red lips. "Bobo, please," she said, and reached over to place her hand over his bulging forearm. "Ask Conchita to bring me my checkbook and the ledger. They're with my other papers in the leather folder on my desk. We'll settle this right now. Mr. Asherfeld, how much did you say my husband owes you?"

"I didn't say and he doesn't owe *me* anything." I looked at Bobo, who had relaxed back into a slouch, and then at Lauren Ellerbee.

"Well, whoever it is," she said, still pretending to be girlish and indignant.

"I don't think you could cover it from your household account." I let things hang in the air. There was a pause. We all sat still. Only the robin on the lawn kept hopping.

"Are you talking about a great deal of money, Mr. Asherfeld?" Lauren Ellerbee finally asked in a softer smaller voice. She was looking away, blinking rapidly; her chin was quivering.

"Yes," I said, and stood up.

"No, don't get up," I said to Bobo, who had shown no inclination whatsoever to get up. "You need your beauty rest." He looked up with a scowl. I had a card in my pocket with my telephone and address. I fished it out and held it in the air. "Why don't you have your husband call me," I said.

Lauren Ellerbee took the card and looked at it doubtfully.

"Thanks for the coffee," I said. "I'll see myself out. You'll give that husband of yours the message, won't you? Tell him that he's swimming with sharks now."

I turned to go back to the front of the house. From the second floor or somewhere I could hear Conchita, the maid, singing something in Spanish. When I turned the corner I could see that Bobo had gotten out of his chair. He still looked as if he didn't know what to do. It was very warm but Lauren Ellerbee had put her sweatshirt back over her buttery brown shoulders.

This Awful Itch

I was five feet from Mad Bad LeRoy when somebody whacked him; I saw his brains fly out of his head.

I had left Lauren Ellerbee and Bobo and walked back to Atherton. My car was like a sauna, the steering wheel almost too hot to touch. I rolled down the windows, turned on the air conditioning, and rested my piles on the leather seat. When the car had cooled a little, I drove to the corner of Montecito and Atherton and parked under the shade of a gorgeous elm and watched Roger Ellerbee's house. Watching things is not one of my favorite activities. I couldn't see over the fence, of course, and I didn't know what I was waiting for. I turned on the radio. Dr. So-and-So was giving medical advice to the usual imbeciles.

Hi, Mary, You're on the air.
Doctor, I have this awful itch.

I could just imagine. The doctor was warming up to Mary and her awful itch when the iron gate swung open and Bobo slouched out. He slouched down Montecito, away from my car. I watched him slouch to the end of the block, slouch into a fire-engine red Trans Am, and slouch off with a dusty roar. I did a U-turn and drove slowly through the bright sunny streets.

I still like the Peninsula. There is something about the light, and the way the sun sits very high in the sky, and the deep blue shade thrown by the trees. I remember when it was a valley of fruit trees in bloom.

I got back to the city just as the fog was rolling in, carrying its strange sullen smells. I parked on the street, blocking The Chairman's enormous black Chrysler. He regarded driving an automobile as an incomprehensibly difficult feat. It was a treat seeing him try to maneuver the Chrysler. He had a genius for turning the steering wheel in the wrong direction and accelerating suddenly at very low speeds. Once he had put the monster into the driveway nothing could induce him to take it out again.

There were four messages on the machine. The ASPCA wanted a contribution; so did the Police Benevolent Association. Years ago I had sent them a check for fifty dollars. Now they called me every month, reminding me of the glory days. Someone named Crystal had a low sexy voice, but she was looking for Charlie, and not me; she kept saying *Charlie, you there, Charlie, it's me, Crystal, pick up.* She wasn't too good with telephone numbers—or with men, from the sound of it. The last message was from Mad Bad LeRoy. He needed *urgently* to speak to me. He was in his car. I called him back right away and His Fatness said can you come right out to Oakland, and I said I was tired as a dog, and He said it was very *very* urgent and could I meet him—no not in his office but I'll be in my car on the corner of Sepulveda and San Pablo just off MacArthur Boulevard and you can't miss it, it's a 1957 black Cadillac, and I said what else? and he chuckled his sour mirthless chuckle.

My eyes felt like someone had rubbed pepper in them. I found an old package of salted peanuts in one of my kitchen drawers and washed that down with a little bit of diet Ginger Ale and a finger of scotch and then a half bottle of stale beer I had forgotten to throw out. I thought of taking a quick shower; I didn't need to be that clean to talk with Mad Bad LeRoy.

It was after eight by the time I got on the Bay Bridge. The traffic had thinned and the sky was that deep royal blue we sometimes get in northern California in the late summer. By the time I crossed the bridge it was dark. Only half the city was covered with fog; the rest of the place sparkled in my rearview mirror. Up ahead Oakland sparkled too, the air bending the light. It was a hell of a night for sparkles.

I drove slowly up Ashby and made a right on MacArthur Boulevard. The neighborhood gets very bad very fast. Two blocks into Oakland and the streetwalkers come out like night owls. They were standing on every corner, dressed in short skirts, or hot pants, or tight jeans and leotards. There were tall ones and short ones and fat ones and thin ones. Some of them looked strung out and some of them looked old and tired of men and some of them were so young and juicy they looked as if they might burst. None of them seemed overly concerned with public health.

I made a right turn a block before Sepulveda and turned left on San Pablo and then left again. Sure enough, there was an enormous black 1957 Cadillac Seville parked underneath a flowering fig tree. I honked twice to let LeRoy know I was there. No one honked back. I slowed down and stopped when I was just even with the door of the Caddy. The street was empty. I leaned over and rolled down the passenger-side window. I could hear a cricket chirp far away. Mad Bad LeRoy was sitting with his heavy arm resting on the window frame; he nodded gravely toward me and patted the passenger seat decorously with his right hand. I drove forward a few yards and then swung in front of the Cadillac to make a U-turn. I wanted to park away from MacArthur Boulevard. I was just even with the Cadillac going back toward Sepulveda when I heard a mild *whump;* it is not a sound you can miss. LeRoy's head snapped back. His car filled suddenly with a pink-red glow; something began to drip on the side and rear windows. A car door slammed and an engine started up with a cough.

I braked hard in the middle of the street and flopped down onto the seat, my arms over my head. My heart was pounding. For no reason whatsoever I began to count the beats, checking my heart against the pulsing square on the quartz dashboard clock. I stopped at fifty. Fifteen seconds had gone by.

Very slowly, I inched up and looked at the side mirror. The street was empty behind me. I could hear the cricket I had heard before. I hunched my head down toward the steering wheel and released my foot from the brake pedal. I let the car drift to the end of the block; I crossed San Pablo, and parked a block further down. I tried to slide down in my seat so that my head was hidden by the seat back. I turned off the car's engine and sat with my hands at my sides. I kept my eyes on the side mirror. I could hear the cricket chirping; I could hear the traffic far away on MacArthur Boulevard; I could hear the wind in the trees. I couldn't hear anything else.

I took out a cigarette, smoked it down to the butt, and smoked another one just after that.

I let five minutes go by and then got out of the car and just stood there, leaning against the door. Nothing. I could see the lights of MacArthur Boulevard in the distance.

I walked back down the block and crossed over to the driver's side of LeRoy's elegant black Cadillac. The window was open. LeRoy's head was all the way back; his arms were at his side. There was a neat brown little hole in his left temple and a huge gout of brains and gore on the right side of the curved leather headrest behind his head. The side and rear windows were

21

covered with red slime. A fly had already gotten into the car and was investigating the interior with a dawning sense of remarkable good fortune. Only the fact that LeRoy was so fat had kept him upright. He had no place where he could bend so that he could sag.

"Hey," I said softly, "you're looking poorly, LeRoy."

I left things just as they were and walked back to my car, the small hairs on the back of my neck prickling. I always imagined that that was a myth. Now I know better. I thought of leaving LeRoy where he was, fat and friendless; but in the end I dutifully called 911 from the payphone on the corner of Sepulveda and San Pablo. Then I walked back to the Cadillac and sat down on the curb in front of the car. I thought I would watch over LeRoy. I thought it was the least I could do.

The squad car was there in no more than sixty seconds; the cops must have been cruising MacArthur Boulevard, looking industriously for teenagers dealing dope or hassling the hookers.

There were two of them in the car, a young man and a woman who looked even younger. The man got out with a heavy professional swagger. He was no more than five-ten or so and somewhat pudgy, with a waxy look on the skin of his untroubled round face. He slid his night stick into his belt and nodded to me. I noticed that his wedding band bit deeply into the flesh of his fourth finger. His name was Hulpnagel. I could read it on his name tag. He had left the overhead light of the squad car on; it continued to rotate malignantly, sending flashes of red and green into the quiet air.

"You call in?"

I nodded and pointed to Mad Bad LeRoy with my head.

"I was walking by."

The second cop got out of the squad car from the passenger seat and walked over to us with a rolling gait. She was pear-shaped, wide-hipped, slow-moving, very deliberate. Her shaggy brown hair spilled out from the stiff sides of her policeman's cap. She was carrying a clipboard. Her name was Mary Tooley. She

22

glanced over at Mad Bad LeRoy and said: "Oh, my God," turned theatrically, and walked back to the squad car.

Hulpnagel stood there for a moment, making up his mind; it must have been like parking a Mack truck. The colored spotlight on the car continued to rotate in the evening air. Finally, he called over to Tooley, who was sitting in her seat, looking straight ahead. "You wanna call in a priority to Satwitch. He's gonna need to know about this." Mary Tooley didn't move at first. "For God's sake, Tooley," Hulpnagel said, "you wanna please call in a priority please."

It took another ten minutes before they got the chief of detectives out and all that time Hulpnagel and Tooley sat in their squad car, staring straight ahead, listening to the static on their police radio, the overhead light above them rotating slowly. I sat on the curb, smoking one cigarette after another, the taste acrid.

The chief of detectives arrived quietly in an unmarked Plymouth together with a police photographer and a Lieutenant named Blinderman. Satwitch was tall and very stooped. He had a high wrinkled forehead, foxy old eyes, with great pouches underneath them, and very big hairy ears. Blinderman had the same high forehead as Satwitch, the same pouched raccoon eyes, the same hairy ears. They might have been brothers.

"This is the ped that found the body," Hulpnagel said to Satwitch.

Satwitch stopped in front of me and gave me his hand. He refused to exert any pressure.

"You pretty lucky about finding things, are you?" he said.

"Sometimes."

Satwitch turned to Blinderman, who was standing over with Hulpnagel.

"You hear that, Lieutenant, fellah says he's pretty lucky at finding things."

Blinderman guffawed.

"Think maybe he can find the wife's earrings. I keep getting grief about that."

23

Blinderman guffawed again.

Satwitch, Blinderman, and the photographer walked around Mad Bad LeRoy's Cadillac and took pictures and asked a few questions and scribbled into their notebooks and looked about as enterprising as the three stooges.

When they were all done, Satwitch walked over to Hulpnagel and told him to go back to cruising the boulevard. He had been standing there, watching. Hulpnagel nodded and said: "Yes sir," in a quiet choked voice.

"Not your first one, is it?" said Satwitch. "What about you, Tooley, first time you see the eggs scrambled?"

Tooley nodded from the front seat of the squad car.

"Well, don't lose your lunch over it," Satwitch said. He turned to face me. "Those things'll kill you." He meant the cigarette I was smoking.

"It doesn't exactly seem the moment to worry about lung cancer," I said.

Satwitch shrugged his thin shoulders. "You know," he said reflectively, "the other day we get a call over in East Oakland, woman lying dead in an apartment on account of someone shoved a broken Coke bottle up her ass. I been on these streets twenty years. One spade more or less, it don't make no difference."

He was of the old school.

He stood for a while in the quiet evening air, thinking things over.

"So how come you're here?" he said to me when he had thought over everything he wanted to think.

I said I was just a citizen out for a walk. Satwitch asked how come I was strolling on MacArthur Boulevard in Oakland. I said I needed some Brie. I said you never know when you're going to want some Brie, especially the runny kind.

"You hear that, Lieutenant," said Satwitch, "man takes it into his head to go out on a Saturday night looking for Brie."

"Takes all kinds," said Blinderman.

Satwitch, Blinderman, and the photographer made a final tour of LeRoy's car, and then Satwitch asked me to sign a copy of his notes.

"We need you, you be somewhere where we can find you?" he said.

I nodded.

"Don't worry," said Satwitch. He was becoming very jovial. "We get the little woman on the telephone we tell her you were out here lookin' for Brie. That right, Lieutenant?" Blinderman guffawed. "We're very discreet out here. We're the souls of discretion. That right, Lieutenant?"

Blinderman guffawed again.

"We got boogies whacking boogies in the middle of the street, we got crack coming out of the old gazoo, we got twelve-year-old hookers in hot pants, and we got you, lookin' for some skanky piece of Brie. Hell of a world. That right, Lieutenant?"

Blinderman guffawed for the third time. He was pretty good at it. Satwitch reached into the Plymouth and picked up the phone.

"Yeah," he said after a burst of static, "we've got a big fat Spade he needs a lift over to County and we got a hell of a nice classic Caddy here."

I didn't say anything else. I didn't know LeRoy and I didn't love him. I didn't know who killed him. I didn't much care.

So Long, LeRoy, and Good-bye

LeRoy made all the newspapers, of course. Grief at his passing was offset by the suspicion that he had been killed as he was about to accept a payoff from some awful drug dealer.

Me? I was out of it. I went to his funeral anyway. I hadn't earned the money he had promised me. I was worried that he might take it with him and spend it on foolishness in the hereafter.

The ceremony was scheduled for three in the afternoon. I drove out to Oakland at a little after two and parked a block away from the church. The sky was hazy, the air still and hot, with the heavy feel of late summer. I tried looking very black. It didn't help much; I was counting on people to appreciate the effort.

I hustled up the polished gray slate steps in front of the church and nodded to the usher standing by the side of the door. I said: "Terrible thing, brother."

The usher looked at me sharply. "I ain't your brother," he said.

Inside, the place was almost full. LeRoy had had a lot of friends or else he knew a lot of people who liked funerals. I stood for a moment at the back of the church and looked around. The reddish exposed brick walls were shaped something like a triangle, opening up toward the rear of the church and tapering toward the front. I liked the way they seemed to hold a tremendous volume of space. Light came into the building from the stained windows and two skylights in the ceiling. I could see the dust moving aimlessly in the air. A wooden pulpit was mounted on the raised stage in front of the church, where the triangle tapered; one of those determined little electronic organs stood by the far wall. A middle-aged woman in a red silk choirmaster's robe was sitting at the console, peering intently at the sheet music on the organ stand. A choir consisting of four monstrously fat pink-robed teenagers stood lined up by the side of the organ.

LeRoy himself was on display in an open coffin just underneath the pulpit. It seemed obligatory once you entered the church to walk down the center aisle and then shuffle past the casket. I shuffled along with everyone else. I didn't much want to see LeRoy again, but when I reached the front, I looked down like everyone else. LeRoy was lying on silk plush. He was wearing a blue sharkskin suit, with a snowy white shirt and a red tie on which little dancing men had been embossed. The undertaker had done a fine job. No one could see that half his head had disappeared.

I walked to the back of the church by the side aisle and took a seat just as the organist began to play softly. She played "Summertime" and a syncopated version of "Sheep May Safely Graze." Just as she was beginning a medley of civil rights songs—"We Shall Overcome," "My Way," "The Battle Hymn of the Republic"—there was a commotion in the back of the church. The mayor of Berkeley was trying to enter the hall inconspicuously and shake hands with half the congregation at the same time. She was a small, rat-faced woman, with bulging black eyes, and stringy gray hair. She was surrounded by four ebony bodyguards. She kept spotting people in the audience she knew and waving at them with a hand she kept curved, as if she were cupping a chipmunk.

After a while, the organist and the choir did a rendition of "Amazing Grace." Then the Reverend Leotis emerged from the wings of the church and moved to the podium.

During the 1970s, the Reverend had managed to direct a great deal of Federal work-study money to the Lamumba Mission, which he directed in East Oakland. He would cruise the streets in an enormous chauffeur-driven stretch Lincoln with elk antlers on both fenders. There was some unpleasantness about bookkeeping. The Mission closed. An associate was disciplined in court. The antlers disappeared discreetly. The Reverend discovered that his genius lay not in work but in faith.

Now he cleared his throat and folded his hands together over his ample stomach and said what a sad day this was. A lot of people in the audience thought so too. They all said Amen. The Reverend went on to talk about LeRoy and how he had prayed and persevered and persisted and prospered. He talked about how proud the Black Community was of LeRoy and how LeRoy was a role model for its young black men. He said that White America wasn't able to accept LeRoy, because White America had a fear of black men standing up and taking what's rightfully theirs.

A lot of people said Amen and rustled their feet appreciatively.

"I know," said the Reverend Leotis, "that there are all sorts of schisms and isms and chasms and spasms in the Black Community; we are stratified by racism, we are oppressed by reaction, we are held back and we are shackled and we are in chains and we are kept down like junkyard dogs."

Many people said Amen.

"Is that right?" the Reverend asked.

The audience indicated that that was right.

It went on like that for a while. I didn't know if LeRoy was married. The dignified elderly woman who sat in the mourner's pew looking straight ahead during the sermon might have been his mother or his aunt. She was with a small boy who kept turning in his seat to look behind him. He had a small round face and dark melancholy brown eyes.

The Reverend Leotis concluded his sermon. He said that Mad Bad LeRoy was a *victim*. There was a chorus of Amens.

I thought to myself that of all the ways to die with dignity, being fat and black and sitting alone in a 1957 Cadillac Seville with your brains blown out isn't high on the list.

New York, It Ain't

The telephone rang sometime after eleven the next morning. I had been cutting my toenails.

"This Asherfeld?" There was no *hello*.

"None other," I said.

"Hey, that's great. A wise guy. You're my first California wise guy."

"Terrific," I said, "what do you do to show your appreciation, burst into song?"

"Hey, don't get your bowels into an uproar. It was a compliment. Listen, this is Hubert Dreyfus. I'm over the Federal Building. I thought maybe you could come down for a while, we could talk?"

I said: "Why should I?"

"Here's why. Listen good." There was a scratching on the line and then a hiss and then I heard myself telling Mad Bad LeRoy that I would be prepared to commit extortion for ten percent of $250,000.

"Hey, no rush," said Hubert Dreyfus. "I'll see you when I see you. It's the tenth floor."

Hubert Dreyfus didn't have a secretary and he didn't have a receptionist. He met me himself by the elevator after the security guard had called from the lobby.

"Coffee, tea, orange juice, you wanna beer?" he said as soon as he closed the door to his office. "I got a fridge."

I sat down and said I was fine and took out my cigarettes.

"Sure, sure go ahead," Dreyfus said, "I like the smell. I can't believe the song and dance you people make out here about smoking. Guy lights up in a restaurant it's worse than if he's pissing on the floor."

"Sounds like you don't much like San Francisco."

Dreyfus walked over to the window and pulled the blinds. His office looked down on the Civic Center Plaza. Sunlight flooded into the little room.

"What's to like?" he said. "You got a lot of sun, an ocean that sort of flops onto the beach, ten million queers, and everyone else they got more time on their hands they know what do with. Listen, the other day I go to this coffee shop the corner O'Farrell and Polk, me and two other guys from the division. There's this dip behind the counter, cook standing two feet from her. First guy says he wants two eggs over easy. She writes this down on a check like she's taking ten on Sinai, pins the check on a wheel, short order cook comes over, takes the check, looks it over like it's this fantastic secret code or something, finally goes over to the grill, starts cooking two eggs. Meanwhile the dip's taking an order from the second guy, goes through the same song and dance, when she's finished she puts the second check on the wheel, the cook he waits until he's *finished* cooking up the first two eggs before he even reads the second order, the eggs he's finished are just sitting on the counter getting cold. By this time smoke is coming out of my ears. When I ask if maybe they could do two things at once, like cook four eggs instead of two, they got a big grill, the dip looks at me like I'm asking her to grow a third arm."

I chuckled. "After a while you'll discover there are better ways to spend your time than working," I said. "Everyone does."

"Take my kid down to Fisherman's Wharf, it's supposed to be this very big deal, right? Place's got nothing but tourists, there's a wind coming off the bay freezing my ass, the sea lions are honking and hopping over the piers like they own a piece of the action, we go get something to eat, this Mex gives me two shrimp in a paper cup with some ketchup over them says that'll be six bucks. Wants to sell me some of this sourdough bread extra for another buck. Stuff tastes like someone pissed into sawdust. New York, it ain't."

"How old are you?" I asked.

30

"Thirty-eight. Why?"

"Pretty soon every place is going to be some other place. You'll get over it," I said.

"Man'll get over anything, you asked me whether I *liked* the place. So you in mourning for the Fatman?"

"No," I said.

"So how come he gets whacked you're with him? I know this on account of the computer crossed our tapes with the Oakland police report. It's something the police should've done themselves only the police here don't know squat."

"He called me. He didn't tell me what was on his mind, he just said it was urgent."

I had no reason to lie.

"So you know the Fatman was a bad guy? I mean we have him into bribery, influence peddling, he was dealing, he was running women over the Alameda. This was one busy creative sharing sort of guy. Am I right?"

"I don't know what LeRoy did. I don't much care. He asked me to run an errand, that's all."

"So that's what you do, you run errands?"

"That's what I do, I run errands."

"It doesn't matter you run these errands for good guys or bad guys?"

"It doesn't matter. You want me to go all crinkly inside?"

"Hey, nothing personal, I was just asking. So what do you think he was doing, the Fatman, with this Ellerbee character? Doesn't sound like a match made in heaven, fat crooked spade and some yuppie dummy. Me, I think LeRoy was putting the arm on Ellerbee. Figure maybe Ellerbee gets up his nerve, takes a whack at the Fatman."

"Sounds good to me," I said.

"That's all you got to say," said Dreyfus, "sounds good to me?"

"That's all I got to say."

"You know, you're a lucky kind of guy. Man gets his head

blown off, you're standing right there, don't even bend a finger-nail. I've got you on tape agreeing to extortion, all sorts of things, and I'm just going to forget I hear what I hear. As I say, a lucky guy. Been married?"

"Three times."

"Maybe not so lucky. Remember you're a white man. Call me you get a hot flash."

Please, Please, Please

Nothing much happened that day and nothing much happened the day after that. A woman called and asked if I did regression analysis. She was convinced she had lived in Carmel in another life. She wanted me to check it out. I asked her where she was now living. "Oh, I live in Carmel, honey," she said. "It's just that it's so familiar." A real-estate agent with a heavy Korean accent asked me to look at some property in Pacific Heights. "I need some place not in fogs," she said obscurely. A man who had been a client of mine in the old days called and asked whether I wanted to be involved in a scheme to sell convection ovens on late-night television. "Can't miss with these little beauties," he said buoyantly. He had missed with everything else; I couldn't see why convection ovens should be different.

On the day after the day after that, I got up and showered and shaved and combed my hair and rumbled around my apartment for an hour or so, putting books away and emptying the dish-washer and making a list of things I needed to get. I believe in making lists. It's a strong, manly activity; it indicates purpose in life.

A little later I went out for a walk. There was a lot of high hazy overcast in the sky above Coit Tower, and a brisk bright breeze blowing in from the bay, the kind that smells of iodine and seaweed. My cheeks tingled pleasantly from shaving. The light was strong enough for sunglasses. The Chairman was still at home, his parking space brimming over with his Chrysler. I remember when a workday morning meant that a neighborhood would be taken over by bustling housewives. Greenwich Street was empty. The housewives had long disappeared. The women who lived in my neighborhood were out hustling in their dopey Reeboks, carrying their high heels in a paper bag.

I walked down Greenwich toward Grant. There is an enormous furniture store called Wonderama at the foot of the street. It sells waterbeds with ornate and corny brass headboards and formica kitchen tables and love seats covered in iridescent zebra-striped fabrics. EZ credit is available. The place is always open and always empty. The same saturnine salesman is always standing in front of the store; his black hair is always slicked back; his hands are always in his pockets; a toothpick is always in his mouth.

Further down the block is an Italian bakery. Everyone in the neighborhood worships the ancient leather-skinned baker and his wrinkled mustachioed wife, both of them dressed severely in black. After seventy years in this country, they still can't speak a word of English. Their bread is awful.

The Café Maudit, which has tables on the street, is at the end of the block.

I stopped there for coffee; I wanted to watch the young mothers saunter across the street toward the park, pushing their baby carriages in that soft languid way young mothers have. I liked them, the young women, but I didn't want to get involved. Anything I wanted I could have by looking.

I dawdled in the sun, smoking, looking out at the park. I had a slice of apricot butter cake; I took an hour to finish two cups of coffee; I thought of walking downtown and decided against it; I couldn't think of anything else I much wanted to do. I had left my list at home. I paid my bill and walked past the Italian bakery and past Wonderama and headed back up the hill.

Lauren Ellerbee was waiting for me. She was standing beside the front door of my house. She was endeavoring to hand a piece of paper to The Chairman, who stood behind the door, expressing himself volubly in Cantonese.

"It's a waste of time," I said as I walked up.

Lauren Ellerbee turned toward me. She was wearing an open white polo coat; underneath, I could see, she had on a very expensive red silk blouse, with a kind of scarf tied at the throat. Her hair had been whipped by the wind; she kept one hand on her head to hold things together. It was the fragile worried gesture of a woman past thirty.

"I'm so glad to see you," she said. "Can we talk? Please?"

The Chairman opened the door a crack, shot out another few sentences in Cantonese, and then retreated toward his own apartment with the awful dignity of a man speaking a language no one understands.

"If you don't mind my apartment," I said.

"Not at all. I'm just so glad you showed up. I called and called and called and finally I just decided to take a chance and come by." She shrugged her shoulders. "I was shopping."

I followed Lauren Ellerbee up the two flights of stairs, noticing as she walked the plush way her hips swayed. I took her coat when we were in the apartment and her perfume, something lilac and lavender, seemed to envelop us both for a moment. She shivered, still standing, and hugged herself with her arms.

I pointed her toward the couch, and she sat primly on the edge of the down cushion, still holding herself.

"Would you like an afghan?" I asked. "There's one right behind you."

My first wife had spent a year crocheting the red and yellow squares that made up the coverlet. The things were everywhere, like mice. When she left she said: "Take the damn thing, Asher, it doesn't mean anything to me anymore." It *never* meant anything to me, but I was glad to have it.

"Afghan? Oh, an afghan," Lauren Ellerbee said with a sudden smile; she reached over to place the heavy shawl across her knees and tucked the ends behind her thighs.

"That's much, much better," she said.

I hung Lauren Ellerbee's polo coat in the hall closet; it looked like a bright white flower between the solid blue of my windbreaker and the drab tan of an old raincoat.

I walked back into the living room and sat down at my desk and swivelled in my chair to face her.

"You said to call," she said.

I nodded absently.

"I gave Roger your message."

Her bright blue eyes puddled suddenly with tears; her chin began to quiver. "I'm so frightened," she said.

I got up and walked into the bedroom.

"Where are you going?" she wailed.

I found a clean white silk handkerchief buried in one of my good shoes. I gave it a shake and walked back into the living room. "Here," I said.

Lauren Ellerbee took the handkerchief. "I can't blow my nose in this, it's silk. Didn't your mother ever teach you these things?"

"Sure," I said. "Blow anyway."

"I feel like a monster," she said, honking into my handkerchief. She looked up at me, her eyes wide, the whites exposed.

"What happened?" I asked.

"I don't *know* what happened."

"Tell me what you know. It's generally the next best thing."

Lauren Ellerbee dabbed at her nostrils with my wadded-up handkerchief.

"I know that Roger said he had go to Los Angeles. He was supposed to talk with somebody from Japan. He was just supposed to fly down and fly back and then he called that afternoon after you left and I said you came by the house and I told him what you told me."

"He know what you were talking about?"

"I'm not sure. He just listened in that kind of I'm-strong-and-silent way he has when he's worried about something."

"Is he the strong silent type?"

"Roger? No, he's the warm and cuddly type."

Lauren Ellerbee smiled the smile that women smile.

"You're lucky," I said. "Did he come home that night?"

She shook her head doggedly from side to side, her chin swinging in an arc. Her smile had disappeared.

"He didn't come home that night," she said, her head still swinging, "and he didn't come home the night after that and he didn't come home the night after that."

"Not very cuddly," I said.

"Not very cuddly at all," she said ruefully.

I tried to look thoughtful, as if I were smoking a pipe.

"When we were married, we promised we would never spend more than one night sleeping away from one another."

"That's very romantic." I had promised one of my wives the same thing.

Lauren Ellerbee patted her nose again with my silk handkerchief. "He's never been away from home this long. He never lets whole days go by without calling me."

There was a long cold silence in the room.

"You call the police, anyone?"

"No."

Neither of us spoke. Her nose blowing and crying had given Lauren Ellerbee a lovely rose-colored flush. She sat very primly at the edge of the couch. From time to time, she patted her nose. "Will you help me?" she finally said. "Please, please, please. I don't know where to turn. He's all alone out there."

I thought of asking her how she knew that, but I didn't say anything at all.

Arnolds

When Mad Bad LeRoy became dearly departed, I thought that Roger Ellerbee might simply come home like a wet lost dog. Nothing doing. He stayed lost. Lauren Ellerbee had told me that he usually booked a room at the Los Angeles Hilton. I called the hotel detective, an alcoholic incompetent named Pryzwyki. I once defended Bottoms Up on a charge of driving under the influence. I argued that only a certifiable lunatic would wave an empty six-pack at a motorcycle policeman and explain that he was speeding in order to purchase another. The jury observed Pryzwyki sitting at the witness table in dopey, thick-lidded bewilderment and voted promptly to acquit. Pryzwyki placed himself in my debt and boasted of my legal skills to a number of dilapidated winos and common drunks. For months I had to fend off their boozy obsecrations. I told Pryzwyki my problem. "Get right to it, chief," he said confidently. Four hours later he called back to tell me that Roger Ellerbee had checked out of the Hilton two days ago.

"Any hookers up in his room?" I asked.

"Nah," said Pryzwyki. "He was a good boy. Spent most of the time with a couple of slopes."

That left me with a glossy picture of Roger Ellerbee taken in the company of a woman evidently prepared to meet his hygienic needs.

I took my supper at The Chairman's Italian restaurant on Columbus. Tino, the French-Vietnamese maitre d' made his usual elegant fuss over me. *Too long,* he said, *we not see you.* Not seeing me was like a cancer to him.

Afterwards, I walked home and changed into a black silk turtleneck and a black silk suit. I put on my gold Rolex, just for show. A client from Hong Kong had given it to me instead of paying his bill. I had looked at the heavy watch dubiously. He assured me it was the real thing. One of my wives glanced briefly at it and said: "You are so pathetic, Asher. Anyone can tell it's a fake."

You live in a city for a lot of reasons. Some people hate the country, can't stand the sight of cows. Others like the noise, or the way the streets look just before dawn, or the fact that Burger King isn't the only place in town to eat.

Me? I've always liked the low life, the mud. If you know where to look, there are things you can get in San Francisco that are not available in Grain Ball City, Iowa.

Or anywhere else, for that matter.

A steady fog was blowing across the city. I took a Yellow from my apartment to Arnolds on O'Farrell; my driver was a Latino transvestite. He had very dark black hair that fell to his shoulders and he wore very pink lipstick and very pink nail polish. He had enormous hands and a swarthy jaw into which he had unavailingly rubbed talcum powder. He thought I was from out-of-town. "You gonna love the show, honey," he said confidently.

In the 1970s, the Arnold brothers built a business empire out of nothing more striking than their obsessive interest in the way women looked without their clothes. They named their theater after themselves. Its official designation was the Arnold Brothers Erotic Emporium. Everyone simply said *Arnolds*.

It was very California. Newspaper advertisements soliciting for strippers described the place as a *caring environment*. The girls were called *erotic performers;* they were supposed to look wholesome. They were said to adore making fools of themselves.

The headliners performed on stage in the Copenhagen Room; for a few dollars more than admission, a man could have one of the girls from the stable sit on his lap and wriggle discreetly. In the Grotto, customers were given flashlights. The girls danced on a raised platform and satisfied vagrant episodes of gynecological curiosity. It was all very open and life-enhancing.

38

The police were there a lot and so were members of the mayor's staff, who frequently used the upstairs facilities for budget meetings. The women got their consciousness raised. There was a lot of grass and then a lot of hash and then a lot of crack and then somehow it turned sour the way everything like that turns sour sooner or later. The women finally figured out that getting their consciousness raised might not be such a great thing. The cops had other things to do. Some solemn crazy shot the mayor.

I walked into the lobby and looked around. The headliner was someone named Vanilla Jugs. Her measurements, a poster announced, were 58fff!-22-34. She looked like she might suffer a hernia holding up all that silicon.

The clerk behind the register was new, some dweebish little guy in a soiled yellow shirt and a bright red vest. He sat primly behind the counter. The bouncer, who was dressed in a red sports coat and tuxedo pants, stood talking to the clerk. There were a few men in the lobby, looking at the video exhibits. They had the sad suburban look of men not used to sin. From far away, there was the sound of music. None of the shows had started. I headed for the stairs.

"Can't go up there, fellah," said the bouncer. "Private."

I was already on the stairs and I didn't stop.

"Hey dickbrain, maybe you didn't hear me. You can't go up there. It's private."

I stopped but didn't turn around.

"I heard you," I said. "I didn't pay any attention."

"What are you, a wise guy?"

"I'm a member of the Vegetarian Police," I said. "We got word someone's eating a cheeseburger upstairs. It may be too late but I've got to investigate."

The door at the head of the stairs opened and Vinnie Arnold poked his head out. He had taken too many drugs and scrambled his brains; it was an effort for him to focus.

"What's going on?" he said, peering downstairs.

39

"Dickbrain wants to go up. I told him it's private."

"It's me, Vinnie," I said. "Asherfeld."

Vinnie turned the phrase over in his mind for a moment; it had a lot of room to move.

"Oh for Christsakes," he finally said, stepping out from the door.

"He didn't tell me he was family, Mr. A," said the bouncer forlornly.

"He didn't tell me he was family," said Vinnie, with a mean mimetic whine.

I climbed up the rest of the stairs and shook hands with Vinnie. His hand shook slightly. He had lost an inch of height since the old days; and his face had collapsed in on itself, like a sagging house. His dark brown eyes were full of mixed messages.

"Still the same old Vinnie," I said, punching him lightly on the shoulder.

"Still the same," he said. "Hey com'on in. We'll smoke a few." He opened the door behind him. Somewhere deep in his eyes I could see a flash of the old furtive greaser.

"I don't want to smoke, Vinnie," I said. "I want to talk."

"No one wants to smoke anymore," he said sadly. "No one wants to shoot up. No one wants to do anything."

"Hard to believe," I said, "seeing where it got you."

"Hard to believe," he said cheerfully.

I followed Vinnie Arnold into his office. There was an enormous fireplace in the near wall; it was big enough to roast a haunch of beef. There were a few smelly, cold-looking logs propped up on the gridiron. Above the fireplace there was a gigantic oil painting of a voluptuous mulatto about to plunge an eleven-foot dildo into herself. She looked as if she couldn't wait. There was an old-fashioned rolltop oak desk by the far wall; it was covered with bills and papers and a few ledgers. A computer stood on a stand by the desk, looking like a sightless eye. There were three or four greasy-looking mattresses scattered on the floor. The place smelled of sweat and potato chips.

Vinnie walked over to the fireplace irresolutely and then walked over to his desk and plopped into his reclining chair. I looked around the room.

"You're preparing a spread for *Architectural Digest?*"

"Nah," Vinnie said with bluff good humor, "we're gonna move to female mud wrestling. We put the mud right on the floor and let the cunts go at it. I want the place to look used. So what's up, Asher? You didn't come hear to smoke, you ain't gonna snort. You need some moistness? You want to get laid? I can fix you up two lesbians. Nothing like it. You want a dog, maybe, a big Shepherd?"

Vinnie no longer made eye contact when he spoke; he kept looking around the room, at the fireplace, out the window. He was still pretty funny, though.

"No, Vinnie, not tonight."

"So what then?"

I had made ten copies of the picture that LeRoy had given me; in each I had cropped out Roger Ellerbee. I walked over to Vinnie and handed him one. I braced myself against his desk. He took the picture and leaned way back in his chair, putting his feet up on the desk.

"What do you think?" I asked.

"Nice knockers," he said professionally.

"You know her?"

"It's hard to tell. I may."

Vinnie looked up at me sadly. I knew what he was trying to say. "Maybe you ask Pussy," I said.

"I'll do that," he said brightly, sitting up in his chair and putting his feet on the ground again. He pushed against the back of his chair with his arm and bellowed, "Pussssy!"

From far down the hall a middle-aged voice shouted back: "What?" It was pretty irritable, that voice.

In the early part of the eighties, Vinnie had fallen passionately in love with an eighteen-year-old dancer professionally named Pussy Willow. They had publicly pledged to one another in a

Shinto ceremony on the western slope of Mt. Tamalpais; they spent the next ten years doing drugs and driving one another nuts. Now she did good work with the dancers, introducing them to witchcraft, feminism, and the Third World. She kept the books for Vinnie.

"Pussssy," Vinnie shouted again; this time he let himself whine.

"Coming," shouted the voice and then there was the flap-flopping of a pair of mules.

Pussy Willow was dressed in a blue silk bathrobe with an embroidered eagle over her left breast. Her dark hair was piled on top of her head and held in place with an ivory pin. She stood by the door, holding her bathrobe closed.

"What?" she said. She had once been achingly beautiful.

"You're looking good, Pussy," I said.

"Asher, what're *you* doing here?" She came into the room and gave me a light kiss on both cheeks; she was still holding her bathrobe closed. I steadied her as she leaned up by holding her hips. Her flesh had the kneaded lumpy feel of cold potatoes; she had on very bright red lipstick.

"I want a career in erotic dance," I said. "I need a caring environment."

"Still the same old kidder," said Pussy. She walked over to Vinnie and sat comfortably on his lap. Vinnie rested his head on her shoulder. "Don't," she said sharply. Vinnie raised his head obediently and reached for the picture he had placed on the desk.

"Do I know her?" he asked.

Pussy looked at the picture critically; her right foot was rocking, the mule flapping against her bare sole. After a moment she said: "I think it's Brown Angel."

Vinnie brightened up right away. "That's *right*," he said, pounding the table weakly with his fist. "It's Brown Angel."

"Friend of the family?" I asked.

"No way," said Pussy, putting the picture facedown on the desk.

"She's not?" asked Vinnie, disappointed to have lost the thread again.

"No, honey, no. Brown Angel was strictly Vegas and L.A. Don't you remember?"

"Oh yeah," said Vinnie.

"Also she was very bad news," said Pussy, looking up directly at me.

I took the picture back from the desk.

"Bad news how?" I asked.

"I don't know," said Pussy, "It's what I heard. She was a different crowd."

"Anyone over at the Palace know her?"

The Palace on Market was a rival to Arnolds. It featured erotic performers who travelled the big-money circuit from Houston to Dallas through Las Vegas and Los Angeles and up to San Francisco. It was run by a no-nonsense Latino named Chico-Chico. I never knew whether he was fronting for anyone else, and never cared to ask.

"They might," said Pussy. "It was her kind of environment."

"Not very open and all about their sensuality," I said.

Pussy looked up at me. She had clear, cold brilliant blue eyes. Nothing could take that away from her. She was still flopping her mule against her foot.

"You know, Asher," she said, "you were always a very big jerk."

I smiled and leaned over and kissed her cheek, holding her head by the back of her neck. She smelled warm and frail, like a kitten.

"Always," I said and straightened up. "Keep the faith, Vinnie."

Pussy Willow was still sitting on Vinnie's lap when I reached the door. His head was on her shoulder again. She didn't seem to mind anymore.

When I got to the bottom of the stairs, the bouncer in the red jacket looked at me with a scowl.

"I was too late," I said. "It was terrible, just terrible."

Good Old Jack

When I heard next from Lauren Ellerbee, her voice on my answering machine was low and calm and self-contained. She said she was sorry she had made a scene; she said she had been beside herself; she said she appreciated everything I had done; she would have gone on appreciating everything she could possibly appreciate if the tape on the machine had not come to an abrupt end.

I called her back in Atherton after an hour or so.

"This is Aaron Asherfeld," I said.

Lauren Ellerbee said "yes?" in a way that suggested she really did not know who was calling; then she whispered: "Let me switch phones."

There was a bang and the clatter of receding heels.

"I'm so glad you called," she said when she had picked up another telephone. "I wanted to ask if you could come down later in the afternoon."

I must have hesitated.

"I'm having a lawn party."

"It's what I like best," I said, "right next to root canal."

"Please," she said softly, "for me."

* * *

It was raw and dreary and damp when I left San Francisco, but the great flowing elm trees on Montecito were still flowing when I got to Atherton, the leaves whooshing from time to time in the breeze, and the sun was still high in the sky, and the season was still summer.

The heavy iron gate at the front of Roger Ellerbee's house was open; Bobo was standing there greeting people. He was dressed in a creamy silk shirt with a wide collar, open at the throat, and tan slacks; he had a gold chain around his neck and loafers with tassels on his feet. He was carrying a Hasselblad by a leather strap. He held out his other hand mechanically. He looked like Wayne Newton's cousin, the one kidnapped at birth by Gypsies.

He stared at me without letting go of my hand.

I said I was the guy from last week. A slow smile of radiant confusion began spreading across his face, only to end abruptly in a frown.

"Oh yeah," he finally said. "You're the guy from last week."

I looked down at my hand which Bobo kept pumping slowly and methodically, as if he were trying to raise oil. "Don't let go," I said. "It'll be worth more next year."

There were about fifty people milling around the lawn in that uncomfortable way people have of milling around lawns. The men looked like lumbering caribou; the women had the loping overexercised look of Greyhounds.

A buffet had been set up on a long white table by the brick wall in front of the house. Conchita, the Spanish maid, was behind the table, sweating in her tight uniform. I walked over and nodded to her. She went into a flurry of activity, pointing at each of the dishes. There were cut vegetables on ice, and platters of bread, and fruit, and heaps of yoghurt, and a bowl with rice and nuts, and another bowl with curry, and ten different kinds of cheese, and a platter with scalloped potatoes, and an enormous roast beef set in a chafing dish—the kind heated by little cans of blue-flamed Sterno.

Lauren Ellerbee intercepted me as I was almost at the bar at the other side of the front lawn. She smelled of soap and shampoo and long rambles down country roads. She took my arm in hers and swayed against me as we walked.

She said: "This is an absolute agony."

We reached the bar, which was being manned by a hired catering service. The barman wore a short bolero jacket with the legend *Hey Ho* stitched in red on his lapel. He had a deformed thumb; he needed a shave.

"What'll it be?" he said musically.

"Calistoga, with a twist."

What else?

I took my drink, the glass sweating pleasantly in my hand, and Lauren Ellerbee took my arm again, and we walked on the flagstone walkway toward the back of the house.

When we reached the yard, Lauren Ellerbee sat down on an iron lawn chair and looked up at the heavy fecund madrone by the corner of the lawn. I stood beside her.

"I've heard from Roger," she said.

I raised my eyebrows.

Lauren Ellerbee opened the white satin clutch she was carrying; she took out a postcard and handed it to me. On the front it showed a series of palm trees receding down a broad sunny street somewhere in Los Angeles. I turned the card over.

"Should I read this?"

Lauren Ellerbee nodded without looking at me.

It said: "Mouse, Trust me. ILY." There was no signature.

" 'Mouse' is Roger's name for me."

I couldn't imagine anyone less mouse-like.

"He's with another woman, isn't he?" she asked abruptly, her eyes blinking furiously.

I thought of the photograph LeRoy had sent me.

"I don't think so," I said.

"That's what you have to say," she said bitterly. "I don't know why I even asked."

After a while Lauren Ellerbee stopped looking at the madrone

46

and turned her face to me; she had wonderful clear skin that looked plumped up, as if there were water underneath the tissue; and clear blue eyes and red lips and white teeth.

"I'm sorry," she said after a while. "That was uncalled for."

"It doesn't matter."

"Can you meet some people?" she said.

I raised my eyebrows. They were getting tired from all that exercise.

"It's all right. They know."

I nodded and said why not. The tension dissolved and Lauren Ellerbee laughed a silvery laugh and said why not and got up from her chair with a fluid graceful gesture. She took my arm and steered me from the little patio and into the big fake tudor house.

Roger Ellerbee's study had been furnished in a style intended to suggest masculinity. There was drum-dyed leather everywhere; and a lot of oiled wood paneling, and heavy maroon curtains that made a statement, and a desk the size of an aircraft carrier, and English prints of horses by Peel, and an illuminated globe almost as big as the real thing. I could just see some dismal little swish running around the place with a bolt of fabric over his arm saying *I just think this is going to be so butch.*

Two men were standing by the desk, talking, their heads inclined.

"Jack," said Lauren Ellerbee, still holding on to my arm possessively, "this is my Mr. Asherfeld."

I shook hands with J. Madford Wunderman. He was one of those men whom goofy women sometimes refer to as a fine figure of a man. He took up a great deal of space. He had a large square head with plenty of thick black hair, turning to white over his ears; he had enormously bushy eyebrows and a florid fleshy nose, the kind that looks as if it should be useful for something besides sniffing the air. He wore an old-fashioned Guard's moustache that turned up at the tips; he was dressed beautifully in an elegant

47

double-breasted blue blazer and gray slacks that just broke over a pair of polished burgundy loafers.

I said How Do and he said How Do and we pumped hands. I remembered his deep bass voice from the telephone, but if he recalled that we had spoken, he didn't let on.

"And this is Marvin Finklestein," said Lauren Ellerbee with a note of maternal warmth. I stopped pumping Jack's hand and pumped hands with Marvin Finklestein instead. He was tall and stringy, no more than twenty-five. He bobbed his head as he shook hands with me and made noises at the back of his throat. He had a long, unused face.

"Please sit down everyone," Lauren Ellerbee said. I sat at one end of the enormous brown leather couch; Lauren Ellerbee perched herself girlishly on the side bolster, her long tapered legs held out in front of her. Marvin Finklestein sat at the other end of the couch, holding his knees with his hands and rocking backward and forward. Good Old Jack sat at Roger's desk in Roger's chair and promptly put his burgundy shoes on Roger's desk.

"Get a lead on Roger yet?" he asked.

"I see you're all eagerness to find him," I said.

"Now what's that supposed to mean?" said Good Old Jack in a voice of doom, lifting his feet from Roger's desk and sitting up abruptly.

"Aaron, please," said Lauren Ellerbee. She put her hand on my shoulder. She let her finger briefly stroke the back of my ear. If my ear had any objections, it didn't register them with me.

"It doesn't mean anything," I said. "I was just acknowledging your pain."

Marvin Finklestein grunted from his end of the couch; it might have been a laugh.

J. Madford Wunderman flushed deeply. I could see the purple veins on his nose stand out, even from where I was sitting. He said: "What are you, a stand-up comedian or something? You think you're on Carson, is that it?"

He didn't have the manner to go with the clothes.

Lauren got up from the edge of the couch and walked over to the back of the big leather chair in which J. Madford Wunderman was sitting; she put her arms over the top of the chair and around his neck.

"Jack, please, for me," she said. "That's enough, please."

Wunderman gave his head a little shake in order to shrug off Lauren Ellerbee's arms. She paid no mind whatsoever. Finally Wunderman patted his hair and lifted his nose up a little bit and managed simultaneously to look hurt and mollified.

"Let's get on with it," he said gruffly. "We're in big trouble here."

Lauren Ellerbee took her arms from Wunderman's neck and allowed a very small smile to play across her face. She walked back to the couch and sat down beside me again.

"I knew I wasn't on Carson," I said.

Marvin Finklestein lifted his face up and spoke to the air without looking at anyone in the room: "Do you know where Roger is?" he asked, his voice squeaking.

"Me?" I said. "No idea."

Finklestein made a strangled sound in the back of his throat, lowered his head, and resumed rocking.

"This isn't what is needed, Lauren," said J. Madford Wunderman. "We are facing some very serious problems here."

"I'm aware of that, Jack," said Lauren Ellerbee. "Don't you think that of all people I'm aware of that?"

I said: "What problems you talking about?"

Wunderman sat up at Roger's big desk, put his elbows on the table top, and supported his square head with his fingertips.

"We've got a quarterly audit coming up in ten days. Our books are a mess."

"You just find this out?"

"This week."

"You're short what?"

49

"It's not a matter of being short. I can't make heads or tails of things."

"Now wait, Jack, that's not fair," said Lauren Ellerbee.

Wunderman sighed deeply.

"You're right," he said. "It's not fair." Then he spoke directly to me. "Roger was a very, very creative type guy. The trouble is that he's the only one that knows where things are and where they've gone. We need him back. You understand what I'm saying?"

"You're saying that Roger was cooking the books."

"I resent that," said Wunderman sharply, bringing his fist down on the desk.

"Jack, this is all so ugly. I won't have it," said Lauren Ellerbee; her voice was trembling.

Wunderman threw his hands in the air.

"Who's doing your audit?" I asked.

"The SEC," he said. "They served Notice of Intent two days ago. Somebody named Dreyfus. But that's not the whole of it. Aztec is also going ballistic."

"Aztec? As in human sacrifice?"

"They've been keeping us afloat for the last six months."

"They're what? Your bank?"

Wunderman nodded but didn't say anything more.

I said: "When do you actually go into production?"

"Ask him," said Wunderman, nodding toward Finklestein.

"A month after we get a variance," he said. It was only the second sentence he had managed to complete.

"No point in wondering whether you've got the variance, is there?"

"It's such a Mickey Mouse racket," said Wunderman bitterly.

"So unfair," I said. "They're probably making you pay taxes, too. I suppose that Roger is the only one knows anything about this variance?"

Wunderman nodded: "He kept a lot to himself. I only found

out about this business two weeks ago. *I've* been marketing my ass off to the Japanese."

I stood up with a sigh. Lauren Ellerbee got up with me and smoothed her skirt. "I've got to go," I said.

"Terrific," said Wunderman.

"You two," said Lauren Ellerbee, as if we were both naughty children. "I'm going to see Mr. Asherfeld out, Jack. I'll be back. You stay put too, Marvin, please?"

Marvin Finklestein grunted from the corner of the couch; Lauren Ellerbee took my arm and we walked out of the study and out of the house and onto the dappled lawn that was now divided into irregular zones of sun and shade.

"I don't have anyone I can lean on," she said.

"Is that what you want, someone to lean on?"

"Doesn't everyone?"

"I don't know."

"Yes you do," she said softly. "You know very well."

"What about Bobo? I thought he was your support system."

Lauren Ellerbee smiled mysteriously. "Bobo is just Bobo," she said.

"Is he a relative or is taking care of him just sort of charity work you do?"

"He's Roger's son," she said. "He's really very dear."

We had walked from the back of the house to the front.

I looked at her. The sun was in her eyes. She lifted a hand to shade them. I could see the fine lines around her full rich mouth.

"Do eat something," she said. "Stay as long as you like. It's comforting for me to know you're puttering around out here."

She disengaged her arm from mine and gave my hand a quick squeeze. I watched her walk toward the back of the house, her hips rolling elegantly against the pleated fold of her skirt.

I walked around the lawn a little and took a few odds and ends from Conchita's table.

I was eating them morosely when Wunderman came up to me. It was like being approached by a super tanker.

51

"Sorry I got a little hot under the collar there," he said.

I said it didn't matter.

Wunderman coughed sententiously and said: "Could we talk someplace alone."

I shrugged my shoulders.

"You know the Angel Waters State Park?"

I shrugged my shoulders again. I was getting good at it.

"There's a wooden walkway, goes right out into the bay," said Wunderman. "I'll meet you at the end."

After a few minutes, Lauren Ellerbee came back out. I walked over to her to say good-bye. She looked at me and said: "I just don't know what to think anymore."

There wasn't a whole lot to see at the Angel Waters State Park and hardly anyone was there to see it. I parked between a rusting green Camaro and a row of overflowing trash containers. The air when I opened the car door was wet and warm and smelled faintly of decay. A boy scout troop of energetic bees was buzzing around the trash. I walked over to the information center and read the plaque that had been mounted on the wooden wall. The place had been set aside to celebrate the environment of the marsh. As far as I could tell, there wasn't a whole lot of difference between a marsh and a swamp. There were pictures of birds on the wall and something that looked like a bobcat without a tail. The something looked pretty annoyed at having lost its tail. Inside the information center you could buy a map of the park by putting a quarter into a little wooden strong box. Restrooms were in the back. Please, said a stern sign, no music on the walkway. No bicycles. No littering. No loitering, either. Do not disturb the wildlife. Respect the rights of others. Take a good fast look and get the hell out of here.

J. Madford Wunderman was waiting for me at the end of the walkway. He turned and said: "Thanks for coming," in his organ voice.

"No problem."

He swept his large fleshy hand in an arc across his chest.

"When I was growing up, there was marsh all the way down to the end of the peninsula. Miles and miles. We used to see elk feeding here in autumn."

"Hard to believe," I said.

I tried to sound sincere and hurt.

Wunderman sighed deeply. "This used to be one of the golden spots, this bay," he said. "Now look at it."

"Pretty awful," I said.

He meant the bridge in the far distance, the refineries on the near shore, the freeway on the Peninsula. It was the sort of complaint that everyone makes in California; no one knows what it means.

A small bird settled itself on a black rotten log some distance from the walkway. Wunderman pointed at it.

"Know what that is?"

"An eagle?"

"It's a kingfisher."

"I knew it wasn't an eagle. The markings are all wrong."

Wunderman looked at me condescendingly. "There haven't been eagles in this bay for thirty years."

"That's very interesting, Jack," I said, "but you didn't ask me here to talk about the wildlife."

"No, I didn't. There are some things you should know. I wanted to avoid speaking in front of Lauren."

"Why's that?"

"Asherfeld, you've got to understand that Roger was being squeezed pretty hard. There was this business with the variance for one thing, then this business about the books."

Wunderman let his hands flutter to indicate how disturbing it all was.

"Roger actually went to the SEC in December."

"Is that a fact?" I said.

"He asked for help, he *pleaded* for help."

"They do anything for him?"

"Not a thing," said Wunderman bitterly. "I'm afraid that after that Roger made a very foolish decision and decided to ask the wrong sort of person for help."

"Kind of a late-lamented fat black person?"

Wunderman nodded.

"But that's not all?"

The little bird Wunderman had pointed out snapped its head forward and into the water. It came up with a tiny fish in his beak, which it swallowed whole.

"You're going to tell me there was another woman. It's something you think I should know."

Wunderman nodded his large head in a glum unhappy theatrical way. "Roger was very worried that Lauren would find out. He was beside himself with anxiety."

"Why is that, Jack?" I said.

Wunderman gave a snort of indignation. "Why is *what?*

"Why is it that he was beside himself with anxiety?"

Wunderman settled his mottled hands on the wooden railing and looked out over the waters. He wasn't about to answer my question.

"He loves Lauren very much, you know," he said sententiously.

"Is that so?" I said.

"Well yes," said Wunderman, shifting his shoulders inside his sport coat.

A breeze had come up, stirring the waters into silver and black ripples. The little bird finished fishing from the rotten log. It looked out over the bay with beady black eyes. It didn't seem too disturbed at not seeing any elk.

Weinberg

It wasn't hard to get hold of the Reverend Leotis—about as hard as getting hold of North America.

I called up the First Baptist Church in Oakland.

"Hallelujah," said a woman with a rich contralto.

"Hallelujah," I said, but when the Reverend Leotis got on the telephone and Hallelujahed himself, I said: "This is Henson Bottlesworth of *The New York Times.*"

The Reverend chuckled and snorted and cleared his throat and said: "Well, well, well."

"I'd like to talk to you about Lawrence Williams, Reverend."

A pause paused.

I said I would be glad to come out to Oakland.

"No," said the Reverend. "Can't have that." He didn't say why. He said he would pick me up in San Francisco, corner of Broadway and Grant. "Forty minutes, sharp, you hear," he said.

I walked down Greenwich in the weak warm sunlight that was just starting to brighten and purchased a yellow legal pad at the Kim Sung market on Stockton. There were high cirrus clouds in the sky; and in the distance a zeppelin featuring an advertisement for Fuji films was floating motionlessly.

Just ten years ago, North Beach used to be the point of intersection of half a dozen topless clubs; now the neighborhood is seedy and rundown, Chinatown washing up sheepishly to its flanks. There are dreary take-out restaurants on Broadway and stores that sell large doughy cookies and tee-shirts with the legend I LOVE SAN FRANCISCO inscribed on the front.

There is still one topless club left; I stood in front of the place and looked over the marquee while I was waiting for the Reverend. Sam and Diana were all set to do their patented love act inside. Sam looked a little like he might benefit from Weight Watchers. I figured Diana belonged in therapy. But then, so does everyone in California.

A barker dressed in a green jacket opened the door of the club and released a whiff of old very stale air onto the street. A pale puffy pudgy little blonde in a miniskirt came out with him. Her legs were mottled with purple splotches. She began to sway to the beat of a stereo in the back of the theater.

"Innerested in seeing a little snatch?" asked the barker.

"I'm a Buddhist," I said.

The barker looked at me alertly. "No problem," he said. "Fifty dollars, she's a Buddhist too."

He turned to the girl, who continued to rotate her hips.

"That right, Charlene."

"Whatever you say," Charlene said, not opening her eyes.

A white Lincoln with opaque green windows pulled up in front of the club. It wasn't any longer than a football field. The rear window rolled down an inch and someone said: "Yo."

I walked over to the window and leaned over the car, my hand on the Lincoln's roof. The window stayed opened by an inch. "You mind," said the voice, "don't want to see no fingerprints on the roof of my car."

"I don't mind," I said. I took my hand off the roof and straightened up. "I'll just tell my readers that I had a terrific time talking to a pane of glass."

The voice gave a low not very amused laugh, but the window went down a little more. I could see the top of the Reverend Leotis' head; it looked like a rhododendron bush.

"Get in the car," he said.

I went to open the door but the Reverend said: "Other side. That way I don't need to inconvenience myself sliding over."

"That a problem, inconveniencing yourself?"

The window went down another inch. I could see all of the Reverend Leotis now. He was sitting primly in the backseat, an ivory-tipped cane in his hands. He was dressed in a dove gray suit and an off-white shirt with a gray silk tie. His stomach and his shirt were fighting it out. His stomach was winning. An enormous Doberman pinscher sat erectly on the floor beside him.

"Depends on whether you consider getting a call from some asshole claims he's from *The New York Times* an inconvenience."

"Think of it as an opportunity," I said.

"I get so many opportunities," the Reverend Leotis said bleakly. "Can't hardly give them away." He rapped at the glass partition and I could hear the locks in the limousine open.

I walked around to the driver's side and slid into the car. It's always a thrill getting into a limousine, no matter how many times you do it. The Doberman waited until I sat down and then thrust its sleek head insistently into my lap.

"He friendly?" I asked.

"He don't much like white folks," said the Reverend Leotis. "Last asshole claimed he was from *The New York Times,* he bit his nuts off."

"What's his name?"

"Weinberg."

"I mean the dog."

"I'm *talking* about the dog," said the Reverend, "Weinberg, it's a Jewish name."

"Jewish?"

"On account of it's a Jewish dog."

He clucked his tongue at the dog and the Doberman promptly withdrew his head from my lap and sank to his haunches.

The Reverend Leotis rapped on the glass with his walking stick and said: "Drive slowly up to the Golden Gate Park." Then he said to me: "That all right with you, we take in the greenery?"

I said it would be fine. The Reverend eased himself into his seat.

"You think a black man can't dial a telephone. That what you think?"

I said I was sure that a black man could dial a telephone.

"Then how come you don't figure I would call *The New York Times* find out if they ever heard of this Henson Bottlesworth?"

"You got me wrong, Reverend," I said. "I figured that's the first thing you'd do. I know you're smart enough for that."

The Reverend Leotis turned toward me. He had a broad fleshy face, with a high forehead. Then there was that bush on his head. It had a life of its own.

"If you figured that's the first thing I do, why'd you claim you was from *The New York Times?*"

"Get your attention," I said.

The Reverend Leotis thought the matter over for a moment.

"Now you got it what you going to do with it?"

"Talk about LeRoy," I said.

"What about LeRoy? White folks couldn't stand the fact he was a successful black man."

I looked out of the window of the slowly rolling limousine. We were driving down Pine Street. The tint of the glass made the world look intimate and green, like hills seen before a thunderstorm.

"It kept us up nights, Reverend, the thought that LeRoy was a success."

The Reverend Leotis rotated his torso toward me; he was still holding on to his ivory walking stick.

"What you know about success?"

"Not much," I said.

"I figured," said the Reverend Leotis morosely. "Why you so interested in LeRoy?"

"Let's just say I'm sentimental. I like old show tunes. I remember girls I used to date in high school. You know how it is."

"You want some of his money," said the Reverend. "Figure you best be coming around here and scratching for it."

We had reached the edge of the park on the Panhandle; the Reverend rapped on the window and told the driver to go down Park Presidio toward the ocean.

"LeRoy didn't owe me anything when he died."

58

"He owe you money later? The man is going to *accumulate* debts in his grave, that what you're saying?"

I smiled and said: "I was doing a little recovery work for LeRoy. A little deep sea fishing."

"And no fish bite?"

"Not yet."

"How much they be biting for?"

"A quarter of a million dollars." ·

The Reverend Leotis turned almost his entire torso toward me; the maneuver involved rotating his stomach. It was like beaching a whale.

"Somebody owe LeRoy a quarter of a million dollars?"

"That's what he said."

The Reverend meditated for a moment. We had reached the end of the Park Presidio. He rapped on the window and told the driver to pull over to the sandy shoulder on the side of the road.

"What you want from me?" he said, "Christian comfort excepted."

"Information."

"Like what?"

"Like who LeRoy did business with?"

"LeRoy was in a lot of businesses." The Reverend Leotis smiled to himself. "When you know better," he said. "Call me. We can talk about donations to the church then." Then he said, "LeRoy was a *careful* man. You understand my meaning? Carry around a needle, people figure you a junkie. Take in the wash, people figure you a wash lady. I'm not saying LeRoy never took in no wash. I'm not saying he did. I'm not saying he didn't make deliveries. I'm not saying he did. I'm saying he was careful."

"That's very interesting, Reverend," I said.

"I know it is," said the Reverend Leotis jovially, "I just know it is."

"But it's not interesting enough."

The Reverend Leotis acquired a look of alertness.

"Enough for what?" he asked.

"Enough for me to even think of making a donation to the church."

The Reverend Leotis deliberated on this point.

"So what you want?" he finally asked.

"An introduction to whoever it is that's handling LeRoy's affairs. Probably be his lawyer."

The Reverend Leotis rapped at the partition with his stick. "Gentleman be getting out now, Carlos," he said. The limousine's locks opened with a click.

We were on the sandy spit of land that ends just before the windmill.

"Reverend," I said, "this is about six miles from where you picked me up."

"I know," the Reverend said happily, "walk'll do you good. Pudgy white fellah like yourself could use a little exercise."

I looked over at His Pudginess himself. The Reverend Leotis patted his stomach tenderly. There was an awful lot to pat.

"It's muscle," he said.

"Muscle?"

"*Soft* muscle. He reached over to stroke the Doberman's head. "Say good-bye to the man, Weinberg," he said.

Weinberg scrambled to a sitting position and snarled at me, his lips retracted over his elegant white teeth.

Wuss Ball

J. Madford Wunderman hadn't given me much; but he had given me the name of LRB's bank. I called Wunderman himself a few days after Lauren Ellerbee's lawn party, and asked him to arrange an introduction. I thought he'd refuse with a lavish display of indignation; he said suavely that actually Asherfeld that seems like a pretty good idea.

"The man you want to speak to is Darr," he said. "I'll set it up for you."

Ten minutes later Wunderman called me back. "Darr'll see you at eleven," he said. "You know where the office is?"

I had no idea.

"Top of the TransAmerica building. Great view."

I said: "Thanks a lot, Wunderman."

"No problem," he said.

He had a note in his voice that suggested there was something he wanted to tell me.

"Something to remember, Asherfeld," he said. "It's a pretty fast-moving crowd over there, if you get my drift."

"I got it, Wunderman," I said.

I dressed in a tan suit that hadn't seen a great view in a long time and a blue shirt with French cuffs; I put on a spiffy yellow power tie and old-fashioned wing-tipped shoes. I stuffed a white linen handkerchief in my breast pocket and slapped some imported cologne on my razor-burned cheeks. I hadn't been this turned out in months. That's what a fast-moving crowd does for me.

I clattered downstairs and walked down to Columbus and over to Broadway. The sun had broken through the clouds; the air was sharp. It almost felt like a fall day, the kind you get in New York.

I could see the TransAmerica tower as soon as I got to the top of the financial district; it was one of those nutty buildings that go up a lot in San Francisco. It was white and shaped like a tapering triangle. It looked like it was designed to spear a giant bagel.

The Aztec Corporation took up the whole of the twenty-third floor. I rode the elevator alone. It zoomed upward to the twentieth floor, slowed, and then stopped with a silky sound, opening onto what was obviously a private landing.

The enormous oiled redwood door facing the elevator had an Aztec ziggurat raised on its front; above, it said AZTEC in letters of gold; below, it said THE AZTEC CORPORATION, and in italic letters, *An Investment Bank.* I opened the door and walked in. The facing wall had a black-and-white photograph of the Aztec ruins at Teotihuacán; the near wall on the right had another golden sign that spelled out AZTEC. A dishy-looking young woman with corkscrewed hair sat at the receptionist's desk. She was speaking on the telephone. She covered the mouthpiece with her hand as I approached the desk and looked up expectantly. The telephone had the AZTEC logo on the receiver.

"Know where I can find the Aztec Corporation?" I said.

She nodded her poodle head and raised an index finger and said to the telephone: "Susyn, I'll call you right back." She hung up and leaned forward, arching her back. "My roommate," she said, rolling her eyes upward. "She keeps getting into these *situations.*"

"She probably needs to take charge of her own life," I said.

"Exactly, but that is *exactly* what I keep telling her. I keep saying 'Susyn, you've got to take charge of your life.' "

"You've got to be your own best friend," I said.

"I *say* that to her, but *exactly,* I say 'Susyn, you've got to be your own best friend.' "

"Before anyone else can love you, you've got to learn to love yourself."

"That's incredible. You must be psychic, I mean you are just *so* intuitive."

"I'm an Aries. We're people people. Darr in?"

"I'll see. He's running late this morning." She picked up the telephone again: "Jimbo," she purred, "there's this very psychic Aries to see you." She looked up at me. "I forgot, what did you say your name was."

"You didn't forget," I said. "I didn't tell you. It's Asherfeld."

"Asherfield," she said into the telephone, and then to me, her hand over the receiver: "Did I get that right?"

I told her she did fine. She hung up and said: "I'll take you back."

She was dressed in a red micro-mini, and a red cashmere sweater with a white bolero jacket. I followed her agile young rump across the reception area and down a carpeted corridor. No Muzak. The citrus smell you get in very expensive men's cologne. Soft white walls, the color almost creamy. Expensively framed prints of the French impressionists. She finally stopped at the corner office, opened the door and poked her head in. "I'm all yours, Jimbo," she said, and then backed away giggling: "Just kidding, just kidding." I stood behind her by the door. She stepped a little to the side. "This is Mr. Asherfield."

"Asherfeld," I said.

"How you doing?" said Darr glumly. He was a man of perhaps my own age. He had a large, square, deeply lined face; his chin was cleft and his beard so heavy that his lower jaw looked almost blue. We shook hands. He reached out to palpate my shoulder, driving his thumb hard into the muscle. His brown hair was combed over his ears; his sideburns were ten years too long. "Come on in," he said.

Darr's office was the sort of place in which a great deal of money had been spent in order to show that a great deal of money had been spent. The carpet was a dense blue weave with irregular gold threads that caught the light. The desk was made of bleached white wood. There was nothing on it except for a brass device in which chrome balls were suspended from a cross-beam. Tap one and it sets the others in motion.

What else? There was a glass and black enamel fish tank; it reached from the floor to the ceiling in hexagonal segments. Each segment had different colored goldfish. There was a bronze statue of a bosomy young woman extending her arms in a swan dive. There was a floor-to-ceiling ficus. There was a gold-colored umbrella stand. There were two imitation Eames chairs.

Darr walked over to the picture window and turned his back to me, his hands folded behind him. He saw the receptionist's reflection in the darkened glass; she was still standing by the open door.

"All right, Cindi, thanks," he said, without turning around.

"No problem, Jimbo," Cindi sang out. She blew a kiss with her pouted lips to Darr's back and closed the door behind us.

I sat down in the Eames chair in front of the bleached white desk and stretched my legs in front of me; Darr kept on looking out over the city that was just beginning to sparkle in the high, clear morning light.

"Fantastic ass," he said.

"An intellectual, too."

"Regular Einstein," Darr said. "We're taking bets on when she's going to catch a pencil in her snatch, those skirts get any shorter."

"Keep me posted," I said.

I noticed that there were a series of handsomely framed military photographs on the wall opposite the fish tank; I thought I could recognize Darr. He was dressed in fatigues cut off at the shoulder; he was carrying a heavy machine gun and looking out at the goldfish. His face looked younger, not different. There was a cigar in his mouth and his chin looked blue, even in the black and white photograph.

"Vietnam?" I said to his back.

"Eighty-second Airborne," he said. "Hell of a good time."

"Good time?"

"The best," he said. He turned from the window and sat down at his desk, his feet extended sideways, legs crossed at the ankles. He had a trick of moving quietly. "So you're over there at Ellerbee, you working for J. Madford?"

"No, Lauren Ellerbee." This wasn't true but I didn't see any reason to let Darr know it.

"You're better off. Wunderman's a wuss. Ellerbee's a classy lady."

The speech seemed to confirm him in his sourness. He straightened up and said: "Maybe Doxie should be in on this."

"Doxie?"

"She's more hands-on than me."

He slid open the side drawer of his desk. A white telephone on a pedestal appeared to float up from its interior. Darr pressed the speakerphone button. I could tell it was the sort of thing he enjoyed doing. "Cindi," he said, "get Doxie in here."

"You'll get a kick out of Doxie," he said.

He closed the desk drawer and the exquisite telephone swung silently downward and out of sight.

Doxie knocked gently on the door and slipped into the room within the minute. She was a tall mournful woman, with wide hips, heavy thighs, and a narrow chest. Like Darr, she was dressed in a grey suit; underneath, she had on one of those furiously ruffled blouses that are supposed to work for women with flat chests. She was wearing Reeboks instead of heels and carrying a clipboard. She had thin lips; she wore no makeup. She had the sharp intent face of a woman prepared to be injured.

She nodded severely to me and said: "Pleased to meet you," after Darr had made the introductions from his desk.

"Asherfeld here is working for Lauren Ellerbee," Darr said.

Doxie said: "I see," as if that explained everything.

"Sit, sit," Darr said, motioning Doxie to the other imitation

65

Eames chair. He had commenced holding up his head with his hands, his cheeks resting in his palms.

"Your show," he said to me.

"Tell me about Roger."

"He's very professional," said Doxie.

"He's a wuss," said Darr.

"I don't think that's really fair," said Doxie.

Darr looked at her with his dead black eyes. "Me either," he said, "but it doesn't change the fact that he's a wuss."

Doxie raised her hands slightly from her lap and turned her head away; her cheeks were flushed. She looked better with a little bit of color.

"Wunderman's a wuss," I said. "Ellerbee's a wuss. How'd two wusses get into so much trouble?"

"That's what wusses do," said Darr morosely, "they screw up."

Doxie dropped her hand back into her lap.

"Screw up how?" I said.

"Site selection, for one thing," said Darr. He turned his face toward Doxie. "Am I right?"

"I don't know," she said. She was coming close to the end of her courage; she didn't have far to go.

"Don't know? You don't *know?* I know. They're sitting on a three-year lease, place is zoned commercial light, even *before* going into production they need a variance. Ellerbee figures this is a great time to take a hike, get up close and personal with a woodchuck, Wunderman goes menstrual." Darr lifted his head from his hands to look at me. "How'm I doing?" he asked. "Sound like wuss ball?"

"Who did your site selection?"

"I did," said Doxie.

"You didn't know about the zoning?"

"We all knew. It was in disclosure. We were *entitled* to a variance. It wasn't supposed to be any big deal."

"See what I mean?" asked Darr, rolling his eyes upward to appeal for help.

"It happens," I said. "These things happen."

"It happens to wusses," said Darr.

Cindi opened the door silently and poked her poodle head in the room. "Jimbo," she said, "you've got everyone in the conference room. They're waiting." She gave Doxie a quick appraising look and said: "I love that gray on you."

Darr got up from his desk. "Got to go," he said. "Doxie'll fax you in on the rest." At the door, he paused to allow Cindi to straighten the collar on his jacket. He had a homily to deliver. Doxie and I swivelled in our seats to look at him. "Two kinds of people," he said, "those who screw up, those who don't."

"You learned that in Vietnam," I said.

"That's right. I learned that in Vietnam."

Darr set off down the corridor, Cindi a poodle step behind him. The large heavy door swung slowly on its pneumatic hinges and closed finally with a muted click.

My Little Rubber Ducky

The woman in the wood-and-glass cashier's box of the Palace Theater was at least nine hundred years old. She had eyes that were even older. She peered out at me through a magnifying cyclops set in the glass.

"What'll be?" she asked. She spoke in a husky whisper through a transom with a slide that she withdrew when she began speaking and snapped shut when she had finished. "Ten dollars for a single, twenty for both shows, thirty for the Naughty Paree room."

"What's the Naughty Paree Room?"

"It's the star's dressing room. You can take pictures."

There were two shows that evening. Someone named Kitten Caboodle was set to do her patented love act at ten; nasty Annie Ample went on at midnight.

I said I wanted to see absolutely everything. It was a professional obligation. She took my money and then had me slide my convexed hand through the transom so that she could stamp my wrist with some sort of fluorescent ink.

"So if you want to go out for something to eat you can come back in," she explained.

"Go out for something to eat? It would be a crime," I said.

Old Eyes just looked at me blankly. "Whatever," she said.

Inside the theater there was a small waiting area, a soiled red carpet on the floor; one wall was given over entirely to photographs of various pornographic stars. The women had lavish impossible bodies and cold hard frozen faces. The place smelled of urine and old paint.

A very tired-looking Hispanic in a red jumpsuit was pushing a carpet sweeper listlessly over the rug. I walked over to him.

"Chico-Chico in?"

"Ina back," he said, not even looking up.

I nodded and walked to the rear door, the one that said Fire Exit, and pushed it open slowly; it gave onto an alley. Chico-Chico kept his office in a basement storeroom. He was a very tough Mexican, which meant he was very tough. He had served in Vietnam and liked it so much he reenlisted when his tour of duty was up in 1967. Something happened to him the second time around. He became quiet and started wearing a crucifix. In 1980, he killed a man in a knife fight, and served three years of a life sentence in Folsom Prison.

I knocked on the door of his office. Someone said *"si"* in a chilly voice.

"Chico," I said, opening the door, "you busy?"

Chico-Chico looked up at me; he was sitting at his desk. The only light in the humid room came from a desk lamp. He may have been happy to see me. It didn't show.

"Sure I'm busy. I'm always busy. I got taxes coming up."

"You're not going to invite me in, offer me a drink, talk about old times?"

"No," he said efficiently. "What you want? You wan' an introduction to one of those cows upstairs. You goin' to the dairy business, is that it?"

"I need to talk to them, Chico."

"So talk, who's stopping you?"

"I just wanted to let you know."

"You let me know."

I thought of saying something clever and thought better of it.

"Thanks, Chico," I said.

Upstairs the show was about to begin. A whole planeload of Japanese tourists had arrived. They took up the front two rows in the orchestra and were busy snapping pictures of the empty stage. There were a few greasers in the back and one or two sad-eyed older men. The music was heavy rock; the amplifiers made the building shake.

The music stopped all of a sudden and a listless drum roll began. An electronic squawk followed. Somebody got on the P.A. and said: "Ladies and Gentlemen, direct from Paris, France, Miss Kitten Caboodle." The lights went down, the music resumed, and a very pretty, middle-aged woman dressed in a red rubber suit with a big yellow zipper on the front pranced out to the center of the stage. The Japanese began applauding vigorously. Kitten Caboodle flashed them a smile that was like a sunburst. Two stagehands wheeled out an enormous translucent tulip-shaped bathtub from the stage wings. Kitten Caboodle began singing a song about how much she loved her Little Rubber Ducky. She began playing with her zipper. It took her twenty minutes to get the thing down to her navel. By the time she was out of the wet suit and into the tulip-shaped tub, the Japanese had experienced a collective spasm of ecstasy and wasted at least three thousand rolls of film.

There was an intermission and then the announcer said Kitten Caboodle was going to do her famous love act.

I passed and sat smoking in the lounge for the next half hour.

When the lights went back on I walked backstage to the Naughty Paree room, which turned out to be the hallway in front of Kitten Caboodle's dressing room; sure enough, there was Kitten Caboodle, back in her wet suit, posing for the Japanese.

I watched them climb all over her. They would have committed *sepuku* if she had asked them to.

Finally she said: "That's all boys, bye-bye," and blew them a kiss, her bulbous lips pursed archly. She opened the door to her dressing room and closed it behind her with a bang. After a while the Japanese drifted away, and so did the three teenagers with acne who were dying to speak to her. They had been too nervous to try.

I knocked on the door. Someone said: "Hold on." A short, tubby man dressed in a pale blue cardigan sweater opened the door. He was bald, except for a horseshoe fringe, and had pale pink skin. He looked like a soap bubble. "Show's over, pal," he said kindly. "You can get pictures of the Kitten at the box office."

"Chico-Chico sent me."

The little tubby man looked doubtful.

"Chico said you should come up?" he asked.

I couldn't see Kitten Caboodle, but I could hear her: "Eddie, please," she said, "trouble with Chico we don't need."

The little man seemed to meditate on this message, and then nodded.

"Yeah, come in," he said. "It's just that Kitten needs her rest after a show. You know what I mean? If it were up to her she'd be out in the hall all evening."

"I know what you mean," I said. I followed Eddie into the room.

Kitten Caboodle was sitting at her makeup table. She was exactly what she seemed to be: A very pretty woman in a rough trade.

"Kitten," said Eddie superfluously, "this here's a friend of Chico's."

"Asherfeld," I said quickly, before either of them could think of calling Chico. Kitten extended her hand primly and I shook it primly.

"Eddie Nagel," said Eddie, extending his own hand, "I'm Kitten's artistic manager." I shook hands with Eddie Nagel. We were getting to be a cozy trio.

"Eddie," said Kitten gently, "maybe you wait for us outside?"

Eddie said that was okeydokey, took a worn leather jacket from the hanger that was suspended from a steampipe, and slipped from the room.

Kitten turned to face me. She was sitting with her legs crossed; she was still dressed in her wet suit.

"So you're a friend of Chico-Chico's," she said without much pleasure.

I nodded.

"I don't do water sports or S and M or scenes. It's five hundred a throw, seven fifty around the world, one thousand for the night," she said mechanically.

I spread my hands apart. "It would be cheap at twice the price," I said.

Kitten snorted and turned back to her makeup table. "You just want to talk, right? I dance my buns off for these Japanese yo-yos and now you want me to sit for a couple of hours over coffee and tell you the story of my life. Forget it. I don't care what that crazy Chico says."

I got out the picture of Brown Angel and put it on Kitten's makeup table. She looked at the picture and then looked up at me. "So?" she said. "Don't tell me. You fell in love when you were both just kids and now you're trying to find her again."

"Kitten," I said, "you're a pretty woman. I like you, I really do. All I want is a little information. That's not asking too much. Now we can cooperate, in which case I'll be out of your life in two seconds flat, or you can give me some more lip, in which case I'll ask Chico-Chico to carve his initials on your ass. Your choice."

Kitten looked at me and then looked at the picture.

"I'm sorry," she finally said, "I get so tired of it all."

"I know you do," I said with as much kindness as I could put in my voice.

"I don't know who she is," she finally said, "she's very pretty."

I picked up the picture. "Thanks," I said.

Kitten looked at me with gray eyes that suddenly seemed sad.

"You sure you don't want to party?" she asked. "I was just kidding about the five hundred. Anything's better than hearing Eddie snore in the next room."

"Another time, Kitten," I said. "I'd be honored."

"Sure," she said.

I had an hour to kill before the next show so I went out to the lounge and smoked some more and then walked over to the videos. The Japanese were lined up in front of the displays, jabbering away.

The lobby began to fill up. Annie Ample was the headliner. Even Chico-Chico made an appearance. He came in through the fire door, looking as if he had been carved from pig iron, and walked over to the Japanese.

"He enjoying the show," he said to no one in particular.

The Japanese stared at him. There was a burst of furious gabble. Finally one of them, their leader, I suppose, stepped forward and bowed slightly to Chico-Chico.

"*Hai,*" he said eagerly.

Chico-Chico smiled his thin-slitted wolfish smile and said: "That's good."

I loitered around the video displays for a few minutes more; when I got into the theater the place was almost full. A short cartoon about safe sex was being shown on a tattered and tiny movie screen that a stagehand had set up on stage. It featured an animated condom. After that, there were a series of announcements over the P.A. about *sinsational* forthcoming attractions, and the usual canned drum roll, and then Annie Ample bounced onto the stage to the music of Van Hamel.

The Japanese applauded, the guys in the back row hooted, and a few men whistled and stamped their feet.

Annie Ample had heavy brown hair that flowed and rippled to her waist; she was thirty or so, with nice features and a thin-lipped mouth. She was dressed in an Indian costume that featured a short, short buckskin skirt, and an open fringed top. She had a cowboy hat on. She had little feet and tanned polished muscular legs; her hips and stomach still looked adolescent; and, of course, she had simply gigantic breasts which stood at right angles to her chest wall. She bounced around the stage a few times, her enormous breasts heaving up and down like dirigibles, two angry red scars still visible when her breasts rocketed skyward. Then she did a low bow, the back of her neck bared, straightened up all of a sudden, and shouted: "Are we ready to party?"

The Japanese certainly were. They went into a frenzy of picture taking, almost standing on one another to get a better shot. Someone from the back of the theater moaned "Oh yeah." There were catcalls and hoots and stamped feet and whistles.

Annie Ample seemed to love it all. Over the next forty-five minutes she demonstrated no discernible erotic talents other than an engaging good-naturedness. She danced a little, and changed costumes on stage three times, disrobing with an artistic clumsiness that was endearing. She lay down on her belly on stage and arched her back and crossed her legs at the ankles so that she looked like a teenager. She bit into a juicy red apple and spat a peel toward the Japanese, who scrambled for the soggy thing; she lip-synched three songs; in one of them she complained about not finding a man *big* enough to fill her needs, and, of course, someone in the audience shouted "Try me" and without missing a beat Annie Ample shot back that she was looking for a *man;* she asked for a volunteer from the audience and did a skit about bull flighting with this clown holding a red cape and a chair and looking dopey; afterward she gave him a kiss on the mouth and his friends began shrieking and slapping their thighs and yelling "way to go, Errol"; she strutted and pouted and pranced and danced and chatted and sang and kept up a line of low-key funny patter and showed her breasts and flashed her rear and when the show was over the audience was happy and relaxed and in a forgiving mood.

Me too.

I had a cigarette in the lounge—my tenth of the evening— while I waited for the mob to clear from the Naughty Paree hallway. Annie Ample was still posing with the Japanese when I got there; she would ask each of the men to stand so that her breasts were resting on top of his head while the rest of the group snapped away enthusiastically. She seemed to enjoy it as much as they did. When everyone had had a chance to stand in the rainshadow of her chest, she sang out: *"Sayonara* boys, go shoo now," and retreated to her dressing room.

I waited for a moment and then knocked once and slipped into the room quickly without being asked to come in.

Annie Ample was lying on the brown imitation leather couch. Her feet were resting on the back cushions and were elevated above her head.

"Hi," she said.

I said hi and she said hi again and we both laughed.

"Sit," she said, pointing to a straightbacked chair with her left hand. She let her hand droop down to the floor as soon as she

74

finished pointing. I sat down. I said I loved the show. She said she was glad. I said I was glad she was glad.

"Chico-Chico suggested I might come and see you."

"That Chico," said Annie Ample without rancor. She might have been talking about a wayward boy. "I don't know what he told you, but I don't do dates, I don't party. I'm sorry, honey, I hope you're not all disappointed."

"Of course I'm disappointed," I said, "what man wouldn't be?"

"You're sweet," she said vacantly. She was still lying with her feet up. "If you knew how my feet hurt."

I got up and walked over to the couch. "Scoot over," I said. Annie Ample slid up toward the head of the couch and I sat on the edge and put her feet in my lap. I began kneading her left foot, first on the ball and then on the heel.

"That feels *so* good," she said.

I took the picture of Brown Angel from my pocket and passed it over to her.

"While you're feeling good, tell me about her."

Annie Ample let out a sigh and took the picture. Then she let it fall to the floor beside her head.

"It's Angelita."

"Friend of yours?"

"Not really. We used to work together in L.A. It was long ago, maybe ten years. There were three of us, Angelita, me, and a blonde, someone named Carmen."

"What kind of work?"

"Double dates. Parties. Receptions. I was always somebody's gift or their surprise. Sometimes they flew us to Vegas, sometimes to Houston. Angelita was kind of a specialist."

I looked at Annie Ample quizzically.

"She did B and D, cross-dressing, training."

I said that I understood.

"It all seemed like fun then. There was the money. And the drugs. No one knew about AIDS. Can you believe it? We thought the worst thing that could happen was you'd get crabs."

"You don't have to explain it to me."

"I'm not. It's a story. Sometimes I tell it."

"What happened?"

"You get used up fast. I got out. After I left L.A. I spent six months in a commune for women. They were nice. Almost everyone but me had a baby and we all took turns cleaning and cooking and we were all good to each other."

I dropped Annie Ample's left foot into my lap and picked up her right foot and began massaging.

"This better?" I meant Chico-Chico and the Japanese.

Annie Ample lifted her head up slightly so she could look me in the eye.

"It's a living," she said calmly and without bitterness. "You doing something that makes you feel like Mother Teresa you look in the mirror each morning?"

"No," I said.

I sat rubbing her feet for a few moments more.

"There's nothing wrong with what I do."

"I didn't say there was."

"No, but you meant it. I can tell."

"I'm sorry," I said.

"I make people happy. So what if it's not brain surgery?"

"What about Angelita? Did she get out too?"

Annie Ample positioned her neck on the cushion so that she was looking up at the ceiling.

"I don't know," she said, "we sort of lost contact. Is she in trouble? Is that why you're asking all these questions?"

"Not that I know of," I said.

"Gee," said Annie Ample childishly, looking again at the photograph she had picked up from the floor, "she's so young in this picture."

"Any idea where she is now?"

"She's around. Somewhere in the Bay Area. I don't know where."

"What about you?"

"What about me?"

A silence formed in the room. Annie Ample lifted her head so that she was looking at me again. Her eyes were filled with tears.

"Sometimes it seems like everything is long ago. Doesn't it seem that way?"

I said that it certainly did seem that way.

Commercial Light

When I awoke the next morning, I lay in bed and watched the hard yellow sunlight move across the concrete wall facing my bedroom window. It was five o'clock. I had never seen sunshine like that when I first came to California. The stuff was everywhere, spilling over the water and lighting up the hills. Now all that was left of it was on that concrete wall. I liked to look at it in the early morning.

After a while, I got up and rumbled into the living room. The copper ashtray on my desk was full. I rumbled back into the bathroom and dropped the stubs into the toilet, where they began to decompose, spreading an alien yellow stain over the unruffled water of the bowl. I brushed my teeth and flossed them dutifully, the cinnamon-flavored strand swishing between my gold-filled molars. I showered and shampooed my hair and shaved with a new blade said to be revolutionary in its implications. I dried off with a hand towel, and combed and brushed my hair. I dressed myself in a pair of cream-colored gabardine slacks with an elastic waistband and a blue shirt with a spread collar.

No tie. Black Ferragamo loafers. No socks. I had coffee with a lot of sugar for breakfast and a donut dipped in maple syrup—the real kind, from Vermont. There was a picture on the tin of a farmer lugging the stuff up a hill in pails. Attaboy. I cleaned the kitchen, stacking the dishes neatly in the dishwasher and running a rag over the counter top, and made the bed. I sat at my desk in the living room, my feet up, and smoked a cigarette. I looked out over the bay, cold in the cool light.

I didn't have a thought in my head.

I worked once for a law firm with an old-fashioned reputation for probity. The partners wore starched white shirts and dark blue suits; when they left their office on Sutter they wore homburgs. One partner named Hexaflim carried a walking stick with an ivory bulb at its head. He had acquired a considerable reputation by beating someone into a stupor with the thing. One day he took me aside and with a roguish twinkle in his rheumy eye said: "Sonny, if you don't know what in hell you're doing, call up the client. Say anything."

I called Lauren Ellerbee in Atherton. "She no in," said Conchita the maid. "You wanna talk weeth Mr. Bobo?"

I said that would be a fine.

Conchita said: "He no in too."

I diddled and doodled a little on the blotter on my desk; I got up and stood by the living-room window with my hands in my pockets and looked out at the bay some more. You can't beat a view of water for wasting time. There were wisps of fog by Angel Island; the hills beyond were gold and brown. An enormous container ship with a black hull was moving sedately toward the Golden Gate. I could just make out the red lettering on its bow. It said TOKAGAWA. The ship was bound for Tokyo. I've never seen a ship under sail without wishing I were on it.

I called LRB from my desk. The line rang a dozen times or so and then someone answered the telephone saying *Hey-lo*.

"Marvin Finklestein. Is he in?" I tried to sound pretty peremptory.

"I'm just covering the phones," said Hey-lo. "I think I saw him somewhere."

That was good enough. I said I'd call back. Instead I got up and tootled down the freeway to Redwood City.

I got off 101 just where Marsh Road crosses the freeway and heads off toward the bay. LRB occupied a suite of offices in an office park named The Highlands. The place was built on bay-fill and still smelled vaguely of wet refuse. A billboard at the end of Marsh Road had a picture of a woman holding a cigarette holder in the air and a man in a top hat; the legend said that The Highlands was a Byword for Elegance. The parking lot faced the bay, which looked low and oily in the hazy light. There were a lot of redwood buildings scattered around. You had to hike from building to building to find the one you wanted.

I finally found a map of the whole place on a redwood post in one of the buildings. LRB was in Building K. I was in Building A. I walked around in the sun for a while until I flagged down a mailtruck and asked the driver for directions. He pointed me back toward the bay. "First building off the drive," he said.

There was an open courtyard on the ground floor of Building K. No directory. No map. Offices on each of the four sides of the courtyard.

I knock-walked into the office of someone named Dr. Heavi-sides; the doctor limited his practice to endodontics and took patients only by referral. I could smell the sinister smell of novo-caine and alcohol and rubber. The receptionist was a stern-looking woman with a bleached moustache. A miniature poodle kept her company in a red basket by her feet.

I said: "I'm looking for LRB. It's a suite of offices?"

She looked at me as if I were asking directions to Tashkent. "LRB, LRB," she said in a singsong voice. It all seemed very baffling and tricky to her.

From the rear of the suite, someone shouted: "Second floor, over your right."

The receptionist brightened up. "Did you get that now?" she said. "Second floor, over to your right."

Get it. Getting it. Got it.

LRB was tucked into an alcove on the second floor. The reception area inside had beige carpets. There were pictures of Switzerland on one wall—the Eiger, looking big, dumb and bleak, some cows on a mountain slope, a bearded nincompoop honking into a flugelhorn—and an enormous reproduction of Manet's "Water Lilies" on the other. Muzak was piped into the room through the ceiling.

There was no one at the desk; and no one else in the waiting area.

I walked through the main doors and down a hallway which let out to a series of partitions. The Musak followed me. Someone was playing "Midnight in Moscow" on a muted trombone. It didn't make me think of midnight and it didn't make me think of Moscow. The hallway ended at a pair of heavy steel double doors, which hissed pneumatically when I pushed them open.

There was a large workroom past the doors. No beige carpets. The floor was concrete. No Musak. No fancy pictures, either. The walls were cinderblock and covered with glossy pictures of naked women from *Playboy* and *Penthouse*. Whoever put up the pictures seemed to prefer women on all fours. They stared out from the walls like Airedales. A length of plywood shelving ran along the one wall. It held computer monitors and consoles. The shelving was wide enough to double as a workbench. The place was chilly and depressing.

Marvin Finklestein was sitting on an accountant's backless three-legged stool, his elbows resting on the plywood shelving. He was staring at a monitor.

I said: "Hoody doody," and sat myself on the stool next to his.

He said: "Hi," without turning to face me.

Neither of us said anything else; he kept staring at the console in front of him.

I finally said: "Lauren said I should come by."

Finklestein nodded vigorously, tried to say something, choked, and made a gulping noise. He had the kind of face that will start to look attractive when other men's faces have begun to fall apart. He didn't know yet that he was lucky. He wouldn't have cared.

"I'd like to know a little more about the product," I said.

Finklestein nodded again. His hands had begun to move indifferently over the surface of his workbench.

He leaned over and turned on the worn gray monitor that was standing next to the one he was using. There was a smudged keyboard by the monitor and a joy stick. The monitor glowed for a moment and then came to fluorescent life. The screen was split by three lines. One of them seemed to recede backward to infinity. There was a small arrow on the screen.

"Try it out," Finklestein said. He pushed the joy stick over to me.

I rotated the plastic ball at the top of the stick. The arrow not only moved up and down and from side to side, but when I pressed the ball forward it seemed to follow the third line on the screen toward infinity. It gave you the impression of having found a kind of sly secret, a doorway to the Back of Beyond.

"Wonderful," I said.

Marvin Finklestein kept looking at the wall. He said: "Thanks." It was an effort for him.

"Do it all by yourself?"

Finklestein nodded his head slowly.

I thought he was pleased, but it was not all that easy to tell.

"Sounds like a lot of work," I said.

Finklestein nodded his head again. "Lot of work," he said.

"That what you do, programming?"

Finklestein nodded his head for the third time. He wasn't about to spoil the effect by saying anything.

The pneumatic double doors behind me opened with a seeping sound and someone said: "Hullo, Marvin."

It was J. Madford Wunderman's unmistakable voice. Finkle-stein gurgled something. I turned on my stool.

Wunderman looked at me with an expression that caused his already stiff eyebrows to waggle upward.

"You're what's-his-face," he said.

"What's-his-face," I said. "Exactly."

"Asherfeld. What are you doing here?" he said gruffly.

"What does it look like I'm doing, Jack?" I said. "I'm sitting here stealing trade secrets from Marvin Finklestein."

"That's not even funny," said Wunderman. "Everything in this room is proprietary and confidential."

"You're right," I said. "I'm going to make a special effort to forget every one of those fifty thousand lines of code I just memorized."

Marvin Finklestein gurgled again and smiled an especially goofy smile. He had irregular green teeth. Smiling was not in his best interest.

Wunderman said: "Come on, Asherfeld, I'll walk you out."

I said good-bye to Marvin Finklestein, and J. Madford Wund-erman escorted me past the long row of doggish women on all fours and toward the double doors.

Once we were back in the suite of offices I said: "You keep the boy on kind of a tight chain, don't you?"

Wunderman sighed heavily and shuffled his shoulders to straighten out his shirt underneath his jacket.

"I've got to," he said.

I said: "No telling what he'd say if you weren't there."

Wunderman looked at me soberly with his bushy old eyes.

It was still midnight in Moscow.

The freeway was absolutely empty. I accelerated into the left lane, eased myself in my seat, and turned on the radio. On KYWN, Ron or Jon or Don was listening gravely to a caller arguing that Cuba was a paradise on earth, better certainly than America, I mean with the homeless and all. On KPFA, someone was talking about a caring space called "Womaneat." "Eating compulsively is *not* about uncontrolled gluttony," said the disembodied fatty. She was addressing herself to the program's host, someone called Mama. She said: "Mama, eating compulsively is an expression of distress deeply rooted in our bodies." Mama said: "I see, I see, I understand," in a darkened, scratchy voice.

I got off the freeway at Broadway and drove through the quiet leafy streets with my window down. I parked on El Camino Real and walked back to the Municipal Building on Cifuentes. The thing is still an imposing structure. It takes up a block. It was designed in the 1930s by WPA architects under the impression that they were building a battleship. Except for the fact that someone had spray-painted *Eltan 47* in red over and over on the creamy sandstone, it has retained a grave majestic air.

I hustled up the steps and through the revolving doors.

I like buildings like this. I like the cool way they feel after the high steady glare of the sun on El Camino Real. I like the tremendous Rafael Sawyer murals in the lobby, with laborers in goofy red overalls staring intently into the future over a field of ripening wheat. I even like the white stainless drinking fountains, which never pump the water up more than half an inch.

I wanted to check the zoning codes. I asked the inevitable old party sitting on a marble bench for directions. "Hall of Records? Second floor, up the staircase, sonny, to your right and right again."

No one had called me "sonny" in years.

The part of the Hall of Records that was open to the public was actually a large reading room. There were legal books and documents on the open stacks against the walls, and a long rectangular desk in the middle of the room, which smelled everywhere of worn binding and paper.

I got down a copy of the City Code and took it over to the table and looked up Z, zoning, see under, Civil Code, rules, regulations of, zoning.

It was all pretty straightforward. Residential meant residential. Industrial meant industrial. But commercial light was trickier. There was a list: Bakeries were welcome in Redwood City just so long as gas-fired ovens were in use only between the hours of six in the morning and midnight (Nocturnal bakers beware); upscale restaurants were fine by the City fathers, ditto catering services, gourmet speciality shops (except those selling sausages or meat products from Hungary, Poland or Romania), meat markets, but not slaughterhouses or dressing plants; you could comb women's hair in any building zoned commercial light, or shave their legs and thighs; but no abortions, please, or podiatric surgery; sell leather goods anywhere you want, but don't dye them or dry them; body shops, hey, welcome guys to paradise, but not if you plan on *painting* that 1957 Oldsmobile; you could make furniture but not press steel or run a sawmill; sell bacon if you wish but piggeries are out and so were chicken processing, chicken plucking, and dairy management.

What about computers? You could *sell* computers, computer products, computer services, computer software, computer chips, computer printers, printer inks and printer drums in Redwood City, but manufacturing, assembling, repairing, adjusting, or fabricating computers, computer disk drives, computer components, floppy disks, computer storage devices or the like was *streng verboten.*

Unless, of course, you had a variance.

I took the book over to the Xerox machine and for a quarter made a copy of the code.

Next, I wanted to see LRB's original lease application. I checked the map above the Xerox machine. Applications and Permits? Downstairs.

I walked down the wide marble staircase. Applications and permits was in the back of the building, down a hall filled with heavy structural scaffolding that had been put up after the earthquake.

The clerk behind the counter was scratching her scalp with the eraser of a pencil. I told her what I needed.

84

"You the attorney of record?" she asked indifferently.

I said yup.

She disappeared into the closed stacks behind her counter and re-emerged a minute later. "Can't leave the desk," she said, as she handed me the lease application.

LRB had filed to lease under commercial light zoning; under Request for Variance, someone had checked *yes*.

"I've got a question," I said.

"Doesn't everyone?" said the clerk.

"Generally speaking, how long do I have to file a zoning variance?" I tapped the application; I was hoping to suggest an attorney troubled by an obvious oversight.

"Generally speaking, ninety days," she said. "Is that all or would you like to take up the rest of my lunch hour?"

The attorney of record listed on the lease application was Seybold Knesterman. I knew him. He was pompous and well-connected. I called him from the payphone that was next to the men's bathroom. I could hear the toilets flush as I dialed the number. Knesterman answered the telephone himself.

"This is Seybold Knesterman," he said. He made it sound very wonderful.

"Knesterman," I said, "I'm surprised you don't have a trumpet fanfare when you announce your name."

There was a long dead silence: "This is Aaron Asherfeld. I argued against you in District," I said.

"I know who you are," said Knesterman frigidly.

"I see here that you were attorney of record for LRB when they filed for lease in Redwood City."

"How disappointing. This isn't a social call," said Knesterman. "I can't hang up on you right away."

"You go right ahead and hang up, Knesterman," I said. "I'll just ask LRB whether they got timely notification from you."

"Meaning what?"

"Meaning this. LRB leased a property zoned commercial light. They needed a variance to go into production."

"I know that," said Knesterman.

"Last time I looked, filing a variance be the sort of thing an attorney might handle. I could be wrong, Knesterman. You might have told the shoeshine boy to take care of it. You know the one I'm talking about. Old guy, sort of shuffles into your office in the morning, snaps his rag, says 'Shine'im up, sir?' "

"Look, Asherfeld," Knesterman went on. "I don't even know why I'm bothering to explain all this to you. This firm *did* take care of this business with the variance. LRB leased in good faith. The city attorney reviewed the business plan. He filed a Letter of Intent to grant a variance with the Board of Supervisors. As you perfectly well know, the filing itself is automatic. It's something that the secretaries at LRB took care of. Now that's not too difficult for you to handle, that bit of legal prestidigitation."

"No," I said, "it's not too difficult at all. Which is the only reason anyone entrusted you to do the job. One thing."

"Yes, what is it?"

"No one actually filed for the variance."

There was a long pause during which I could hear Knesterman snuffling quietly into the telephone.

"Are you sure?" he finally said.

"I'm sure." I hung up the telephone just as Knesterman was beginning another round of perplexed snuffles.

It wasn't a very dignified exchange.

Racist Remarks

I drove home as the yellow light was fading from the freeway; when I got into the city I could see it was going to be one of those evenings when everything would seem dark and glowing and mysterious and filled with promises. We get those evenings sometimes in San Francisco and then any place seems better than home.

I parked in front of my house and walked through North Beach and over to Nob Hill. The streets were crowded with good-looking young people; everyone was in a hurry to meet someone before the deep purple went out of the sky.

I had no one to meet and nothing to do. I thought I'd get a drink in the lobby of the Stanford Court. It's a great lobby to sit in; the place is snobbish and expensive and well-run. Every few minutes, a bellboy in a red uniform comes by and empties the heavy sand-filled ashtrays standing by each table. Then he rakes the sand with a tiny wooden rake as if it were a Japanese rock garden. I sat in one of those old-fashioned green leather chairs they have in the lobby, the kind with brass grommets holding down the leather, stretched out my legs, and smoked a cigarette. I once knew a maid who worked there; she was from the Dominican Republic. She said to me: "You wanna know whad I think of those peeple?" She made a vigorous face. "I speet on thaim." She had never acquired an appreciation for wealth.

I thought of her as I watched a rock group endeavoring to register. There were five young men in tank tops lined up at the desk, and a sullen, none-too-clean-looking blonde. She was acting as their interpreter.

"The artists are very tired," she kept repeating to the man

behind the desk; he was dressed in a creamy gray and black cutaway; I could see that he was perspiring.

"I understand that, madam," he said with a passive upward shrug of his shoulders, "but your reservations aren't until the twenty-fourth."

"Piss on the reservations," said the blonde loudly. "Are we going to get some freakin' service or do I call the manager."

"Madam," said the manager sadly, "I *am* the manager."

I smoked another cigarette and when I wasn't smoking, I ate the mixed nuts on the table, one after the other. I admired the way that someone had managed to fill the bowl chiefly with big nuts. That gave a nice illusion of nut largesse. I wondered whether someone in the back spent a lot of time sorting through huge bags of nuts. It must have been a tough job to fill. They probably needed an attorney to fill it.

After eating almost the whole bowl, I got up and left the lobby and started to walk back home through the darkening streets. I never did get a drink. I felt pretty good anyway. The sky above me had pink-tipped clouds and had held its deep purple color. My mouth tasted pleasantly of peanuts and I wasn't thirsty yet. At the top of Nob Hill I stopped in the little park behind the cathedral and sat down on one of the green wooden benches. There were a couple of pigeons marching solemnly on the walkway; every now and then one would peck at something on the ground. Out over the bay the foghorns had already started to sound, but there was not much wind and I could still feel the last warmth of the day come rising out of the pavement.

A pretty young girl in an oversized turtleneck and baggy jeans walked down the park path and then stopped by the concrete wall below the grass, leaning with one lush hip braced against the pitted ledge. She had a head of very full shaggy brunette hair. She looked like the kind of girl who shampooed a lot and liked to leave the shower door open when she did it. She looked like the kind of girl who would spread that hair out over a pillow and say things like: "Is this what you wanted, lover?" She had on very

88

dark red lipstick that made her large mouth look indistinct, smudged and fuzzy.

She consulted the oversized watch on her thin wrist ostentatiously and crossed her arms and then pressed her chin into her chest to brush something from her sweater and then uncrossed her arms and lifted up her chin, her eyes closed. It was too chilly to sunbathe and there was no sun left in the sky but she didn't seem to mind at all. She just liked to show the universe her face.

I sauntered down one slope of Nob Hill, past a couple of restaurants that called tuna fish *ahi*, and down the flank of Russian Hill, and over to Grant and up Greenwich.

There was a SFPD squad car parked in front of my house. One of the policemen had gotten out of the car and was looking at the building with the air of a man confronting a very great mystery.

"Looking for someone, officer?" I said.

"Move along, buddy," he said, "police business."

The cop's name was Tszienck.

"Okeydokey," I said and jogged up the stairs to the front door.

"Hey, wait a minute," said Tszienck, "you live here?"

"Me? No way," I said. "I'm just sort of trying the front doors in the neighborhood, see if I can boost a few tea sets before dinner."

Tszienck narrowed his little eyes; he knew a wise guy when he met one.

"You wanna show me some identification?" he said. "Something maybe with your picture on it?"

"No," I said.

Tszienck shifted his stubby torso so that he was better balanced on the balls of his feet. He raised his hands up to his webbed belt and hunched his shoulders. He looked as menacing as a turtle and about as bright.

His partner got out of the squad car and hitched up *his* webbed belt and sauntered over to us. He was a Vietnamese named Nyguen. He had a row of police department commendations arrayed next to his name tag. He was little but he looked fit and tough. He nodded at me.

"You have identification, sir?" he said.

I said: "Yup," and turned away from the two cops and started to open the front door.

Tszienck said: "Step back from that door. Put your hands in the air."

I still had my keys in my hand, but I put my hands in the air without putting my keys back in my pocket.

"You're a credit to your race," I said, still facing the door.

"That's a racist remark," said Tszienck.

"Couldn't be," I said, "you're not black."

"You hear that? You hear what he said?"

The little Vietnamese said: "Mike, you letting him get to you."

"I take it back," I said, "you're not a credit to your race. Can I put my hands down now?"

Nyguen climbed up the steps. "You plenty big lip. Put you two hands against wall," he said, "spread legs wide."

I did what I was told to do. Nyguen patted me down and threw my wallet to Tszienck. Then he said: "Hands behind back," and cuffed me.

I turned around and watched Tszienck pawing through my wallet. "Hey," he said, "you're Asherfeld."

"Some people'll believe anything they read," I said.

"Could have saved us a lot of trouble you show us this when we ask for it." He held the wallet in the air as an object lesson.

"That's assuming I'm interested in saving the police any trouble at all."

"Mister," said Tszienck regretfully, "you got one heavy attitude."

"Show me a good reason for the hassle and I might change my attitude."

Tszienck walked back to the squad car and reached for his clipboard on the front seat. "Got a bench warrant here for your arrest," he said, but the meanness had gone from his voice.

"A bench warrant?" I said, "you're pulling in citizens on a bench warrant? What is it? I forget to pay a parking ticket in Daly City in 1982?"

"It's legal," said Tszienck, but I didn't think his heart was in it.

"Mind if I read it?" I asked.

"Hell no," said Tszienck. He walked up the steps still holding the clipboard and held it out for me. It was a bench warrant all right; it was signed by Judge Henry Wachtler of the Magistrate's Court of San Francisco.

I said: "All right," in a tired sort of way. Nyguen said: "Maybe we take cuffs off, you be good boy, oakay?" He had a real command of idiomatic English. I said fine whatever and Nyguen slipped behind me and took the cuffs off.

Tszienck pointed to the rear of the squad car and said, "Inna back."

I got in and sat down heavily on the cloth seat with its scuffed leatherette head rest. The back of the car smelled of vomit and alcohol.

We got to the station house on Potrero Hill, and Tszienck and Nyguen escorted me up the smooth marble steps, but instead of processing me at the front desk they hustled me up a flight of metal steps behind the front desk and over to the office of a Captain named Oberfleisher.

Tszienck knocked tentatively on the glass panel of the office door; someone inside said: "Yes, what is it" in a pleasant unhurried tone of voice.

"Got the man you wanted to see, Captain," said Tszienck deferentially.

I could see a shadow advancing toward the glass. The door swung open.

Oberfleisher looked as if he had been made of three soccer balls stacked on top of each other. He wore his blue shirt cuffed back at the wrists. He had thinning sandy hair and wore gold spectacles.

91

"Thanks, boys," he said to Tszienck and Nyguen. "How you doin'," he said to me, sticking out his hand. Even his hands were round.

"Tip top," I said, "couldn't be better."

"Glad to hear it," said Oberfleisher, "come in the office."

He waited for me to walk in and then closed the door behind himself and walked over to his steel desk.

"Go on," he said, "sit down. Make yourself comfortable. Hope you're not burned about coming down here. Have to get your statement. Take a couple of hours, you be home for the news at seven."

"What statement?" I asked.

Oberfleisher looked confused for a moment. He consulted the pile of notes on his desk and began glancing through them. He finally found what he was looking for.

"Statement explaining how come you're in Oakland during the commission of a crime."

"I already gave that one to the Oakland police."

"That a fact?" said Oberfleisher.

"That's a fact," I said.

"Reason I sound so skeptical," said Oberfleisher not sounding skeptical at all, "is that it looks to someone like some of what you told the Oakland police is maybe not so true and some of what is true you didn't tell the Oakland police."

"So?"

"So?"

"That's what I said. So?"

"Mister," said Oberfleisher without rancor, "didn't anyone ever tell you that lying to the police is a crime?"

"Sure they did. They just never made me believe it."

"I'll make a believer out of you," said Oberfleisher.

"You could probably make me believe that black is white. It wouldn't make it true."

Oberfleisher rested his forehead in his palms and said: "Why does these things always happen to me?"

92

"You don't floss," I said. "It's all that tartar."

"You're right," said Oberfleisher.

"Tell you what," I said. "Let's make a deal."

"I'm all ears," said Oberfleisher morosely. "What do you have."

"You tell me who asked for the bench warrant and let me call them."

"What's in it for us," said Oberfleisher.

"I don't call *The Chronicle*. I don't sue for false arrest. I don't go on the ten o'clock news and say that someone named Oberfleisher worked me over because I support gay rights. Is that a deal or what?"

Oberfleisher sighed deeply. "My mother always said I should go to law school. 'Be a policemen, be a schnook,' she said. Did I listen?"

"You're better off," I said.

"Absolutely," he said. "Lawyer gets to spend his nights in some high rise, go out for lunch to one of these restaurants charges two hundred dollars to open the menu, choke down that French food, afterwards spend a couple of hours getting fitted for a nice custom-tailored suit, maybe he knocks off early and has a thousand-dollar hooker meet him at the St. Francis. No life for a man. I get to sit here, listen to guys like you come in tell me how much they like pissing on the police."

"You're right," I said, "you should have listened to your mother."

Oberfleisher sighed again, a kind of world-weary, thin flute sigh. "Near as I can figure out," he said, "someone named Deukmajian over in district signed the request."

Imbiss Deukmajian was the deputy assistant district attorney for Alameda County.

I reached for Oberfleisher's telephone and said: "You mind?"

Oberfleisher nodded his head and leaned back in his chair. "Why should I mind?" he said. "If I want to make a call, I can use the pay phone in the hall. Hell, take the desk if you want."

I called Deukmajian at home. His wife Inez seemed to remember me. She told me that the poor dear was still at work. Before she hung up she said: "Give my love to that sweet woman of yours." I said that I would.

I reached Deukmajian at his office without any trouble.

"Where are you, Asher," he said. "I'll get right back to you."

"No rush, Imbiss," I said, "I'm at the Potrero Hill Station. Police brought me in under a bench warrant you signed."

Deukmajian cleared his throat melodramatically. He had a lot to clear and it took him a long time.

Oberfleisher said: "What's he say?"

I cupped my hand over the receiver. "He says to ask you which idiot went and served a bench warrant."

Oberfleisher cupped his head in his hands and said: "Why should I be surprised?"

"Asher, no hard feelings, I hope," said Deukmajian, when he finished up with his throat.

"No feelings at all," I said.

"Good, good, why don't you put your captain on."

I handed the telephone to Oberfleisher who listened and said *uh* a few times and hung up.

"You're free to go," he said, "ROR."

I got up and said thanks.

"Were up to me," said Oberfleisher, "you'd be in the tank."

"That's why it's not up to you," I said. I reached the door and edged out.

Deukmajian told me he'd meet me in front of the station house; but it was evening and traffic was heavy, and an hour slipped by without even breathing heavily. I waited out front at first and then I sat inside on the wooden visitors bench just past the ancient double doors that led into the station house. The police came in two by two, looking tense and tired, and fat and friendless.

Imbiss Deukmajian showed up a little past eight. He came into the station house with a flourish. He moved gracefully. He was thin and very tall: he had a walnut head, with very wiry black hair and an enormous nose, a wide prominent forehead, recessed and hooded eyes. His cheeks were concave and his mouth was reticulated by fine lines.

We shook hands and Deukmajian nodded and smiled his aloof tall-man smile.

"Come with me, Asherfeld, we'll have a drink at the Shamrock."

The Shamrock was an Irish bar at the foot of Potrero Hill. Imbiss Deukmajian wasn't much on asking you where you wanted to go or what you wanted to do.

We walked out into the cool evening air. Deukmajian didn't rate a limousine, but he had a driver and a car. He told his driver to park the car in the departmental lot. "Get me at eight-thirty," he said. He didn't have a leisurely evening in mind.

The Shamrock had green walls and green table cloths; it was run by an Irish family of almost legendary taciturnity. Every other tavern in the neighborhood had long since become an upscale bistro, brasserie, or trattoria. Not the Shamrock. They still served beer by the sweating pitcher and catered to the police coming off duty from the Potrero Hill station. Whenever the IRA launched an especially revolting action in northern Ireland, drinks were on the house. The owner of the tavern, a pasty-faced evil-looking man with small dark eyes, would wander the floor, making sure everyone was drinking to the lads. A miniature English flag had somehow been fastened above the toilet paper in the men's bathroom. It was considered fashionable on Potrero Hill to declare your affection for the Shamrock.

When we were seated, the waitress placed a pitcher of beer on the table, and a platter of heavily salted peanuts. She appeared offended when Deukmajian waved it away. He ordered a tomato juice with a twist of lime. The waitress regarded him with amusement. "Twist of lime?" she said. "You want a doily, too?" Deukmajian smiled that weak smile people smile when they're slumming and found out. I told the waitress that hey I'd have whatever the big guy was having.

Imbiss turned to me and said he had heard things hadn't worked out. He was sorry. It didn't matter.

He looked sharply at me. He was debating whether to launch into a lecture. I beat him to it. "Let's get on with it, Imbiss," I said.

He nodded and swallowed. He had a way of breathing calmly that made everyone around him feel calm as well.

"You know," he said, "I didn't think much of Lawrence Williams."

"How come?"

"Being black doesn't give a man a licence to be rotten."

"You figure LeRoy was rotten?"

"I didn't say that, Asherfeld," he said.

"You didn't have to."

Our drinks arrived, and Deukmajian took his wedge of lime and bit into it; seeing it made my gums ache sympathetically. When he had finished, he began playing with the plastic toothpick that had held the lime to his glass.

I said: "You're going to tell me that whatever LeRoy had rubs off on me. Work for someone dirty, get dirty yourself."

"Those are your words, Asherfeld, not mine."

"They might as well be yours."

"I'm asking only because I got a fax from a man named Dreyfus."

"Very aggressive civil servant," I said.

"So I gathered. He sent me the fax as a courtesy. Is it true that you didn't give the Oakland police any cooperation at all?"

"None whatsoever," I said.

"Don't you believe you owe them that?"

"I did once. I don't anymore."

Deukmajian looked at me disapprovingly. He was the sort of man who considered his rhetorical options in advance.

96

"Is it worth my while to start looking for Roger Ellerbee?" he finally said. "I'm asking this professionally."

"I don't know, Imbiss. The prevailing opinion is that LeRoy was shot in some sort of drug deal."

"That's the prevailing opinion whenever a black man is shot."

"Possibly because it's so often true," I said.

"I don't approve of racist remarks, Asherfeld," said Deukmajian. "I won't tolerate them."

"You're right, Imbiss," I said. "Most black men shot over in East Oakland are probably shot as the result of a dispute over English grammar. No telling what a black man will do when he hears the subjunctive misused."

"Why do you do these things to yourself, Asherfeld?" asked Deukmajian.

"Low self esteem," I said. "I was abused as a child. It's all that denial."

"You're not going to give me anything, are you?"

"I'll give you what I can, not what you want. You want more, you shouldn't have had me arrested."

"You're wrong," said Deukmajian, "the only reason you're even talking to me is that bench warrant."

He was right, of course, and I knew it.

"I've never met Ellerbee, never even spoken to him. Some men, they think a high-powered rifle is a solution to a credit problem. It doesn't sound likely to me, but maybe Ellerbee was that sort of guy."

"I'm sure that's true," said Deukmajian. "On the other hand, there is the matter of that photograph."

"Which one is that?"

"The one showing Ellerbee in the company of a trollopy young woman. I happen to have a copy here."

Deukmajian reached over to the briefcase that he had placed at his feet and withdrew a copy of the same photograph LeRoy had sent me. It was printed on the same heavy dense paper as the one I had.

97

I looked at it briefly. I was surprised to see it.

"Nice knockers," I said.

Imbiss finished up his drink and then chewed some more on his lime.

"You always had standards, Asherfeld," he said, "I'll say that for you. The trouble is they're private. They don't mean anything."

"It just worked out that way," I said.

Deukmajian sighed to indicate that our business was done.

"I'd suggest another drink," he said, "but I have to be over at the Fairmont by nine."

"What for?" I asked to be polite.

"Steering Committee meeting of the ABA," he said.

The ABA was the American Bar Association. He wanted to make sure that I knew where he was going.

Out of the Closet

The next day was zip. No one called and no one bothered me. LeRoy was resting. Roger was busy staying lost. I had dinner that evening at a Chinese restaurant; afterwards I went to a kung fu movie at a theater on Geary. The hero spoke English with a farcical French accent. He regularly dispatched men three times his weight and twice his height. Good-looking women kept toppling blood ripe into his lap. Sinister Asiatic drug lords offered him vast sums of money in tribute. He was about to consummate a carnal relationship with a young woman when she was set on fire by someone evidently indifferent to the kung fu code. I walked out just as the hero indicated, by means of his solemnly twitching blue jaw, that this turn of events was apt to provoke his wrath.

I should have stayed; I might have learned something. I might have saved myself a beating.

There was a strange smell in the hallway before my door when I got home, a disturbing odor; the brass doorknob to my flat was a little warmer than it should have been.

I opened the door, walked into my apartment, and closed the door behind me with my shoulder. Chico-Chico was sitting on the sofa; someone I didn't know and had never seen before was standing by the window. He looked as if he had been carved out of stone.

"You home," said Chico-Chico, "we been waiting." He nodded toward the gargoyle. "This here's Hector. He's an Indian. He don't talk so good. He helps me with my work, you know what I mean?"

Hector gave me a sinister smile showing four gold teeth. He was short and dark and fat.

"Hell of a smile you got there, fellah," I said. "You show those teeth to America's Funniest Home Videos yet?"

Hector grunted.

I took my coat off and loosened my tie.

"You get him off a cathedral ledge, Chico?" I said, pointing with my head toward Hector.

Chico-Chico got up lazily and pulled one of my kitchen chairs from the table in the alcove and put it in the center of the room.

"Sit," he said, "or Hector here he break your back."

"Chico," I said, "you certainly know how to motivate a man."

"You know why I'm here, greaseball?"

"Let me guess," I said, "you and the Gargoyle are coming out of the closet. It's a matter of Gay Pride. You want I should be the first to know. I'm with you, Chico, it's the right thing to do."

Chico took a solid step toward me and slapped me across my

99

left cheek with his right palm. He put plenty of force into the blow. It wasn't intended to do a lot of damage; it just hurt.

"Look," I said, "don't just come out of the closet, make a statement, affirm your sexuality. Let the Gargoyle wear a tutu. Your friends will support you. You'll get a spread in *The Guardian.*"

"What's this closet you're talking about?" said Chico-Chico, baffled.

"If you're not planning to come out of the closet, I respect that too," I said.

Chico-Chico said something in Spanish to the Gargoyle, who looked perplexed and shook his thick shaggy head.

Chico-Chico walked back toward me and without pausing at all slapped my right cheek with his left hand.

I shook my head. "Hey," I said, "it's gone, my headache's gone."

"You know," said Chico-Chico, "I don' know what you talking about but I don' think I like you."

"It's my breath, isn't it? You can tell me, Chico, man to man. I don't know what to do, I mean I've tried everything, mouthwash, Dentyne, Listerine, Scope in the morning, nothing works. I'm thinking of having an air freshener surgically stapled to my tonsils. What do you think, Chico. Should I go for the gusto?"

This time Chico-Chico slapped me twice, with the same leisurely and methodical blows.

"Listen good," he said, "I got a message for you. Stop sniffing around the talent. You come to my place like a dog, you sniffin' so bad. You wanna see the talent you buy a ticket like anyone else. I catch you sniffin' around my talent again, Hector here he's gonna do bad things to you." His face was inches from mine.

"I get it," I said, "you don't want me sniffing around the talent."

"That's right," Chico-Chico said. "Now Hector here's going to give you something make you remember." Chico-Chico nodded to Hector, who smiled grandly, showing all his teeth.

100

"No need, Chico, I have a wonderful memory." I said, "Look, give me a list of numbers, I'll show you."

"Shut up," said Chico-Chico. He walked behind me and grabbed my shoulders and pulled me up; he was terrifically strong and knew how to move. Then Hector balled up a meaty fist and drove it into the soft tissue below my sternum. There is no way to protect yourself against a blow like that and no way to prepare for it. My knees gave way. The acrid ugly taste of bile came into my mouth. Chico-Chico let me drop. I lay there on the floor, gasping for breath; as I lay there he and Hector kicked me a dozen times on my legs and back. They were pretty careful not to do any real damage. The kicks hurt less than the feeling of not being able to get enough air. I felt them from far away. I tried to concentrate on breathing. After a while, I got some air back into my lungs. I pulled my knees up to my chest a little.

"Chico," I said.

"What? What you wanna say?"

"Have you discussed all this with your therapist?"

ABC

I came awake at two in the morning, feeling my ribs ache with each breath. I felt cold and then I felt hot and then I felt cold again. I might have called one of my wives; I might have rolled over and died.

I climbed out of bed, shuffled to the medicine cabinet and swallowed two Percodans and a Tylenol tab with codeine. I was warm and fuzzy and happy within the hour. I could see things

101

clearly. I wanted to tell Chico-Chico that I held no grudges. He had done what he needed to do. I understood that.

When I awoke again, the dawn was gray. My ribs still hurt. So did the back of my legs. I thought of Chico-Chico. I wanted to hammer his ugly Hispanic face into the urine-stained pavement.

I read *The Chronicle* while the cold light filled up the room and then I dressed myself in a pair of tan slacks with an elastic waistband and an old turtleneck sweater.

At a little after eleven, someone rang from downstairs. I shuffled over to the intercom and said: "Whatever it is I don't want it."

From downstairs, Lauren Ellerbee said: "Are you sure?"

I didn't say anything. I wasn't sure.

"Can I come up?" she said. "Please."

I finally said: "Come on up." I opened the door and stood with my head leaning against the door frame. The wood felt cool on my temples.

Lauren Ellerbee was wearing a lilac jacket over a pale pink silk blouse and a pink skirt; she came up the stairs like a wave, her perfume filling the hall. She stopped at the head of the stairs and looked at me.

"My God, what happened to you?"

"I was jumped by a group of militant gays."

"You're going right to bed." She took my forearm in hand and propelled me backward toward the bedroom. I flopped onto the bed. Nausea came over me.

Lauren Ellerbee tugged at the covers; she wanted to get me under them. I wanted to get under them myself, but I couldn't move. "Can you scoot over?" she asked. I moaned dramatically. "I'll get the comforter," she said.

I could hear her heels receding from the bedroom on the hardwood floor and then coming back again. She was all waves that morning, coming in and going out. She placed the coverlet over my legs and then she fluffed up the pillows underneath my head. She ran a cool calm finger over the skin underneath my eyes.

"You've been in a fight," she said.

"There were six of them," I said. "They jumped me when I did my Judy Garland imitation."

"Asher, must you always be so cynical, so empty?" She sat down beside me on the bed, touched my forehead with the back of her hand to see if I had a fever; then she stroked my hair backwards.

I looked directly into her wide blue eyes. I don't know what I was hoping to see there. Looking into her eyes was like looking at the ocean floor.

"I can be very positive," I said. "For example, I like the way you walk up a flight of stairs."

Lauren Ellerbee placed a finger over her lips.

"Hush," she said.

"What are you doing here?"

"Taking care of you," she said. "You seem to need a lot of taking care of."

"Do I?"

Lauren Ellerbee gave me a look intended to suggest fond contempt—eyebrows slightly arched, lips pursed, cheeks flushed.

"I like you," she said. "I don't want you to be hurt."

"There's nothing you can do about it," I said.

Neither of us said anything. Then she said: "Why is it so hard for you to be happy?"

"It's hard for everyone," I said.

"I know," she said, looking away, biting her own lip gently. She let her hand drop over mine. Then she said: "I think he's run away."

"Roger?"

Lauren Ellerbee nodded and turned to look out my bedroom window.

"Run away from me, from everything. I don't know."

She looked at the print that was hanging on my bedroom wall;

103

it was a copy of van Gogh's sunflowers, the one in all the bookstores.

"Can you sleep?" she asked.

"Probably not."

"Could you fall asleep if I lay beside you? Would you let me hold you and not do anything or say anything or want anything? Could we just be happy for a little while?"

I rolled over on my side. Lauren Ellerbee lay on the bed beside me and put her arms around my chest and rested her head sideways against my shoulder. I fell into a dark, dreamless sleep and when I awoke she was gone.

It was cool and gray when I got up and cool and gray when I sat sipping coffee and cool and gray again when I opened the front door and looked down Greenwich Street and saw what I usually see when I look down Greenwich Street. I had no idea really of what I was looking for, but I was pretty sure I'd know it if I found it. It's amazing how much time you can waste under the influence of this philosophy. I bought a paper at the Korean's by the corner and read it over a second cup of coffee and a cigarette at the Café Maudit. The second lead was entitled "The Myth of Homosexual AIDS."

I dawdled for a while, waiting for the sun to strike through the low-lying clouds; when after a half hour the damn thing just kept to itself I paid my bill and got into the cab that had been sitting parked in the bus zone, its driver, swarthy and no-necked, busy with a book of crossword puzzles.

"Where to?" he said mechanically, putting the book beside him on the seat.

"Market and Fifth," I said.

The taxi swung off smoothly from the curb.

"Say," said No Neck, "what's a seven-letter word beginning with 'a' means lawyer?"

I thought of 'advocate' and 'attorney' but they had eight letters.

"Asshole," said the driver in a burst of chuckles. "Asshole. You get it? It's pretty good." He looked in his rearview mirror to see if I was smiling. "You an attorney? If you are, no offense," he said. "See the way I figure it the lawyers are getting a bum rap all these jokes and such."

"The lawyers and the taxi drivers," I said.

"Hey yeah?" said No Neck. "What are they saying about the drivers?"

"Same thing they're saying about the attorneys," I said. "Only the guys saying it are generally making twenty times what the drivers are making and don't suffer a lot from hemorrhoids."

"Yeah, well go figure," said the driver philosophically.

Go figure.

I got out on the corner of Fifth and Market and sauntered slowly toward the Palace. I had on my dark glasses. Absolutely the last people I wanted to meet socially on the street were Chico-Chico and the Gargoyle. I knew it was too early for either of them to be around; still, there was no sense in taking the chance of having them decide that a little more work needed to be done on my aching ribs.

At the theater itself I stopped to look over the coming attractions. Lotta Top was in town. She certainly did have a lot on top. I thought for a moment of a picture of a Saurosaurus that I had seen in *Newsweek*. It depicted a creature as large as the Empire State Building. Its brain was no larger than a walnut. The activating principle seems to have slithered up the evolutionary tree.

The box office wasn't open yet, which was fine with me. Someone was sleeping sitting upright against the rear wall of the theater's lobby. He had covered himself with a pile of old newspapers. I could smell him from where I was standing. He came to snorting life abruptly and seeing me began to shamble to his feet.

"Don't move, fellah," I said, "and it's worth a buck."

"Hey, what, yeah?" he said, and sank back down.

I looked over the marquee pretty closely and then I looked over the ticket price information that was pasted to the glass front of the wooden ticket booth. Every theater in California is required to have a statement of corporate ownership somewhere. I found what I was looking for pasted to the bottom of the glass. It was the bottom half of a ripped legal form. It said that the Palace Theater at 545 Market was a wholly owned subsidiary of the ABC Corporation.

I was about to go when Shambles reminded me of his existence by rustling his newspapers about ostentatiously. I dug into my pocket to see if I had any change. No good. You never have what you need. The ride down from Telegraph Hill had cost me five and I only had another five and two tens in my wallet. I took out the five, creased it sharply, and then folded back wings to make a plane.

"Yo," I said, and sailed the five toward the pile in the corner. He watched it land a foot or so from where he was sitting and then skid almost to his hand. He picked it up but did not open the note.

"That's a five, pal," I said.

"Well, sure," he said with vast dignity, still without looking at the bill, "I knew you was good for at least a five."

I walked down Market and then over to the cable car turnaround at the foot of Mason. There were the usual assortment of louts and deadbeats standing around, punching each other on the shoulder, smoking grass, drinking wine from paper bags. They all had long dirty blonde hair and wore earrings on their ear lobes. Someone had set a ghetto blaster against the retaining wall of the Bart station. It was doing what blasters do, blasting everyone within half a mile.

A little further up the street, just at the point where the music from the blaster faded, another unwashed teenager was endeavoring to hustle a few bucks by playing the guitar and singing. Actually, the boy was playing both the guitar and the harmonica, which he had fastened around his neck by a metal collar. He would strum his guitar gracelessly and stomp his feet and honk into the harmonica; then he would pull his head back and sing in that squealing way made popular by Bob Dylan. He was singing about the times they were a-changing. They couldn't change fast enough for me. Or for him, by the looks of it. He had a hat on the ground in front of him. It was empty.

A block further I heard a cable car come rumbling up behind me and caught it on the run. The gripman saw me hop on board and gave me a sideways glance but didn't say anything. I rode the cable car to the top of Nob Hill, hopped off, and walked home.

I didn't know anything about the ABC Corporation, but I knew that an attorney named Shmul Wasserstrom represented many of the slumlords in the city; he handled fictitious properties and set up dummy corporations and generally did legal work no one else would touch.

I called him up at his office and left a message on his machine.

"Shmul," I said in a familiar voice, "listen up. A certain very well-connected Japanese person has a group lined up wants to buy one of your properties, turn it into a spa, something like that. I'm taking top dollar but I'm talking now. Call me."

I left my number but didn't leave my name. An hour or so later the telephone rang.

"So who'm I talking to?" said someone even before saying hello.

"You're talking to me, Shmul," I said. "You dialed my number, remember."

"Whose the me I'm talking to?"

"You want to play twenty questions," I said, "or talk business?"

"How come you know who I am and I don't know who you are?"

"I'm smarter," I said.

"You're so smart, you don't need me."

107

I let this linger for a moment and then I said: "You're right. I'll tell my people talking with you was a mistake."

"Wait a minute, wait a minute," said Shmul, "don't be in such a hurry. You're talking about which property?"

"Theater on Market," I said.

"You have someone wants to pay top dollar for that place?

"Japanese group," I said. "They figure they'll go in, do a total restoration, soft lights, new furniture, steam baths, the works. Main thing, though, they have money's looking for a good home."

"You're talking Five-forty-five Market, am I hearing right?"

"That's what I said, Shmul."

"They know it's not up to code?"

"They know. They don't care."

"So when you say top dollar, you can tell me how top is top?"

"Are you a player, Shmul?" I said.

There was another pause on the line.

"I represent the players. So talk to me."

"Can't do it Shmul," I said. "I'm ready to deal, but I deal only with players."

"Look," said Shmul, "my people don't exactly want they should be involved in selling these kind of theaters, you follow my meaning."

"Pretty sensitive group of guys? Think they're too sensitive turn a handsome profit on a sewer?"

Shmul wasn't the world's greatest negotiator.

"Look," he said, "give me an hour to call my people. I'll get right back to you."

"No can do, Shmul," I said, "I talk to your people direct or my people they start looking in L.A. Of course your people might be pretty ticked they find out what their sensitivity cost them."

"All right already," said Shmul, whining. "You want you should speak to a man named Darr, James Darr. You tell him you spoke to me and I told you to call."

108

I said: "Gotcha, Shmul," and hung up abruptly even before Shmul could give me Darr's number.

I love dealing with tough Israelis.

Seen Too Much

Mick Shaughnessy was an insurance agent in the Sunset with a secondary practice in social relations. I thought I'd ask him about Angelita. It was the sort of thing he'd be likely to know. I got him right away. He didn't believe in answering machines and he didn't believe in ever leaving his office. "I'm not here, Asher," he told me once. "I don't do business."

I told him what Angelita looked like and described her special expertise.

Shaughnessy listened calmly. "So the way I understand it," he said when I had finished, "you're looking for a spade hooker with great knockers does S and M."

"That's about the size of it, Mick," I said.

"Can't help you out," he said. "I don't do jungle work."

Shaughnessy had very refined racial sensibilities.

"Know anyone I can call?"

"I know a lot of people you can call. Your best bet be Irma Kupfenberg. She runs a dungeon out in the Inner Mission somewhere."

I asked Shaughnessy for Irma Kupfenberg's number; he gave it to me after I promised to make a contribution to Boy's Town, his favorite charity.

"Only thing, Asher," he said before hanging up, "don't go

109

calling her Irma or Mrs. Kupfenberg or anything like that. Remember, she's the Mistress. She's pretty sensitive about her name on account of the fact that her father had a string of candy stores in the city way back when."

"I'll remember that, Mick," I said.

Later that afternoon, I walked down Valencia with my hands in my pockets. The neighborhood was pretty much empty. The Korean grocery stores were little patches of fluorescent light, elderly Koreans eating noodles with chopsticks by the counters, the same wrinkled unsmiling face in each store. There were a few scuttling blacks on the street, some Korean children walking rapidly home with the stiff-legged walk Korean children have.

Years ago, one of my wives had acquired a spiritual counselor. "He's in touch," she said ominously. I met him at a cocktail party in Mill Valley. He was a small man, with small hands and small feet. He was dressed in a Nehru jacket and very shiny patent leather boots.

"What do you do, man?" he asked. He held a plate in his hand and was endeavoring to conceal the eagerness with which he was eating the appetizers.

"I'm an attorney."

"Bummer," he said.

"Why?"

The small man with small hands and feet stopped eating.

"Too linear," he said. He moved his free hand—index finger extended, fork pointed upward—in a series of perpendicular straight lines. "Doesn't flow."

I kept walking. After a while, Valencia becomes progressively more Hispanic; there are cheap rooming houses on the side streets, and bodegas, and pawnshops. The small grocery stores are run by black-eyed, heavy-haunched women. The streets are filthy, with blackened chewing-gum spots on the sidewalk.

At 16th, I saw a beggar squatting in front of the Bank of America. He was dressed in a padded army jacket; he had a woolen cap over his head. The sign that he held in his lap said: *Seen too much.* I dropped a quarter into his hat.

He looked up. "No paper?" he asked. He seemed genuinely put out.

"Pretty fussy for a beggar," I said.

"I'm not a beggar," he said with a good deal of obviously offended pride. "I'm an entrepreneur."

I like this part of town. Rents are cheap. The houses are dilapidated. The fog stays back. There are wild wisteria vines hanging over the porches of those dilapidated houses. The hookers come home here, and so do the drag queens, and the MUNI conductors, and the garbage collectors, and the walnut-eyed mailmen who keep gun collections and spend Saturday mornings drawing beads on the pedestrians below their window.

After a while, Valencia ascends steeply up a hill. By the time I got to the top, I was breathing heavily. The sun had already set, leaving streaks of pink and gold in the air.

The dungeon occupied the lower half of an enormous ramshackle Victorian in the middle of the block; the top floors were empty, the windows boarded. Someone had managed to paint a black swastika on the peeling woodwork above the third floor. The first-story windows facing the street were covered with red paper, giving the house a lunatic bloodshot look. The rear windows must have had a fantastic view of the city below.

I stood in the walkway for a moment in order to catch my breath. The concrete, I could see, was chipped and pitted. I tucked my shirt into my pants and ran my fingers through my hair and walked up the two little steps to the dungeon's door.

There was no name, only a hand-lettered sign that said RING in spiky inked letters.

I rang. Ding, dong, dong. Nothing. I rang again. Nothing again. I rapped the door with my knuckles. By and by, I heard a heavy no-nonsense tread from the interior of the house. Someone said: "What?"

"I called," I said.

111

"Hold on." Half a dozen locks—I counted—began tumbling and clicking. The door finally opened, throwing a red light into the evening air. The woman who opened the door was very stout, with putty-colored skin that lay on her face in slabs. She was dressed in laced black leather boots that reached up to her knees, a black leather skirt that just covered her dimpled thighs, and a leather motorcycle jacket, cut short at the cuffs, with a death's head insignia on the shoulder. She wore a black leather cap high on her head. She seemed to like leather.

She said: "I need some identification, something with your picture on it."

I showed her my driver's license. She looked at it in the red light.

"You got a major credit card?" she asked.

I showed her my American Express card. She peered at it and then again at my driver's license.

"You sure you don't want a blood sample?" I said.

The Mistress smiled one of those improbably intimate smiles that some women have. She had irregularly spaced teeth and when she smiled her pasty fat face acquired a mysterious look of enigmatic sadness. "Come on in, dearie," she said. I followed her roiling haunches into a tiny entrance way. An oak staircase led up into the darkness. A sampler hung on the wall. It said: GOD BLESS THIS HOUSE.

The Mistress conducted business from her parlor. There was an oak desk in the middle of the room. A curtain of red beads separated the sitting room from a hallway beyond.

"You sit right over there, dearie," said the Mistress. She motioned to the oak chair with a leather seat in front of the desk. "First time?"

I nodded.

The Mistress sat herself at her desk; she sighed heavily. There were papers on top of her desk, a pair of reading glasses, and a copy of a book entitled *Spanish in Seven Days*. She rummaged about the papers. She finally found what she was looking for.

"Here," she said, pushing a legal form toward me, "for insurance."

The form said that the House of Bondage was an *educational* institution. It said that it was meant to help people *explore* their sexuality. It said that I had sought out its services *voluntarily*. It said that I was over twenty-one. It said that in the event of injury or disability I was to hold *harmless* members of the educational staff. It said that I was of sound mind and body and in witness thereof and pertaining thereunto and furthermore and furtherless. It was all gibberish. I signed it anyway.

"I can't be too careful," said the Mistress. "Last year, someone sued me because he said he lost all sensation down in you-know-where."

I looked around the little room. There were whips mounted on the walls, and handcuffs hung from hooks, and brown leather ropes curled into loops around nails, and pictures of men in chains bending low to kiss the feet of very large, very fat women who did not look as if they enjoyed Tupperware parties.

"I can see how you might be a little exposed," I said.

"That's good, dearie," said the Mistress, stuffing the legal form haphazardly into the drawer. "Now let me ask you this. You all right? One of my regulars last year he had this attack, the paramedics couldn't untie him. It was very awkward."

"I can imagine. I'm fine."

The Mistress folded her ample arms across her bosom and looked directly at me with something like amusement in her heavy hooded eyes. She inclined her head to the pictures on the wall.

"Your pick."

"I'd like to know a little more about who you've got working, Mistress," I said.

"Seeing how you've never been here before, I can put you in with Doreen, dearie. She's very good, very firm. Unless you want something special. Then I'd have to make arrangements."

I attempted to look dubious. "What's Doreen look like?"

The Mistress rotated her haunches on her chair and shouted: "Dough-reen." She turned back to me and said: "She'll be right here, dearie."

The bead curtain rustled and Doreen came halfway into the room. She posed dramatically by the beads, one hand raised to hold onto the curtain, the other at her hip. She was a very tall, very thin young black woman; she was dressed in a black camisole top, silk panties, stockings with garters, and high heels. She looked like Abraham Lincoln. I thought she might suffer from Marfan's syndrome. She stood by the bead curtain, swaying gently. I shook my head. Doreen frowned from her great height and slipped back behind the bead curtain.

"I had someone else in mind, Mistress," I said softly, and slid Angelita's picture over to her. She looked at it briefly and looked up at me.

"I look like I run a dating service?" she asked.

"It's for the prom," I said.

The Mistress leaned back in her chair and crossed one leg mannishly over the other, ankle to knee; she compressed her chin professorially with her thumb and forefinger.

"What makes you think I know her?"

"A birdie told me."

The Mistress appeared to retreat into placid deliberation.

"It's two hundred to make the call," she said finally.

"Fifty," I said.

I thought the Mistress might be inclined to haggle; she shrugged her heavy shoulders to indicate her contempt for detail. "Whatever," she said. "Leave me a number. If she's interested, she'll call you."

I patted my pockets for a pen. "Here," said the Mistress, "use this." She handed me a beautiful silver pen with fluted sides.

"Nice pen," I said, as I wrote down my telephone number on the back of a check I had found in my wallet.

"My father gave it to me," said the Mistress.

I folded the check into two twenties and a ten. The Mistress took the money and the telephone number and tossed it into the middle drawer of her desk.

"Don't hold your breath." She looked at me sharply and then let go of the tension in her face. My eyes were still black from the beating I had taken. "I don't think Doreen would have been your type after all," she said, smiling her smile.

Afterward, I walked up Twenty-first and back over to Valencia. The night was black and velvet. I could smell the wisteria everywhere. The skin around my eyes was tender and my ribs ached every time I took a breath.

A real beating puts bondage in perspective.

The Atheneum

Seybold Knesterman needed two days to become curious about what I had told him and a morning in which to swallow his pride. His secretary called me on Thursday. It was a little past eleven.

"Mr. Asherfeld," she said archly, "Mr. Knesterman would like you to lunch with him at his club."

"Swell," I said, "you mean the YMHA over on Geary?"

Seybold Knesterman's secretary allowed herself the tiniest of titters.

"Actually," she said, "it's the Atheneum on Jackson."

The Atheneum had been built before the earthquake of 1906 by railroad men who had long ceased to think of money as a valuable commodity. It was San Francisco's oldest and snootiest club. It did not willingly admit Jews, Blacks, or women. Or just about anyone else.

115

"As long as they serve kosher," I said.

"I beg your pardon," said Seybold Knesterman's secretary, putting as much arctic into her voice as possible.

"If they don't serve kosher I can bring a brown bag. Tell Knesterman I'll pick up a couple of liverwursts on rye, some cream sodas. That way we won't be taking any chances."

"I'm sure that won't be necessary," she said.

"That's what they say on the airlines, but you know the last time I flew United they served pig's knuckles as the main course. Can you believe it?"

"Talking with you, Mr. Asherfeld, I could believe anything."

She hung up without waiting for me to say good-bye.

I walked over to Pacific Heights from Telegraph Hill because I thought parking would be a bother. Foolish boy. At the Atheneum there was someone to park your car when you arrived, and someone on the broad marble steps to help you get up them when you left your car, and someone by the enormous gold and glass revolving doors to swing them open for you when you reached the top of the steps. If you'd ask, someone would do the breathing for you.

I caught sight of myself in the glass as I was trudging upward. Brown suit, white shirt, red tie. No hat. No handkerchief. No overcoat. Brown hair. And those pouches underneath the eyes.

I revolved through the revolving door, which opened onto an enormous rotunda. The floors were polished marble. On the far side of the rotunda there was an open terrace with a delicate ironwork grill and a spectacular view of the bay. The place was calm and soft and quiet in the way that only an old expensive building can be calm and soft and quiet.

The reception desk was a semicircular arc of deeply polished mahogany with a maroon leather inlay. The man behind the counter was dressed in a cutaway. He had thin aristocratic features. A name plate on the desk said: Colonel Rudintsky. San Francisco was full of Russian refugees who had discovered their aristocratic calling.

116

"Asherfeld," I said. "I'm here to meet Seybold Knesterman."

Colonel Rudintsky smiled by spreading his lips a little bit and looked at me with a milky expression. He managed simultaneously to suggest that I was expected and unwanted.

"Of course, Mr. Asherfeld," he said with a slight but very elegant Slavic accent. "Mr. Knesterman asked that you join him in steam room. Henriquez will situate you."

He rang a little bell with a peremptory tap of his manicured finger. "Enjoy your stay with us," he said.

Henriquez swam up to me.

"You follow me, Sir," he said.

We walked out of the rotunda and down a marble flight of stairs with a polished brass bannister and across a gloomy basement hall and past a room that said BILLIARDS and into the guest's locker room, which smelled briskly of disinfectant, soap and liniment.

There was a little desk by the door. A tubby man dressed in a polo shirt, spotless white ducks, and white shoes sat in a chair behind the desk. He stood up when we came in.

"Boris here, he'll take care of you now, Sir," said Henriquez.

Boris nodded vigorously and said: "Come this way with me, sir." Henriquez turned on his heels and walked away.

"First time, sir?" said Boris, as he padded back into the locker room. I said Yup. Boris fetched a cherry red bathrobe with a sash, and a fluffy white towel, and a little imitation leather toilet kit from a wooden closet. "Your locker is right over here," he said, pointing to a floor-to-ceiling locker with an oiled white birch door. "You finish changing, I'll take you to the steam room."

I looked at the locker door. There was no lock on the door. Boris took in my glance. "No locks, Sir, members wouldn't hear of it, this being a gentlemen's club."

I said: "You don't get too many attorneys in here, I take it?"

Boris smiled a surprised smile. Then he gave a wet laugh.

117

Then he snuffled conspiratorially. "Hey," he said, "what do you call fifty thousand lawyers at the bottom of the ocean?"

"What?"

"A beginning." He guffawed and slapped his meaty thigh.

"Pretty funny," I said. I was almost undressed.

Now that Boris had broken the ice he asked: "What line of work you in, Sir?"

"I'm an attorney," I said.

I dropped my undershorts into the locker and fixed the towel around my waist. "I'll take you down the steam room now," Boris said soberly.

We padded down the hall in front of the guest locker room until we came to the steam room. Boris opened the door and shouted: "Got a guest here, Mr. Knesterman," through the thick gray steam, which came hissing into the room from vents in the ceiling.

"Thank you, Boris," said Knesterman gravely.

I groped my way through the mist and gloom and sat down on the lower marble bench.

Seybold Knesterman looked a good deal more imperious in his clothes than he did sitting naked on a towel in the steam room. He was long and thin and had no muscles whatsoever; he had a thin man's potbelly; there were varicose veins crawling on his legs and age spots on his shoulders. He had large, mournful ears, like an elephant.

"You do this often?" I asked.

"Every day," said Knesterman with satisfaction.

"It'll be wonderful when you get the women in here," I said. The Atheneum had fought a losing battle with the city attorney to keep women out of the club. "I can just see them scampering up and down the halls on their little club feet."

Knesterman reached over for the bottle of eucalyptus oil and began spraying it into the air.

"I'm not looking forward to it, Asherfeld," he said. "I see no reason why I should have to share this facility with women."

118

"Hell, Knesterman," I said, "I don't see any reason to share this *planet* with women."

Knesterman was not amused. "No matter what you may think," he said, "I am not a sexist."

"Me either," I said. "We're just a couple of guys think the world be better off if women couldn't talk and didn't vote."

Knesterman got up and walked over to the glistening steel shower head in the corner of the steam room. He turned it on and stood under the water for a few seconds. Then he went back to his seat.

"Try it," he said.

I got up and stood under the shower. The water was cold. When I got back to my seat, steam was pouring out of the vents. The room was full of the stuff. It was about as much fun as standing over a manhole.

"Do you a world of good," said Knesterman.

The door opened and some of the steam floated from the room. Boris poked his round head in and said: "Bring you gentlemen something cold to drink, something to eat?"

I was about to ask for a beer but Knesterman beat me to it. "Thank you, Boris," he said, "we'll take lunch by the pool."

He got up and cinched his towel around his convex waist and opened the door of the steam room. "Coming?" he said to me.

I fastened my soggy towel around my waist and followed Knesterman down the hall and through the wooden double doors that opened onto the swimming pool.

It was pretty much one of those jobs that are meant for exercise and not much else—six lanes with lane buoys separating the lanes. There was an Olympic timing clock on the wall at the far end of the pool and a pile of floats and kickboards underneath the clock. There was a glass-enclosed patio at the other end of the pool with deck chairs lined up in a row.

No one was in the pool; no one was lying on any of the deck chairs.

Knesterman opened the glass door to the patio, took a new

towel from the pile by the door and spread it out on a deck chair.

"We can catch a little sun here, if you like," he said.

"Sun?"

Knesterman pointed toward the ceiling with his long thin finger. An array of tanning lamps had been mounted on a white wooden beam.

I lay down in the chair next to Knesterman. "I'll pass," I said.

Boris came into the solarium pushing a cart. "Some refreshment, gentlemen," he said heartily.

"Just leave it there, Boris," said Knesterman, "we'll serve ourselves."

"Yes, sir, Mr. Knesterman," said Boris.

For a moment we both lay on the wooden reclining chairs; it felt good to cool down after the steam room.

Finally I said: "So tell me, how did things get screwed over at LRB?"

"I have no idea," said Knesterman. He got up from his chair and walked over to the lunch trolley.

"That what you're going to tell the SEC?"

Knesterman looked at me with fixed stare. He had a slice of rye bread in one hand and a knife in the other.

"What do you mean by that, Asherfeld?" he asked petulantly.

"Me? I don't mean anything. I was just asking from a sense of intellectual curiosity."

Knesterman stopped looking at me and began making himself a sandwich with great deliberation.

"Go easy on the mayo, Knesterman," I said.

Knesterman finished making the sandwich and placed it on a plate. He handed it to me with an exaggerated display of courtesy.

"So as I was saying," I said, the plate on my lap, "I view all this as a puzzle, a little bit like a Rubik's Cube sort of thing, but over at the Federal Building, I think it's going to look very different."

I took a bite from the sandwich.

"Nice sandwich, Knesterman," I said, "you may have missed your calling."

Knesterman finished making a second sandwich.

"Different how?" he asked after he had taken a bite and chewed it reflectively.

"If it were me looking at things over the SEC I'd say LRB missed filing for a variance because someone told them to miss filing for a variance."

Knesterman looked up again; he was still chewing thoughtfully. I watched him swallow, his prominent Adam's apple sedately rising and then falling.

"Why on earth would anyone stop them from filing?"

"To collect a quarter of a million dollars in consulting fees. How's that sound?"

"It sounds fantastic."

"That's what they said about sushi bars."

Knesterman took his plate in hand and walked back to his lounge chair. He seemed a little lost in thought. He sat down and rested the plate on his stomach.

"I suppose you know who this someone is?"

"I have no idea, Knesterman," I said. "I'll tell you what I do know. Consider it a professional courtesy. Lawrence Williams claimed LRB owed him a quarter of a million dollars. He asked me to collect it."

"You're not talking about that fat fool, the one found with his head shot off."

"Yes, that's the fat fool I'm talking about. I was standing next to him when he lost his head."

"How very shocking for you," said Knesterman.

"More shocking for LeRoy."

"Yes, of course," said Knesterman. "I didn't mean to be flippant. But look here, Asherfeld, there's something I don't understand. Why would anyone even think of paying this fellow Williams a quarter of a million dollars to arrange a variance?"

"You got it wrong, Knesterman," I said. "I didn't say anyone was about to pay Lawrence Williams anything at all. I said that's how it would *look.*"

"A nice distinction," said Knesterman. He finished his sandwich and put the tray back on the trolley.

"I don't suppose you'd be interested in taking a sauna after lunch?" he said. "That's dry heat, you know."

"I know what a sauna is, Knesterman," I said. "And no, I'm not much interested."

"Very well," said Knesterman. "I'll have Boris bring you back to your locker."

He got up and padded over to a panel by the glass door and pushed a button and padded back to his lounge chair. Boris was there in a flash.

"Mr. Asherfeld will be leaving us, Boris," said Knesterman.

Boris said: "Yes, Sir," with a great deal of heartiness, "right this way, Sir."

As I was walking out, Knesterman said: "I appreciate what you've told me, Asherfeld."

"I knew you would," I said.

Praise Jesus

I walked back to Telegraph Hill from the Atheneum; it was after three when I got to St. Mary's Park. I sat down on one of the green wooden benches by the park entrance and stretched my feet out in front of me. An elderly Chinese man was doing t'ai chi exercises on the shabby square of grass behind my bench. Two lithe teenagers were tossing a frisbee to one another on the lawn, their scruffy brown dog running between them, its pink tongue lolling from its mouth. A young woman in a motorcycle jacket passed me. She had inky black hair and a ring in her nose that she was turning tentatively with her thumb and forefinger. Over on Stockton, whoever it was that was forever standing in front of Wonderama was forever standing in front of Wonderama.

After a while, I grew tired of sitting and walked up the hill to my apartment. The Chairman had just finished parking his Chrysler in the driveway; he stood beaming, as if he had berthed a super tanker. He greeted me with a gabble of Cantonese and a curt inscrutable nod.

I had the rest of the day left and I wasn't hungry and I wasn't sleepy and I didn't feel like sitting down and learning how to paint in oils or speak in German.

Some months ago, a fat man with a tendency to sweat violently had given me a copy of his book; it was entitled *How to Plan for Your Own Retirement*. I had done him a favor. He had never written a book before and believed in what he had done. "I really think this is going to make a difference, Asher," he had said. I trudged up the stairs to my apartment, smelling the deep woodsy smell of the hall, and let myself in. I found the book lying on its side on my desk. It hadn't moved. I got myself comfortable and read the first chapter. I must have been desperate. The secret to planning for your own retirement, it turned out, was having a pot of money before you retire.

I closed *How to Plan for Your Own Retirement* and sailed it toward the couch. I noticed that I had two messages on my machine. The first was from a new friend one of my wives had acquired. His name was Bruiser. He was a woodcutter. "You're dating a woodcutter?" I had said to her when the news was imparted to me. "Somebody who spends his time making cute little chipmunks?"

"You are so sick, Asher," she had said.

From time to time, Bruiser called me; he was eager that we

meet in the spirit of the great woods. As soon as I heard his slow stupid voice I fastforwarded the machine.

The second message began with a chuckle. "I give lessons to bad boys," said someone whose message was a lesson all its own. "Call me."

I wrote the number down and erased both messages. There was a certain satisfaction in having Bruiser gone from my tape. I gave it a few minutes; when I called, Angelita answered the telephone with a brisk, businesslike, "This is Angelita." I didn't say anything. "This is Angelita," she said again. "Who is this?"

"Asherfeld," I said, "you left a message on my machine."

She chuckled her low throaty chuckle. "I understand you've been a very bad boy," she said.

"The worst."

"It sounds to me like you need some serious training."

"It sounds that way to me too," I said.

I asked where I should go, Mistress, and she told me to go to the Excalibur, Dog, and I said Yes, Mistress, and I asked what name I should ring, Mistress, and she said Houston, Dog, and I said, Thank you, Mistress, and she chuckled a chuckle and hung up.

I started out at a little past seven. Downstairs, the Chairman had commenced polishing his Chrysler with a chamois. He worked slowly, with round placid strokes. For me, an automobile was just a car; for The Chairman it was a symbol of the inexhaustible capacity of things to change. He stopped working and straightened himself up and nodded severely. He almost never smiled; his expression was one of serene satisfaction.

There was a light chill breeze blowing down the streets, carrying the wet evening fog along with it. I tucked my chin in my chest as I scuttled down Greenwich and tried to walk briskly.

I could see the Excalibur as soon as I turned the corner onto Grant; I could probably have seen the damn thing from Mars. It's an enormous spooky pink high rise on the very summit of Russian Hill.

I crossed Columbus, still walking briskly, and slowed to a dull trudge when I hit the flank of the hill, my breath coming in copper-tasting pants. Someone once told me that the way to climb a very steep hill is to lift your knees sharply with each step. I tried it. It didn't do any good.

There's a semicircular driveway in front of the Excalibur and a little concrete pavilion for the doorman to strut across. I stopped for a moment to catch my breath. The place is built on a rise so that all of the apartments have at least one window with a view. What's left of an old park is behind the building; the front seems to reach out toward the bay, dark in the dark night.

The doorman watched me cross the driveway. He was dressed in a peaked cap and a greatcoat that had Excalibur stitched in red over the breast pocket; the thing reached his shoes.

"Help you, sir?" he said. "You goin' up, I'll have to announce you." He pointed to a gleaming silver intercom mounted on the marble wall.

"Tough line of work you're in," I said amiably.

He tried to figure it out.

"Bettern' welfare," he finally said.

"You're right. Can you ring Houston for me?"

A smile played across his face. He was looking for something sly to say.

"Whose calling?" he asked. The "Sir" had disappeared.

"Tell her I'm with the Jehovah's Witnesses."

"You want I should ring Houston and tell her you're with the Jehovah's Witnesses?"

"Tell her it's Asherfeld. Tell her I have good news from the Bible."

He turned to the silver intercom and punched in a code. There was a far off ringing and then a neutral voice said: "Yes."

"Gentleman here to see you, Miss Houston," said the doorman with exaggerated clarity. "Says his name is Asherfeld. Says he's a Jehovah's Witness. Says he's got good news from the Bible."

"Send him up," said the neutral voice.

The doorman hung up the telephone and stepped to the side. "It's the penthouse," he said.

I said: "Praise Jesus."

"Praise Jesus," said the doorman.

Inside the lobby there was a faintly electrical smell from the fluorescent lights. A mosaic mural on one wall depicted a group of Greek nymphs running gaily from a satyr. On the other wall a sheet of water fell from a fluted pipe into a little pool with pennies at the bottom.

I got into the elevator and pressed P for the penthouse. The walls were redwood. Someone had taken a lot of trouble to keep them oiled and the brass railing polished; there was a legend in graffiti carved into the wood beside the brass mountings for the elevator buttons. It said: NIXON IN 84.

Angelita was waiting for me when I got out of the elevator.

She stood leaning against the open door of her penthouse; she was dressed in a demure black chiffon hostess gown; she had her hair swept up in a chignon. Her dark caramel skin had the exotic luster that some black women have, a sort of shimmer. I stopped and looked at her full in the face. Nothing in her photograph had prepared me for the shock of her beauty.

"Asherfeld," I said.

"Jehovah's Witness?" she said. "You think that's funny?"

"Wait," I said, "you haven't heard the good news from the Bible."

She looked at me bleakly and flattened herself against the door and I walked past her into the penthouse; it was like walking past a landmine.

There was a very expensive shag white rug on the bleached hardwood floor. The walls were exposed brick that had been painted white. An oil of Angelita dressed in a black riding outfit hung above the fireplace. Another oil of Angelita dressed in a sombrero and playing a guitar hung on the facing wall. A semi-circular wrought iron staircase rose from the corner of the room

126

like a snake and disappeared to the penthouse. I could see the lights of Berkeley twinkling from the window, and far away the lights of Marin, smudges now in the night fog over the bay.

Angelita sat on the white leather couch, her legs crossed primly underneath her gown. I sat on the facing white leather couch. There was a glass coffee table between us.

A beautiful Siamese cat strutted across the living room and after an untroubled leap made itself comfortable in Angelita's lap. Angelita buried her nose into the animal's neck.

"A quarter inch more cortex and an opposable thumb and they'd rule the world," I said.

Angelita looked at me blankly.

"The cats."

"That's not the good news you were going to tell me, is it?" She looked ostentatiously at the diamond watch on her wrist.

I took out the picture of Roger Ellerbee and Angelita that Mad Bad LeRoy had sent me, and smoothed it on the glass table in front of the couch.

"I'm looking for Roger Ellerbee."

"You try Macy's?" said Angelita.

"Not yet."

Angelita put her hand underneath the silky Siamese and lifted it to the floor; then she stood up and walked over to the white piano in the corner of the room. She took a cigarette from a silver cigarette case that played the first few notes of "La Cucaracha" when opened, and lit it with a gold lighter.

"Maybe that's your best bet, honey," she said, blowing a stream of smoke toward the white ceiling, the curve of her neck lifted for a moment toward me. "This isn't exactly the lost and found here."

I watched her draw the room's light toward her.

"Terrible thing," I said. "The man who gave me this picture was shot in the head not five feet from where I was standing."

"Is that a fact?" said Angelita.

"And the man you're with in the picture has been disappeared for more than a week."

"Honey," she said, "maybe I didn't make myself clear. Whatever it is you want, I'm not going to give it to you."

"Aw, you're just saying that," I said.

"Asshole," she snapped, and then she shouted, "Kong, baby, I need you."

I felt the slight draft of the bedroom door opening behind me and I turned around. Whatever it was that was coming through the door was at least six-foot-eight and must have weighed two hundred and fifty pounds. It gave a grunt. I got to my feet.

"Say, he's a big one," I said. "You plan on showing him?"

"The gentleman is leaving," said Angelita. "See that he bounces on the way out."

I stepped around the coffee table and moved to the back of the other couch.

Kong stopped behind the couch I had been sitting on and put his hands on his hips. He was dressed in an Army shirt, the sleeves cut off at the shoulders. He looked enormously strong but he didn't look mean and he didn't look smart.

"Time to go, cupcakes," he said.

"Me? I'm not going anywhere. I just got here."

"Look, cupcakes," he said, "either you go peaceful-like or I'm going to have to rough you up a little. I don't want to do it, but that's the way things are."

"Is that the line you used in Vietnam?" I said. "No wonder you guys lost."

That brought him up short.

"What?" he asked in irritation.

Angelita said, "Kong, get on with it," with a whine.

"See, Kong, the way I see it that was your big mistake in Vietnam. All windup and no delivery, if you catch my drift."

"I'm going to kill you," Kong roared, his face turning a furious deep magenta.

"Just get him out of here, baby," said Angelita.

"I know," I said, "we'll play war games. You be the grunt and I'll be the Vietcong."

Kong lurched toward me from the door; I didn't have a game plan at hand, but with Kong I didn't need one. As he stepped on the white shag rug he lost his footing all of a sudden, grunted *uh,* and went crashing onto his back.

"Kong," shouted Angelita, "are you all right, baby?" She ran to his side and dropped to her knees.

Kong moaned deeply and dramatically and tried to raise himself to a half sitting position; he lapsed back and moaned again. "My back," he said.

"I knew I shouldn't have been worried about your head," I said.

"Oh baby," Angelita cried, cradling his head in her lap and stroking his forehead. She twisted her torso to face me.

"It's his back," she said. "He's got this bad back. Help me to get him to the bed."

"Are you crazy? He said he was going to *kill* me."

"He didn't mean it, for God's sake. Oh don't just stand there like an idiot, help me to get him to the bed."

I walked over to King Kong and squatted down beside him. "See what I mean," I said.

Kong moaned again and said: "Later. I'm going to take care of you later."

I got to my feet. "In that case," I said, "I think I'll just kick you in the head a few times and be on my way."

Angelita shrieked: "You mean son of a bitch, you touch him you deal with me." Her eyes were flashing and she was breathing in shallow pants.

"That's different," I said. "That's a threat worth listening too. See, Kong, the way I see it you would've been better off you stayed home, sent the little woman over there instead." Kong moaned again.

"Now!" said Angelita. "Help me now."

I squatted down again and managed to get Kong's arm

129

around my shoulder; the thing felt like a teak log. Somehow we got him upright; snorting furiously with each step, he managed to hobble back to the bedroom, where he collapsed with a massive grunt on the king-sized white bed with a white fur bedspread.

"You lie right there, baby," said Angelita, "I'll get you something." She disappeared from the room.

There was a chaise lounge in the corner; like everything else, it was white. I sat in it and then stretched out, my feet over the edge. Kong was staring at the mirrored ceiling.

"What, you wait in here while she's out there whipping the dogs?" I asked.

Kong looked at me with brown eyes. He had a curiously innocent face. His eyelashes were long and curled, and his eyes were wet from the pain and the surprise of the pain.

"I'm here in case she needs me," he said.

"I can see how you're a big help. Probably every woman should have one."

"Did I do anything to you?" he said. "Did I?"

There was no arguing with that.

Angelita came back into the room with a syringe and a pharmaceutical vial. I raised my eyebrows.

"Demerol," she said, "it's the only thing that works."

"Can I have some?" I said. "Please."

She said: "Funny. You are such a funny man," and injected the bolus into Kong's massive upper shoulder.

"That's better, baby," he said.

Angelita stroked his forehead. "You just rest," she said.

In a minute, Kong was asleep, his breathing regular, a buoyant bubble forming childishly on his lips. Angelita motioned me from the bedroom. We left the room carefully, Angelita closing the white door gently behind us.

"He'll be all right," she said with a sigh. She walked over to the coffee table and put the hypodermic back into a leather case.

She sat back down on the white couch. "You might as well sit down," she said.

"Did he do that to his back in Vietnam?" I asked.

Angelita snorted. "He did that to his back trying to show me he could lift that piano all by himself." She pointed to the white piano in the corner. "He spent his time in Vietnam getting high and getting laid."

"What outfit?"

"Eighty-second Airborne."

"You have to feed him, too? I mean he must eat three big boxes all by himself." I held my hands up to show her how large those boxes were.

Angelita lifted her lovely head and looked toward the piano and the window that faced all those twinkling lights.

"I take care of him," she said. "Let's just leave it at that."

"What about Roger," I said. "We were talking about Roger when King Kong made his entrance."

"You're really not going to stop until I tell you something, are you?"

"I'm really not going to stop."

"He was a nice man."

"Nice?"

"All right, he wasn't a nice man. He wanted to wear diapers and have me whip him when he made a mess. Is that what you want to hear?"

"How'd you two find each other?"

"LeRoy set it up."

"Just so he could have the picture?"

"No," said Angelita thoughtfully, "he wanted the picture for insurance. It was the sort of thing LeRoy did. He introduced people."

"Regular matchmaker," I said. "How long ago was this?"

"Three years, maybe a little less."

"What happened, I mean with you and Roger?"

"He fell hard. You know how it is."

"Sure," I said. "I know how it is. He spend a lot?"

Angelita looked at me with a hard appraising look.

"You work for free, honey," she said.

"No."

"Me either."

"And then one day he just walked out of your life?"

Angelita sighed again and looked down at her elegant hands. Her nails were long and tapered and frosted ivory.

"He said he was in trouble."

"What kind of trouble?"

"He didn't say," said Angelita. "He wanted me to go with him."

"Where?"

"Who knows? He never figured out that he was just somebody else."

A small white clock mounted on the far wall began musically to chime the hour. It was ten o'clock.

"I think you'd better go now," Angelita said.

I got a card from my wallet and placed it on the glass coffee table.

"Call me."

She didn't get up from the couch; but she picked up the card and looked at it. "So many men," she said. "Not one of them smart."

"Sure," I said, "it's all that testosterone. Ask any woman."

Angelita lifted her head again and looked into my eyes. "I'm not all ice," she said. "Let me know if you find Roger. I hope he's all right."

I nodded and said: "Take care of King Kong. Don't overload him with brain work."

For the first time that evening, Angelita smiled. She had dramatic even white teeth.

"I never do," she said.

I let myself out the white door.

The night air downstairs was soft and full of promise. The

same doorman was pacing the concrete pavilion in front of the building.

"Give Miss Houston the good news from the Bible?" he asked.

I stopped and looked at him. "I told her that the Wages of Sin is Death. I said *you* said to tell her. I made a particular point of saying that." I looked at the name stitched in red on his great-coat. "I said: 'Miss Houston, *Larry* said to tell you that the Wages of Sin is Death.' "

Counselor at Law

The Reverend's voice was plump and hearty, the way everyone's voice is when they wake you up.

"What you doing in bed this hour?" he asked.

"Sleeping," I said, "would you believe it?"

The Reverend uttered a bull-frog chuckle and said: "The Devil has work for idle hands, don't you know."

"Is that a fact?"

"You can depend on it," said the Reverend. "I've been up two hours, taken my run, had my breakfast."

The thought of Reverend Leotis in a flaming pink running suit, his stomach bouncing up and down as he jogged solemnly through the streets of Oakland, cheered me up.

"I'm coming awake, Reverend," I said. "I'm going to make today the first day of the rest of my life."

"That's good," said the Reverend, "you plan on doing that. Maybe you also want to make today the day you see LeRoy's attorney."

I swung my legs over the bed and said: "Hold on a sec, let me get a piece of paper."

I found a felt-tipped pen wedged between two books on my bedstand. No paper. I decided to write on the inside cover of a paperback entitled *Living through the Loss of Love*. A client had sent it to me on the theory that it was consoling.

"I'm back," I said.

"That's good," said the Reverend Leotis, "now listen up. Man's name is Sharpton, Leonard Sharpton, that's S-H-A-R-P-T-O-N."

"I can spell, Reverend."

"Talking to a white man, you never can tell. Now Leonard, he'll see you at eleven. Here's the address."

The Reverend Leotis gave me an address somewhere in Oakland; and then said: "Don't you be going back to bed, now. You need to be moving get anything done in this world."

"And here I thought you had to be connected."

"Well," said the Reverend, "you ain't connected and you ain't moving, so how you going to succeed?"

"You've been an inspiration, Reverend," I said.

"I know I have," he said. "I just know I have."

I got up and shuffled into the bathroom and shuffled into the kitchen. For a moment, I sat quietly on the kitchen bar chair looking things over. There was the refrigerator, right where it was supposed to be. It was a hard-working and dependable appliance. It was white and glabrous and committed to cold concepts.

I made coffee and ate a donut. A report in *The Chronicle* had indicated recently that everything that tasted good was in some way deeply dangerous to eat. Sugar was the exception. You could eat the damn stuff by the carload and all that would happen would be you'd get fat and your teeth would rot.

I finished up breakfast, washed the dishes, and walked out into the living room. It was perfectly clear over the bay, the sun already radiant, the water all cool blues and grays, the hills beyond a calm summer gold. The air was blue and white. The sailboats were out.

It was no more than ten or so when I got to the Bay Bridge, but one lane was closed, and it took me almost twenty minutes just to get across. A lane is always closed on the Bay Bridge. Traffic is always backed up. The same slow-moving radiantly stupid CalTrans workmen are always standing by the side of the road, doing nothing and staring off into space. I was getting pretty tired of driving into Oakland.

Leonard Sharpton had an office in a building on Jack London Square. I parked in one of those honor systems lots: After you park you're supposed to squish your money into a numbered metal slot. A lot of people evidently parked without squishing. Violators, an angry red sign affirmed, will be towed. I took up ten minutes sauntering from the parking lot over to Sharpton's office. I finally decided he wouldn't mind so much if I were ten minutes early; if he minded, I didn't care.

The building was an older building that had been carefully retrofitted to look like an older building. There was a sign outside on the wall beside the revolving doors. It said: THE EDWARD PHREMIL HAMLIN BUILDING. They're pretty reverential over in Oakland about that sort of thing. There was wood everywhere in the lobby and a lot of brass and even a couple of curved cuspidors that had been filled with sand so that they could serve as ashtrays. The automatic elevators still had seats for an elevator operator and a wooden operator handle and brass gates that you had to shut by hand. It was all very authentic. It must have cost a fortune. I could just see the architect going on and on to the developer: "Well frankly, Sam, if you want something excellent you are going to have to pay for it." I looked over the glass-and-bronze address box in the lobby. The building was half empty. Some people in Oakland didn't care a whole lot for period restoration. "Sam, I said it would be *excellent*, not popular."

Leonard Sharpton, Attorney at Law, shared an office on the fifth floor with Wilemina Lloyd Franklin, CPA.

135

The moon-faced security guard standing in front of the elevators looked happy to see me. Company at last. "Right this way, Sir," he said, pointing to the third of three empty elevators. He would have hoisted the thing himself if he could.

I went up in the elevator, and walked down one empty hallway and over to another. Sharpton's office had frosted glass on the front. His name was lettered on the glass in heavy black ink. I knocked and walked in.

The reception room was empty and the typewriter at the secretary's desk was discreetly covered with a plastic shroud.

Someone shouted: "Be right there, hold your horses," from the inside office.

"Take your time," I said.

Leonard Sharpton came into the waiting room. He was carrying a file underneath his arm. He was dressed in gray slacks and a gray vest and a white shirt and a red tie. His shirt was held up at the wrists by old-fashioned gold shirtsleeve collars. He was short, no more than five-feet-four or so. His face was full of planes and angles. It was a mean, sharp, intelligent face.

I told him who I was and said, "Sorry, I'm early."

"That's all right," said Sharpton, "you still get the same fifteen minutes." He looked around his reception area. "Hope you don't want coffee," he said. "Girl's out sick again."

"I don't want anything," I said.

He turned and walked back into his office. There was a basic law library on one wall, and a desk in front of the casement window on the other wall, and a chair in front of the desk. Nothing else. The window looked over Jack London Square. Sharpton kept a neat desk. There was nothing on it. He sat down lightly and looked at me with his shrewd dark eyes. I sat facing him, my forearms on my knees.

"You a friend of LeRoy's?" he asked.

"I only met him once. He meant nothing to me."

Sharpton nodded. "Least you're honest," he said. "I've got people comin' in here, swear they were thicker than thieves with

136

LeRoy. One guy swore him and LeRoy in the Army together."

"Not possible?"

"Oh, LeRoy in the Army all right. He in Vietnam. This fellah he got the outfit wrong. Man'll make a lot of mistakes, he won't forget the outfit he served with."

"Eighty-second Airborne?"

Sharpton looked at me alertly.

"How come you know that?"

"Lucky guess, Counselor."

"LeRoy didn't exactly brag about his military service, you know what I mean?"

"They probably would have lynched him over in Berkeley they know he served his country."

"Black man gets it coming or going."

"Counselor, LeRoy didn't have to go to Berkeley. There are places in this country where a man can run for office even though he served in Vietnam."

"In those places," said Sharpton, "no one would have voted for LeRoy." He looked ostentatiously at his watch. "You had fifteen minutes. You used up seven."

I got up from my chair. "I didn't realize you were so busy, Counselor. I'll come back when you don't have so many clients waiting outside."

Sharpton looked at me. "The Reverend said you were a hard-ass."

"I'm not a hard-ass. I just get tired of it all."

"What's that tiring you out?"

"The attitude."

"The attitude?" Sharpton was incredulous. "The attitude? You spend five minutes in the company of a black man and you tired out on account of his attitude? Talk about attitude, I spend my whole life with white men."

"It's not my problem, Counselor," I said. "I don't care if there are crack babies over in East Oakland. I don't like rap. I thought the Willie Horton commercial was terrific. Hell, I see a black

137

man coming toward me late at night I figure he's either going to mug me or sell me some dope. On the other hand, I don't see you or the Reverend doing a whole lot about finding out who shot LeRoy."

"That's a pretty nice speech," said Sharpton, "you all through, now?"

"I'm all through."

"Why you so interested in what happened to LeRoy?"

"I was working for him. He owed me money."

"You putting in a claim against the estate?"

"I will if I collect what I was supposed to collect."

"How much is that?" asked Sharpton, his voice not so edged. It's amazing how much a man will forgive when money is at stake.

"A quarter of a million dollars."

"That's a lot of money," he said.

I nodded.

"You going to tell me who owed it to him?"

"I don't know, Counselor. Did LeRoy have a lot of juice over in Redwood City?"

"Man was a councilman," said Sharpton, without committing himself to anything.

"You think he would have fixed a variance for two hundred and fifty thousand dollars?"

"A variance? You mean a zoning variance?" Sharpton was incredulous again. "Asherfeld, for a quarter million dollars LeRoy could have *bought* Redwood City."

"That's what I thought. Do you know of any other deals he was involved in."

Sharpton considered the matter for a moment. Then he said: "Man like LeRoy's involved in a lot of action."

I said: "How about a list of his investments. The sort of thing you'd file with a probate report?"

"Don't you think that be confidential?"

"LeRoy's dead, Sharpton," I said. "He doesn't need your confidence anymore."

Sharpton nodded and said: "You've got a point. I can let you see Statement of Probate. That do you?"

I said that be fine, great.

Sharpton said he'd send me a copy.

"Listen, Asherfeld," said Sharpton, "you think LeRoy was shot because some dude owed him two hundred and fifty thousand dollars?"

"Counselor," I said, "it really wouldn't surprise me if he were shot because some dude owed him ten dollars. It's that sort of world."

"Let me ask you something, Asherfeld. You tracking this thing down for LeRoy or you tracking this thing down for the money."

I let a moment go by. "It isn't even close, Counselor," I said.

No Cheese

When I got the Statement of Probate from Leonard Sharpton I called Herbert Dreyfus at the Federal Building.

"Hey," he said, "the wise guy."

"Free for lunch?"

"I'll be at Macy's," he said. "Need some underwear. You know a place near there?"

I said how about the Chuckwagon at the Sir Francis Drake, and he chuckled and said the Chuckwagon? fine I'll be there in an hour.

I had time to spare, so I walked from Telegraph Hill over to

Chinatown. I like the strange vegetables heaped up on sidewalk stands and the sad golden ducks hanging from hooks in the market and the Chinese newsstands with their exotic ink-smeared newspapers.

I loitered about, looking in store windows and down empty alleys, with their memories of tong bosses and concubines, and then after half hour or so, I crossed California and ambled through the financial district to Union Square.

The Chuckwagon was one of those hotel-chain restaurants intended to suggest man-sized portion and Hmm-good all-you-can-eat victuals. There was a gay chuckwagon painted on the window. Lunch was called the roundup. The host said: "Howdy, partner," when you walked in.

Dreyfus was already there, sitting in a booth by the window. I slid in opposite him.

"So how you doin'?" he asked.

I said I was doing fine and he said that that was good.

"It's better this way," he said. "You deal, I deal, we both come out ahead."

Our waitress was a tall girl with disorganized black hair. She said her name was Trish; she said she would be our waitperson and do we want to hear the specials today?

Dreyfus said Nah, just get me a pastrami on rye; I said I'd have a cheeseburger and fries. Trish wrote it all down with a tremendous show of concentration, sounding most of the words out loud.

I said: "California treating you any better?"

"Hard to tell," said Dreyfus. "The other day, I take my kid fishing, we're out there in the fog, I'm sicker than a dog, don't ever want to see a boat again, my kid he catches a fish *this* long, tells me *he* had a great time."

"Pretty soon you'll be talking about personal growth and eating lot of fiber."

"Not going to happen," said Dreyfus.

I lit a cigarette, caught the no-no look from the manager, Mr.

Chuckwagon himself, who was standing by the cashier's desk, and stubbed it out on the floor.

Dreyfus nodded in amusement. "They got you trained," he said. "So you still involved in the Fatman's affairs, or what?"

"I don't know," I said. I tried to sound thoughtful. "I'm still looking for Ellerbee."

"I understand it might kind of be in his best interest to stay missing."

"It's hard to say what's in a man's best interest."

"For sure," said Dreyfus, "but you're not out there looking for Ellerbee out of respect for the Fatman's memory?"

"No," I said, "he owed LeRoy money, LeRoy owes me."

Dreyfus nodded comprehendingly.

Trish arrived at our table, carrying the plates on her forearms in that weirdly efficient way waitresses have.

Dreyfus looked down at his sandwich and said: "What's this?"

"It's pastrami," said Trish, baffled. "Isn't that what you ordered?"

"No, I mean what's this stuff on *top* of the pastrami?"

"It's cheese," said Trish, "it's pastrami and cheese."

"Trish, sweetheart, didn't anyone ever tell you that cheese don't go on pastrami? It's a sacrilege."

"You didn't *say* to hold the cheese," said Trish.

"Trish, sweetheart," said Dreyfus, "I didn't say you should go on breathing either, but you did that anyway. Some things you know without being told."

Trish took the plate from Dreyfus without another word and Dreyfus pursed his lips and then smoothed them with his fingertips.

"So how come you're working with Ellerbee, aside from the fact that she looks good and smells good and probably told you you're the greatest thing since the invention of the corkscrew."

"No other reason," I said. I was surprised that he knew about Lauren Ellerbee. I hadn't told him.

141

"I figured," said Dreyfus. "So you know who hit the Fat-man?"

"No," I said.

"Me either," he said, reaching over to take a fry from my plate. "Roger, he's got the motive, though. Probably too much of a Yuppie to do hit work. Fries are good, at least."

Trish returned with Dreyfus' plate. "Pastrami on rye," she said, with injured dignity, *"no* cheese."

Dreyfus looked down at his plate. "Probably still smells of cheese," he said, taking a bite of his sandwich that separated the thing in half. "What do you want to talk about? Hey, you mind if I take couple more of your fries?"

"What do you know about Aztec?" I asked.

"You mean aside from the fact that they're keeping LRB afloat?"

"Aside from that."

"Serious movers and shakers. Made out like bandits in the eighties. You meet Darr, he's a real sweet fella?"

"The other day, I met him. He told me Vietnam was a thousand laughs."

"Happens," said Dreyfus between wolfish bites. "Hear they had a happy place down there. Very eighties. Happy food, happy bimbos, happy things to sniff and snort."

"I sort of figured."

"You know whose dealing them?"

"No idea. We don't do pharmaceuticals."

I thought all this over for a moment.

"You know that LeRoy was a silent partner there?" I asked.

Dreyfus looked up from his plate. "No," he said. "That I didn't know."

"He and Darr served together in Vietnam."

"They spit on his grave they find out about this in Berkeley."

"That's probably why LeRoy wasn't too interested in having the world know about it."

"How come you know this?"

142

"It's what I do. I know things."

Dreyfus had finished his sandwich. He looked at my plate. "You gonna finish your burger?" he asked.

"No, go ahead." I pushed my plate toward him.

"They tell you we're doing an audit?"

"You mean over at LRB? They told me."

Trish came over to clear the dishes and said: "Will that be all or is there something else?" She was offended beyond words. The speech amused Dreyfus.

"No, Trish sweetheart," he said. "I'll take some coffee black. That means hold the cream, hold the milk, no sugar, don't put apple juice or yoghurt in the coffee."

Before Trish could think of anything to say, I said: "Me too, just black and I'll have a slice of apple pie." She was preoccupied enough remembering two black coffees and a slice that she forgot to make a scene.

"How much you think it would cost to fix a variance in Redwood City?" I asked.

Dreyfus looked up thoughtfully. "You mean like if someone was zoned commercial light and needed to have someone forget they were putting together computer parts?"

I nodded.

"Figure ten thousand should do the job. Any more than that makes sense to take the hit, break the lease."

"You know that LRB missed filing for a variance?"

Trish came over and placed our coffees and my pie on the table. They were black.

"That we know," said Dreyfus thoughtfully.

"It makes sense to think that LeRoy was asking two hundred fifty thousand dollars to repair the damage?"

"That amount of money, the boys over in Redwood City turn the entire district into a parking lot."

"You know that, and I know that," I said, "but maybe Roger Ellerbee didn't know that."

"Or maybe the Fatman figured he asks for something fantastic, he gets something a little better than he's worth."

"Maybe," I said.

"It's a theory," Hubert Dreyfus said, nodding toward the food on my plate. "You gonna finish up that pie or what?"

Dog's Night Out

The night went by the way nights go by. I thought of Lauren Ellerbee and decided not to think about her anymore. It was like giving orders to a rock. I got up at first light and stood for a while looking out at the bay. I've never been past the Golden Gate Bridge, not even in an airplane. The sullen inky waters surge across the Pacific; beyond, there is only Tokyo or Hong Kong or Singapore, alien gabbling places. Come to San Francisco and there's no place left to go.

After a while, I made some coffee and read the newspaper and clambered back into the day.

I called Doxie at Aztec at a little past nine. She struck me as the sort of woman who would stride into an office early. Poodle-Cindi answered the telephone and said, "Oh, you're that Aries," and told me that Doxie was working at home, "at least that's what she *said* she was doing." I asked her for Doxie's home number. It took Poodle-Cindi a while to find it: "I mean no one's ever asked for it before," she said.

Doxie picked up the telephone on the second ring with a very exasperated *what?*

I asked if she'd be able to get together. "Just to talk," I said.

"You're the person who's interested in Roger Ellerbee."

"That's me."

"I mean is there something you need me for?"

"It's hard to say."

"Let me get my book," she said.

It must have been pretty full, that book. "Well," she said, "I *could* fit you in during my workout." She made it sound like a lucky break. "I'm doing low-intensity this week."

Ugly women are all alike.

"Two o'clock," she said, "it's the only time the place is empty."

"That'd be great," I said. She said she'd leave a pass for me at the desk of the Bay Club. I said that'd be great too. Everything was great.

I had the morning to kill, so I drove across the Golden Gate Bridge and took the old army road up to the Marin headlands.

I parked by the Ranger station at the beach and walked down to the water's edge.

There were a few surfers in wet suits out beyond the breakers. The waves seemed heavy moving and sluggish to me; even after they got on top of their boards, the surfers never seemed to go very far. They would rise for a moment, crouch on their boards, shoot sideways, and then topple into the water.

A starfish had been left high and dry by the receding tides. I thought it might have been dead already; when I picked it up, it gave a faint twitch. I threw it after the soapy waves, which were in a hurry to reach Japan. When they returned they took the starfish with them.

One of my wives had a great passion for walking along the beach. She would take off her shoes and dig her stubby toes into the wet sand. The open air and the sun and the sound of the surf invariably made her melancholic. "I feel the hand of doom on us," she would say.

She was right about that.

I thought of climbing to the top of the headlands, but I didn't much want to hear my heart pound in my chest and I didn't think I could see anything there that I couldn't see from the beach.

I had lunch in a Sausalito restaurant that served terrific hamburgers. Each burger was handcrafted by the proprietor himself and then placed on a revolving stainless steel grill suspended over charcoal. A small flag was stuck on each patty. You got to chose which flag you wanted when you ordered. I asked for Tanzania. "You got it," said the proprietor.

By the time I finished up, it was a little before two. I drove back to the city with the high slanting sun on my right.

When I got to Sansome street on the east side of Telegraph Hill, I parked in the blue zone in front of the Bay Club that was reserved for cripples.

The valet parking attendant looked me over and looked over my car. He was a weedy Black with sad round eyes.

"That's for them handicapped," he said.

"I'm handicapped."

"You? What you got wrong with you?"

"I was born white," I said.

He took a second to take it in and then smiled and said: "Cain't argue with that."

The inside of the club was furnished in chrome and imitation leather. There was a lot of gold and blue paint on the walls and a semicircular formica desk in front where members were supposed to check in. A bulletin board behind the desk had pictures of the fitness trainers. The women looked as if they could snap an oak two-by-four with their thighs. They looked eager to try.

I told the hefty young girl behind the counter who I was. She said Asherfeld, Asherfeld, Asherfeld, as she rifled through a sheaf of slips. "Here you are," she said buoyantly. She was tremendously pleased to have discovered my name. She heaped two towels and a key on the counter.

"Men's locker rooms are upstairs."

I pushed the towels back to her. "I won't need these," I said.

"Not working out?"

"Not in this life."

She shrugged her round shoulders carelessly and took back her towels. No one likes to have a gift refused. Not even towels.

Doxie said to meet her at the coed workout room. I followed the wall signs past the squash courts, where a lot of sweating men were running around, crashing into the walls and shouting explosively, and past the indoor swimming pool, which smelled of chlorine, and across the basketball court. A portly middle-aged man, stripped to his shorts, was running around the perimeter of the court, his elbows held high, his torso jiggling.

There were ten Stairmasters in the coed workout room, and something called a Gravitron, which didn't look like a whole lot of fun, and a lot of exercise bicycles, and a couple of treadmills.

Two girls were trudging on the Stairmasters. They were dressed in iridescent tights and the sort of black leotards whose thongs disappeared unappetizingly between the cheeks of their buttocks. They were hanging from the railing of their machines.

"What does Darnel say about the whole idea?" asked one of them, a pretty young Oriental.

"He doesn't *have* anything to say about it," said the other, wiping the sweat from her eyes.

In a little while, Doxie walked in efficiently. She was wearing the same outfit as everyone else; it made her chest look narrow and her hips wide. Her hair was pulled back by a yellow sweat band. She had very large feet.

"Sorry I'm late," she said. "It took forever."

She stepped onto the pedals of the Stairmaster and adjusted the machine for her weight by pressing various squares on a translucent panel. She began to step slowly up and down. Unlike the other women, she did not support herself with her hands. I stood in front of the awful machine, feeling conspicuous and out of place.

"Do this often?" I said.

"Every day?"

It was a depressing answer.

"It's something I do for myself."

Doxie smiled as she trudged up and down. I was hoping she would have a pretty smile, but the thing was crooked and made her look shifty.

"Is it bad?" she said. "I mean what's going to happen?"

"Depends."

Doxie adjusted the machine so that her steps became slightly more rapid. She was breathing heavily now and sweat had begun to form on her upper lip and at the margins of her tiny breasts.

"Depends on what?"

"I don't know, Doxie. Luck maybe."

Doxie looked down at me from the Stairmaster and shook her head sharply upward to snap the sweat from her forehead.

"What do you want to know?" She asked the question in the tired voice of someone used to being used. "I'm not exactly part of the inner circle at Aztec."

"Who is?"

"There's a group," she said, trying to adjust her speech to her breathing, "they like to punch each other on the shoulder and say things like *How about those Niners* and talk about how short Cindi's skirts are."

"It must be hard."

"It's very hard," she said.

She didn't say anything for a moment and then she said: "Is this where I'm supposed to betray the people I work for?"

"That's a pretty strong word."

"You want me to tell you things about Darr I wouldn't say in front of him, isn't that right?" It was meant to be a bitter speech: It sounded sour.

"That's right, Doxie," I said, "that's what I want you to do."

Doxie adjusted the machine downward by a fraction.

"Why should I?" she asked.

"You can go down with him or you can watch him go down. Your choice."

148

"Great," she said.

She adjusted the machine so that her strides again became more rapid. She kept her elbows close to her sides and moved her feet with a shallow twittering motion. Her face was flushed.

"I understand a lot of people over at Aztec had a serious habit," I said.

Doxie kept twitching on the Stairmaster; then she adjusted the machine again so that her strides became slower. Her breathing became easier.

She looked down at me with her sour disappointed smile.

"I thought you were classier than that, Mr. Asherfeld."

I looked right back up at her.

"You were wrong," I said.

"Evidently."

"Now that we're in agreement about my character, why don't you tell me who's using over there."

Doxie stared straight ahead.

"Everyone," she said. "They thought it was terrific. Darr and the others."

"Was? They're all pure now? Spent a few weeks at the Betty Ford Center, did they?"

"Darr quit, I know that. I don't know about the others."

"Who did the deliveries, you know?"

"One of Darr's war buddies, this *enormous* person with a bad back."

"How do you know he had a bad back?"

"He was always asking Cindi to help him carry things into Darr. Said his back was just killing him."

Doxie set the Stairmaster up another notch, and raised her elbows to her chest; she was pumping vigorously.

"Was Darr dealing and using," I asked, "or just using?"

The Stairmaster must have come to the end of its cycle. Doxie slowed her steps and then stopped pumping altogether. She stood still on the steps of the machine. She looked like a queer pale-armed bird.

"I don't know," she said. "I think it was more complicated than it seemed. There was someone else involved. I mean outside of Aztec."

"Know his name?"

Doxie shook her head. "He was Asian or something," she said. "Darr called him the Buddhist."

"Go on."

"There isn't any more."

Doxie stood still with her hands at her sides. She was trying to blink back tears.

"I'm sorry," she said. "I guess I don't feel very good about myself."

"No one ever does, Doxie," I said. "Don't tell anyone. It's kind of a secret."

All the Difference
in the World

The hotel lobby was almost empty when I walked in. A bellman in a red-and-gray uniform was endeavoring to push a trolley filled with luggage into the elevator. A miniature poodle sat on top of the luggage, looking down malevolently with beady red eyes. I rode the elevator along with the bellman and the poodle.

"Still a lot of countries civilized enough to eat dogs," I said companionably.

"Don't get me started on dogs," said the bellman.

"Forget I said anything," I said.

"Other day, this lady hands me a leash, this Doberman on the other end, says 'Be nice to Bruno when Mommy is out.'"

"Bruno? Mommy?"

"Yeah, thing is the dog will only, you know, do his business if his mommy is with him, only his mommy don't know this. Couple of hours go by, I figure it's time for Bruno go doo-doo. I take the mutt over the park. Nothing. He just sits there looks at me like he's thinking of taking a huge bite out of my ass, right? I tell him: 'Look Bruno, my shift's coming up, let's get on with it.' Nothing doing. So finally I take him back to the room, lock him up. Two hours later I go back to check on him, what do I find? Bruno's taken a dump one end of the suite to the other, carpets ruined, place smells like a sewer, Bruno's spent the time rolling around in the stuff. Lady comes back, she has a fit, day manager he has another fit, Bruno, he's happier than a clam."

We reached the fourteenth floor. The bellman pushed his trolley out ponderously and wiped his brow.

"Dogs," he said.

The elevator doors closed with a silky woosh. I rode up to the nineteenth floor. The doors opened again—*woosh*—and closed behind me—resub*whoosh*.

The Top of the Mark is still a beautiful room. No loud music, a circular bar on a raised dais, plenty of tables facing the huge plate glass windows.

The hostess was a demure Korean, with lustrous oiled skin and black hair cut in bangs.

I told her I'd be meeting someone and I'd like a table by a window.

She said: "Right this way, sir," getting the English wrong, the way they all do, so that it sounded like *light this way*.

I followed her trim square back around the bar and over to a table facing the bay and the lights of Marin.

I remember evenings when it seemed twilight would last for hours. The sky would fill with pinks, pastels, deep purples. I would take the cable car up from Union Square and have a drink at the Top of the Mark. Everyone was dressed. Beautiful women sat in their evening clothes at the small tables by the window. They were always sipping sweet red drinks and waiting for someone. They had mysterious smiles. Anything could have happened.

It's gone now, that feeling. I never know whether it's because I can't feel it anymore or because it isn't there.

I ordered a Dubonnet on the rocks for myself, and another for Lauren Ellerbee. I ate a handful of peanuts and chewed on a flap of loose skin on the inside of my lip.

Two tables away, a couple of chunky brokers were discussing mutual funds. It's always sad to hear grown men talking about mutual funds.

Lauren Ellerbee came up to the table in a civilized cloud of lilac. She was wearing a pale green suit over a white blouse with a lot of lace bunched up around her throat.

I stood up and told her she looked lovely. She leaned over to allow me to kiss her cheek. It wasn't hard.

She sat down and said: "I'm glad you could come."

I said I was glad she was glad.

"I've heard from Roger again," she said.

"Is he coming in from the cold?"

Lauren Ellerbee smiled at me. "No, he's evidently very happy out there in the cold."

She held her drink up to the light before she sipped at it.

"It's so strange. You live with a person and you think you know them."

"I wouldn't be too hard on Roger," I said.

"Why not? God only knows what he's doing wherever he is. What he's doing and with whom."

Lauren Ellerbee frowned and composed herself and smiled again. "I really didn't want to spend the evening talking about Roger."

"Me either."

"I've always loved twilight," she said.

I looked out the greenish plate glass windows. The city lights were twinkling and so were the lights far away. The bay was a cold and alien presence between two sets of lights.

"What happens at twilight?"

Lauren Ellerbee had been looking at the view; she lowered her eyes to the table.

"It depends," she said. "I don't believe that things have to be horrid and matter of fact all the time."

"You're right," I said. "They don't have to be. It just seems to work out that way."

"Don't," Lauren Ellerbee said sharply. "Don't answer everything I say with some smart arrogant comment. It isn't becoming and it isn't appropriate."

"I'm sorry," I said.

"A little consideration would go a long way," she said, pushing her lips into a pout, "that and a little tenderness."

I didn't say anything. She sipped at her drink and looked out at the view.

"Is that asking so much?"

"It depends," I said.

"On what?"

"On who you're asking it from."

"You're not going to let me approach you, are you?"

"Should I?"

Lauren Ellerbee brushed the air impatiently with her hand.

"I'd be good for you, Aaron," she said. "I could make you happy."

It was getting to be one of those conversations. I didn't want it to go on.

"Doesn't that mean anything?" she asked, her voice soft and bruised.

"I don't know what it means. It's something women say."

I looked at her directly. Her face was luminous, bathed in light.

The cocktail waitress came by and asked if she could freshen up our drinks. I told her nothing needed to be any fresher than it was.

The moment was gone. We talked about other things. We left the hotel a little past eleven. Lauren Ellerbee had the bellman bring up her car, the elegant red Jaguar. She seemed sad, but there was nothing I could do about it.

The bellman swung the car smartly up to the front entrance of the hotel. Lauren Ellerbee sat stiffly in the driver's seat for a moment, one leg extended so that her skirt was stretched over her thighs. She looked up at me with her level cool blue eyes.

"Are you sure you won't change your mind?"

I looked into her eyes and saw the ocean floor again.

"It would have made all the difference in the world," she said.

She closed the door and gunned the engine.

I watched her car make a right turn on California, the red turn signal winking in the evening air.

After that I walked home. The purple had gone from the sky and the foghorns had started up over the bay.

Taps at Reveille

I don't much like being called at two in the morning; someone is either dead or dying or they want to speak to Wanda-Sue and become fretful when you tell them that Wanda-Sue doesn't live here and never did. It was two in the morning that morning. I had just clambered out of one beautiful dream and was about to sink back into another when my bedside telephone rang. I picked up the telephone and said, "Wanda-Sue's gone. Learn to forget her."

Someone said: "Asherfeld, that you?" in a nervous husky voice.

"You were expecting Richard Nixon? He works the day shift."

"Asherfeld, listen, don't hang up, it's me, Kong."

I came completely awake and sat up in bed and squished my pillow up so that it supported the small of my back.

"Hell of a time for a social call," I said, but I tried to say it gently.

"I don't know who else to call. I'm in the Crypt. I got one call."

The Crypt was the holding facility of the state courthouse on Fourth. Suspects were arraigned there until charges were filed or bail posted.

"Where's Angelita?"

"She's working."

"What's the charge?"

"These two cops, see, they stopped me on Geary, did a search, found a rifle in the trunk."

"They have probable cause?"

"They just pulled me over."

"Whose rifle?"

"I don't know," said Kong with an explosive whine. "I never saw it before."

"Listen to me, Kong," I said, "I'm going to get dressed and come out there and see if I can make bail for you. The only thing is when you get my bill I don't want to hear peep from you or from Angelita about how steep it is."

I hung up with Kong and called Angelita. I left a message telling her to meet me at the Crypt.

I dressed slowly in that thick-fingered way you dress at two in the morning, ran a brush through my hair, rinsed the gunk from

155

my mouth with mouthwash, and tried to close the door to my apartment without making any noise.

I drove with the windows open, hoping that the cool foggy air would wake me up; I knew I'd be sleepy later, though. Twenty years before I could miss a night's sleep and never notice; now I notice everything.

The Crypt takes up a whole block on Fourth between Folsom and Mission. It's a massive building, hunched and ugly and alive. In the middle of the night, only whorehouses and jails look alive.

I walked up to the main hall and looked up at the great seal of the State of California; then I walked down the first-floor corridor to the flight of stairs that led to the holding tanks. I hadn't been there for years; I still knew my way around.

The tanks are built from the first floor down so that there is never any daylight anywhere at all. Older policemen swear by them. I was in the company once of a deputy assistant prosecutor named Ampleforth and a police sergeant just a year away from retirement. The sergeant said: "Forty-eight hours inna tank a man'll discuss the assassination of Abraham Lincoln."

"Get him to sign the statement," Ampleforth said, "and I'll run with it. Take it up to the D.A. Be a hell of a case."

I was always glad to get out of there.

The stairway to the tanks empties out into an enormous holding room. A staff sergeant is on duty there behind a big chipped wooden counter. A warren of offices for detectives takes up the space behind the desk. The tanks are off to the left, behind locked, steel doors. You want to see someone, they bring him up from the tanks in chains. You get to talk across a screen. It's very civilized.

The sergeant on duty that night was named Fetzer. I nodded to him. I was beginning to get sleepy again.

"I got a call," I said.

Sergeant Fetzer nodded back to me and said: "Who from? He come in this evening?"

I realized for the first time that I didn't know Kong's name.

"Big, big guy," I said, "calls himself King Kong."

"Goes around with this little blonde in his palm?" said Fetzer. "I know who you mean."

"Must have been booked around midnight," I said, "you'll remember him, he's so big."

"I come on at two," said Fetzer. He pushed a handful of arrest reports at me. "Here," he said, "see if you can spot your boy."

I found Kong right away. His real name was Patrick Minnewasser. He did not look happy in his mug shot.

"Here he is," I said to Fetzer. He nodded and stifled a yawn and took back the arrest reports. He prepared himself to fill out the official visitor's form that they keep at the desk. He needed a lot of elbow space in which to write. He kept moving his hands and elbows in a warm-up.

Finally he said: "You the attorney of record?"

I said Yup hoping he wouldn't check; and he didn't. Fetzer laboriously filled in the rest of the visitor's report, pausing several times to undergo a literary flourish with his elbow.

"Your boy'll be up in three in a couple minutes," he said when he had finished.

There were ten interviewing cubicles cut into the wall that joined the main room with the tanks. I walked over to the third one and sat down heavily on the hard plastic chair. The double thickness glass screen in front of me was cloudy; the wooden ledge had once been a beautiful young slab of oak; now it was pitted and chipped and covered with black initials: GG had been there in '79, and the avenger had thought to write "The Avenger" in '75. Someone in 1959 had written "Help Me" and "1959" with the tip of a ballpoint pen.

The door behind the glass opened and King Kong shuffled in heavily; he had manacles on his wrists. I picked up the black telephone that was mounted on the wall and jerked my head to Kong to pick up his. Getting the receiver to his shoulder with the manacles on wasn't easy for him, but he finally managed, and

157

then he cradled the receiver on his massive shoulder, keeping his hands in his lap.

"Thanks for coming," he said. "Must be a drag."

"It's what I do," I said, "I get up middle of the night, go out and sniff underwear. Now tell me how you didn't do it."

"I didn't do it," Kong whined. "These cops pulled me over, searched the car, I wasn't even speeding."

"Kong," I said, "listen to me carefully. Only person cares if you're innocent is your mother, and she doesn't count. You want me to help you, you stop whining about how you weren't doing anything and start telling me what I can use."

Kong looked sulky and then said: "Whatever."

"First thing, the cops pull you over, did they *ask* to search the car?"

"No, they pulled me over, made me get out."

"They tell you why they're searching the car?"

"No."

"So they search the car, what happened?"

"I'm in the position, one of the cops, little guy, opens the trunk and right away he sings out 'Look at what we got here.' "

"What he have?"

"Hunting rifle some sort, it was in sections."

"Look like they were looking for the rifle?"

"They sure found it in a hurry."

"Not what I asked you, Kong."

"I don't know, it's hard to tell."

"Then what?"

"Other cop, fella with a gut, he reads me my rights, they put me in the squad car, take me down here."

"Your rifle?"

"Never saw it before," said Kong stolidly.

"You know you're booked for suspicion?"

"I didn't do anything."

"It doesn't do any good to tell me."

"I know," he said, "all the same, I didn't do anything."

After a while I told Kong that I would see about bail.

"There's something else," he said. His face was open and stupid and troubled.

"What?"

"Can you do a pick-up and delivery for me? It's gotta be done, I don't know who else do it without cheating."

"Drugs?"

"No, I swear."

I don't know why I bothered asking.

"Where is it?"

"Greyhound locker, it's got to go to The Toilet."

I looked at Kong quizzically.

"It's a club over on Folsom," he said. "You give the package to the guy runs the place, Larry Momo."

I asked Kong for the locker number and combination and he whispered it to me. I said It's gonna cost you. He said I know. I pushed the dirty button on the wooden ledge that called a guard; when he came into the cubicle Kong got up and then shuffled off like some sort of shaggy bear.

At the desk I asked the sergeant who was on duty that night.

"It's Captain Feibish," he said, "Morton Feibish."

"Can I see him?"

"Door's open," said the sergeant, and pointed with his ballpoint pen to the offices behind his desk. "I'll buzz you in."

The buzzer by the little half door gave an energetic cheep, and the door swung open listlessly. "It's in the back," said the sergeant.

I walked back along the corridor. There were cops in all the offices. They were laboriously typing up arrest reports or talking on the telephone in that hushed paranoid way cops have of talking or drinking bitter black coffee or just leaning back in their wooden chairs with their hands behind their heads. The hallway smelled of harness leather and sweat.

The captain's duty office had a metal plaque that said FEIBISH on a removable brass plate. The day captain got to slide his name

159

in the plaque in the morning. Next to the name plaque was a little framed scroll. It said Sensitivity Training and Community Outreach.

The door was open, but I knocked anyway. Feibish looked up. He was eating a sandwich and drinking a glass of milk. He had a smooth untroubled face, soft watery eyes, and a high glistening forehead.

"Can I speak to you, Captain?" I said.

"Don't see why not," he said mildly, after swallowing what was in his mouth, "everybody else does. Come on in. Take a seat."

He got up from his chair in a half-crouch and leaned over his desk, his hand extended: "Morty Feibish," he said, "good to meet you."

We shook hands and I sat down in the cold metal chair that was in front of his desk.

"You mind if I just finish this," Feibish asked, "haven't eaten all night."

"Go ahead," I said.

Feibish finished his sandwich and his glass of milk, and carefully swept the crumbs on his desk into his palm and deposited them in the metal trashcan by his side. Then he folded his hands together in front of himself and looked at me with a frank, open expression.

"How may I serve you?" he asked.

"I got a call at two o'clock in the morning from someone claims two of your boys arrested him on suspicion. He's in the tank now, pretty upset. I'm trying to find out what it's all about."

Captain Feibish nodded agreeably and said: "Why don't I just get the arrest report?" I told him Kong's real name and he nodded mildly and went off to get the report; he came back into the office reading it over, the pages separated by his heavy thumb. He sat back down on his wooden swivel chair, still looking over the report. Finally he finished with the thing, and set it neatly in front of him.

160

"You here as the attorney of record?" he asked with a small smile. His voice had lost just a little of its affability.

"No," I said, "Kong called me because he couldn't think of anyone else to call at two in the morning."

"He's lucky to have a friend like you."

"I hardly know him, Captain."

The captain raised his heavy black eyebrows.

"It's what I do. I get up in the middle of the night when people call."

The captain nodded sagely, making small precise movements with his pleasant round head. He rested his forearms on the arrest report and allowed his fingertips to touch so that they made a pyramid.

"You get a lot of calls late at night from people riding around San Francisco with high-powered rifles in the trunk of their cars?"

"Not too many," I said.

"Didn't think so."

"On the other hand, Captain, carrying around a high-powered rifle isn't a crime in this state."

"No it isn't," said Feibish thoughtfully.

"Then why's he in the tank?"

"We have reason to believe that that particular rifle was involved in the commission of a crime."

"That's very interesting, Captain, and it may even be true, but somehow I have this feeling that when your boys stopped Kong's car, they didn't have probable cause."

The captain nodded.

"You know," he said, "a lot of citizens are under a misapprehension as to what constitutes probable cause."

"I'll bet. They probably read the fourth amendment, got totally confused."

"I'd think you'd be a little more concerned with what we found than how we found it."

161

"That's what the police always think, Captain, and they're always wrong."

The captain flushed and then recovered himself. It was all that sensitivity training.

"I understand that you're upset," he said.

"I'd be upset if I were surprised," I said, "but I'm not surprised."

The captain continued to look at me with a pleasant open expression.

"I can arrange a meeting with Dr. Bleiki," he said. "She's our Conflict Resolution Specialist."

I stood up. "I'm really not much interested in resolving my conflicts, Captain."

The captain nodded affably. "I can relate to that," he said. "I'll be here if you need me."

I nodded and walked out of the room and back down to the sergeant's desk.

Angelita was waiting on the scruffy brown bench. She was sitting next to a pregnant woman trying to fill out a bail form. She looked tired; her makeup was smudged and I could smell the cigarette smoke as I approached her. She looked up at me.

"What happened?" she asked. "Where's Kong?"

"He's in the tank. They found a rifle in the trunk of his car."

Angelita looked at me with an unbroken gaze.

"He's such an idiot," she said.

I said: "No argument there."

"Do you know anyone I could call, Asherfeld?" she asked.

I thought about it for a moment. "Call Seybold Knesterman," I said. I wrote the name down on an old credit card chit. "Tell him I said to call."

The Toilet

The Greyhound station is on Mission by First Street. I walked in and ordered coffee and a frank at a snack stand by the main entrance. The woman behind the counter put the frank inside a microwave. When it emerged, it looked hot and wet and disgusting. I pushed the thing back across the counter and said, "This stuff has sort of died. Why don't you just toss it?"

"Suit yourself," said the woman.

I sipped my coffee and looked over the crowds. No one wants to go anywhere by bus and all bus stations look alike. I sipped some more at the hot bitter coffee and left it on the counter, half full.

I walked over to the lockers with my hands in my pockets and looked thoughtfully for the number Kong had given me. I was just a citizen out for a stroll. I found Kong's locker and opened it up. There was a large paper bag inside, with the top taped down to the sides. I didn't have to ask what was in it.

I got out of the terminal without any trouble and walked over to the lot on Mission where I had parked my car.

The snappy Filipino kid got my ticket and ran to get my car; he brought it up from the lot back of the main lot with a tremendous squeal of brakes. He looked pleased with himself for not having totalled the car.

I tossed the paper sack onto the passenger seat and drove over to Fourth and Folsom and parked on the sidewalk next to a long white stretch limousine. I watched the color seep out of the sky without getting out of my car. Leaving New York or Chicago or Trenton, New Jersey, is easy. Nothing prepares you for the beauty of California, and nothing makes up for it when you are somewhere else.

163

The Toilet was one of those places that was hard to get into because it was hard to get into. Kids from the suburbs came there to dance and snort coke in the bathrooms; and so did motorcycle hoodlums and stockbrokers and strange girls with nose rings who were vague about their personal hygiene.

It was only nine-thirty in the evening, but a line had already formed in front of the open white door with the red rope stretched across it. A bouncer in tight-fitting jacket was looking over things. He had the kind of puffy face that young guys get when they don't get a lot of sleep. He had a pretty simple system for admission: Good-looking girls skipped the line and walked right up to him and said Hi Eddie and got right in. Everybody else got to stand on line and shift from one foot to another. I couldn't see why anyone would do it if they didn't have to.

I walked up to Eddie and said: "Hi Eddie."

"On'a line," he said, "just like everyone else."

"That's not fair," I said, "you let in that girl with the cute ass."

"Yeah," said Eddie, "only thing is you don't have a cute ass."

"I got something much cuter."

"What's that, fellah?"

"This," I said, tapping at the paper sack underneath my arm.

"Got your Teddy in there? That's nice."

"I got about ten thousand dollars in here, something for Mr. Momo. I'll come back another time, seeing how you're so busy and all."

"Hey," he said when I started down the steps. "You trying to dick me around?"

"Dick you around, me? Never. I know when the competition's too tough."

"Hold on a sec, I'll call."

Eddie picked up the white telephone on the wall beside the red rope.

"Yeah," he said, "some guy wants to see you."

I stood patiently on the steps, the sack underneath my arm.

"What you say your name was?"

164

"Asherfeld."

"Asherfeld," said Eddie to the telephone, "that's right." Then he turned to me: "Mr. Momo, he says he never heard of you."

"So many people say that."

Eddie turned his back to me and gabbled into the telephone. When he hung up he turned back to me. "I'll take you in," he said. He dropped the red rope by the door and motioned for me to go on through. A tall, gangly kid at the front of the line shouted: "Hey." Eddie turned to him and said: "Shut your mouth."

It wasn't too loud in the club—no louder, say, than a 747 at takeoff. The place was dark, except for the flashing colored strobe lights. There was a dance floor in the center of the club and two bars on either side. In front, there was a semicircular stage. The rock group was called The Pierced Nipple. A sign said so. The lead singer was a skinny kid who wore fuchsia lipstick and was stripped to the waist. He was pretending the microphone cord was a whip. The dance floor was packed with a lot of hippy young women who wore too much makeup and tended to confuse dancing with undulation. The whole place held a sour smell.

Eddie took me by the elbow and turned me toward the bar. "Mr. Momo, he says to have a drink, be right out."

I said: "Thanks Eddie, you've been a prince." Eddie said: "Sure, don't mention it."

I sat down on a bar stool and leaned an elbow on the bar and watched the dance floor.

A heavy-set young woman came over to me. She had on black combat boots, black socks, white tights, black shorts, a translucent white short skirt over the shorts, and a black velvet jacket. She was carrying a tray with drinks for somebody else. "What'll it be?" she said in a low bored voice. Her hair was greased and spiked. She had an angry boil on her neck. She had two nose rings in her nostril. "Got cheese dips if you want."

"I'll pass," I said.

"Cover's eight bucks."

"What happens if you don't get it?"

Nose Ring said: "Excuse me?" in a fretful voice. I said: "Forget it," and put a ten dollar bill on her tray. "Love your nose ring," I said. Nose Ring said: "Thanks," and lumbered off with her tray and drinks.

I took a toothpicked maraschino cherry from the collection on the bar; it's the kind of thing that you always think is going to taste better than it does. I was going to go for another one when the door at the end of the bar opened. A compact man wearing a dark-blue business suit adjusted his cuffs and walked down the bar toward me. He wore heavy black glasses that hid his eyes but not his bushy eyebrows. He had very thick coarse black hair that he combed straight back from a low forehead. He looked as if he needed to groom himself carefully.

"Asherfeld?" he said politely, extending his hand. "Larry Momo. Thanks for coming."

I shook hands with him. He was wearing an elegant platinum pinky ring. His grip was cool and professional.

He gave the bar and the dance floor a satisfied once-over: "Why don't you come with me?" he said. I slid off my bar stool and followed him back along the bar and into his office. Once he had closed the door behind him, almost all of the noise disappeared.

Someone with enormous shoulders was sitting on the couch with his legs awkwardly crossed at the knee. He had shaggy dyed-blonde hair. The roots were black and starting to come through. He was chewing gum in a way that suggested it was like breathing to him. He looked familiar. I stared at his face for a moment.

The office was empty, except for the couch and a closed rolltop desk against the far wall and a worn easy chair with a pink floral slipcover. Larry Momo walked to the chair and leaned against one of the armrests.

"This here's the Terminator. You seen him on television."

I nodded. "California Wrestling Association," I said, "you were always beating up the kung fu guy, what's his name?"

"Doctor Doom," said the Terminator happily. "You watch a lot?"

"When I was laid up with neuralgia," I said, "every day. How come you're not on anymore?"

The Terminator uncrossed his leg by lifting the thing from his knee with his hand. It evidently didn't move easily by itself. He rolled up his pants. A terrible jagged scar ran from his ankle over his shin and up to his knee. "Messed me up real bad," he said sadly.

"Doctor Doom do that?" I asked politely.

"Hell no," said the Terminator. "Couple of Spades thought they were tough jumped me over in East Oakland one night."

I thought of asking what happened to those tough Spades. I decided I didn't want to know.

Larry Momo nodded at the manifest injustice in the world. "Real shame," he said, "could have been another Hulk Hogan."

"Better," I said. "I hear that Hogan dyes his hair."

The Terminator chortled. "He's a pussy," he said, "always was." For a moment, he lost himself in memory. "Hey, you see me against that kid from the Bronx, what he call himself?"

"The Ripper?" I said.

"That's right," said the Terminator, "the Ripper."

"Guys," said Larry Momo, "we could be here all night talking wrestling."

"Beats listening to them pukes outside," said the Terminator.

Momo held up his hand. "Asherfeld, you said something to Eddie about my favorite subject."

I tapped the paper sack with a finger. "I'm making a delivery for a sick friend."

Momo said: "I see." Then he said: "Who's that, your friend I mean?"

"King Kong. He asked me to make the pick up and do the delivery."

167

An expression of surprise crossed Momo's unmoving face. It must have been the glasses lifting slightly on his nose. "Sorry to hear that the Kong is ill."

That brought a snort from the Terminator. "Probably got heat stroke trying to figure out how to tie his shoes."

"Some people don't have the highest regard for the Kong's brain power," said Momo, chuckling.

"Any regard at all," said the Terminator.

"Or his judgment," added Momo thoughtfully. He had taken off his heavy black spectacles and was rubbing his lips with the frame. "How come the Kong didn't tell me he was sick himself?" He wasn't chuckling anymore.

"He's in jail."

"What for?"

"Police found a high-powered rifle in the trunk of his car." Momo continued to look at me evenly.

"No crime in that," he said.

"That's just what I told them."

"But they don't see things our way?"

"They never do," said the Terminator with a grunt.

I said: "Bummer," and the Terminator looked strenuously at his shoes and Larry Momo continued to stare out at me while rubbing his lips with his glasses.

"Look, Mr. Asherfeld," he said, "it was swell of you to come. Why don't you just take your little package and go. Have a drink at the bar if you like. Listen to the group."

That brought the Terminator up straight, but he didn't say anything.

"I'm not here to put the arm on you, Momo, and I don't want this," I said.

"I know you're not here to put the arm on me, but I guess I'm the kind of guy don't care deep down what you want," he said. "Maybe you're just doing a favor for the Kong. It's real nice your being concerned and all, help a sick friend out. I still can't take anything from you."

"Fussy, fussy," I said, "I didn't know you needed an introduction to launder a little bit of drug money."

No one spoke and no one moved and no one breathed.

"Now you know," said Larry Momo without moving his lips.

I thought it might be a good time to go; I backed toward the door. I had the thing half opened when the Terminator said: "Hey, you can get me in reruns in San Jose. Channel 32 evenings."

"I'll make a point of it."

"You do that," said Larry Momo.

I edged out of the room, closing the door behind me. The music hit like a thunderclap. The Pierced Nipple was still on stage. The lead was singing, "Bend over Little Girl," and everyone on the dance floor was clapping their hands and undulating at the same time. Nose Ring was behind the bar, counting her tips. I walked from the club into the cool evening.

Eddie was still manning the rope and the same crowd of kids was still standing in line. The sun had dipped behind the horizon. The night air was cold.

Kidnapped

I turned on the television and tried to interest myself in the local news. The mayor was explaining how it was that his administration had made the streets cleaner even though they looked dirtier. It was a pretty complicated explanation. He was asking for support from those who believed in his mission. He had the open, honest face of an imbecile. I'd support a mission to launch him into outer space.

But then I'm that sort of guy.

Somebody named LuAnn, who spoke with a lisp, had just finished asking the mayor a complicated ten-part question, when the downstairs door buzzer rang.

I got up and lumbered across the room to the front door. I shouted down. Someone shouted up. It sounded like Candlestick Park. I buzzed them in. It was James Darr. He was with the Terminator. I didn't think they had come to drink tea or ask me questions about my new novel.

They reached the landing. Darr stood still for a moment to catch his breath. "Got to talk," he finally said.

"I'm not stopping you," I said.

I moved away from the door, the Terminator moved forward in that elephantine way big men have, and Darr said: "Come on, Asherfeld, don't make this any harder on yourself than it has to be."

Once we were inside the apartment, the Terminator sat on the couch, and Darr sat at my desk, and I sat on a kitchen chair.

"You know," said Darr, "two kinds of people in this world."

"I know, I know," I said, "you told me."

It didn't make any difference. It never does.

"Those who screw up and those who don't," he said. "Know what kind you are?"

"Aries," I said. "I'm an Aries, ask Cindi, she'll tell you."

"You're the kind of guy that screws things up. First time I set eyes on you in my office I said to myself: This is a guy screws things up."

"Me too," said the Terminator loyally.

"Say," I said, "we'd all be a little more comfortable if you didn't rev the engine too much."

"I'd have no trouble at all twisting you into a pretzel," said the Terminator.

170

"What? You can hardly walk across a room. How you going to twist me into a pretzel?"

"Be easy," said the Terminator, shifting his bulk on the couch and sighing.

"That what they all say."

"Shut up," said Darr. "I'm trying to think."

"We could be here for years, then. Mind if I go get a beer?"

The Terminator glowered at me. "You stay where you are," he said.

"I love it," I said. "I love it when two meatballs march into my apartment and tell me what to do."

"Get a beer if you want," said Darr morosely.

"Now it's no fun," I said.

"You know the SEC is doing a Level One on us," asked Darr, "thanks to you."

"Why thanks to me?"

"You put a bug into Knesterman's head. He put a bug into the SEC. He's very worried about bugs."

"Regular entomologist," I said.

"Guy charges five hundred dollars an hour to sit down and talk with you, when you need him he's out ding-donging with people he shouldn't be ding-donging with. Not only that, that moron Kong gets caught with a hot rifle in his car."

"Next thing you know, police are likely to think he shot someone."

"Now I find out you're out at the Toilet trying to make deliveries."

Darr was trying to make sense of things. It was like watching a monkey examine a stopwatch.

"The Fed would have got to you anyway. You know that. They're already doing a Level One on LRB."

"They did it."

"And?"

"The worst."

"How so?"

171

"Money's gone. Books are a mess. I told you those guys are wusses. If you do business with a wuss you got to figure on wussing yourself up. Something I knew and should have remembered."

"Come on, Darr," I said, "save that for the book."

"What book?"

"The one you're going to write after you're indicted."

Darr stood up. He motioned to the Terminator and then to me. "Get a jacket. We'll talk on the way."

"Me? I'm not going anywhere."

The Terminator said: "Wanna bet?"

"You know that kidnapping's a federal offense, Darr? You're going for a matched set. Racketeering and kidnapping, is that it?"

"I don't know what to do with you, Asherfeld," Darr said, "can't let you just run around putting ideas in people's heads."

I put on my blue windbreaker. Darr stood behind me and the Terminator stood in front of me and we walked downstairs. I thought of making a run for it; it's not something I'm good at.

Darr and the Terminator had arrived in a big blue Oldsmobile; they had parked behind the Chairman's Chrysler.

Darr slid behind the wheel and the Terminator held the seat back for me and sat heavily in the front after I got in the car; Darr snapped the locks shut.

"You know I don't want to be doing this?" I said.

"Me either," said Darr.

"Darr, listen to me," I said, "you turn this car around all you stand to lose is maybe money. Kidnap me and you're facing life in federal prison. You wouldn't like it. Trust me on that. No coke, no French cooking, showers once a week, and guys like Godzilla who're gonna think you're the cutest thing they've ever seen."

Darr said: "You're probably right," and turned over the engine. The Terminator turned on the radio. Linda Ronstadt was singing "You're No Good." The Terminator ran a none-too-clean hand through his blonde hair and said: "Hey, she's singing about me. That right, Darr?"

"If you say so," said Darr morosely.

"She's talking about your wrestling, though" I said. "All those dives in the tank."

The Terminator thought that was pretty funny; he snickered and then he chortled and then he slapped his thigh.

We crossed the Golden Gate Bridge. Darr didn't change lanes much and he didn't speed. The Terminator kept the radio on and had his head back on the head rest; whenever a song with a heavy bass line came on, he would beat time on his thigh with his hand.

The hills of Marin were old and gold. I wasn't frightened yet, but I wasn't too happy to be going wherever we were going.

Darr turned off at the Sausalito exit and followed Alexander Avenue into town.

Generally speaking, Sausalito is a place I avoid. It's supposed to look just like an Italian fishing village. I never thought that was much of a recommendation. Now the place is full of shops selling horrible pictures and furniture made of redwood and sheepskin and upscale ice cream and designer watches and cute little stuffed animals. It's very popular with German tourists who come here and walk along the Bridgeway in short pants.

The Terminator was dozing, his shaggy head lolling over the head rest.

Darr maneuvered the clumsy Oldsmobile carefully through the center of town and then turned right at the road that led to the piers. We stopped in front of a line of houseboats.

Darr cut the motor and opened the door. "Everybody out," he said tonelessly. The Terminator shook himself awake and got out of the car with massive deliberation. He held the seat back for me when I got out.

"No hard feelings," he said.

Darr led the way along the pier, walking slowly because the Terminator needed to drag his leg.

The third houseboat on the pier was called *The Foreskin*. A little wooden plank connected the boat to the pier. Darr hopped up on the plank and jumped onto the deck of the boat and then motioned the Terminator to bring me across. I could feel the gentle ocean swell underneath me as soon as I stepped on board.

Darr fumbled with his keys for a moment before opening the door to the main cabin.

Inside there was a big room with an old-fashioned potbellied stove, a couple of worn easy chairs, and a ratty old couch with a spring poking up through the seat on one side. Up ahead, there was a smaller room; the kitchen must have been in the back.

"This is where you live?" I said. "You make, what? A quarter of a million dollars a year and you live on a garbage scow?"

"You should see his place in Belvedere," said the Terminator. "Could lose an army in that house."

Darr looked at him bleakly. "Did anyone ask you?" he said.

"Sorry," said the Terminator.

Darr was standing by the desk, absently fingering his keys. "In the front," he said.

The little room in the front had a space heater on the floor, and two chairs. The Terminator shuffled heavily into the room and sank gratefully into a chair. Walking was an agony for him. Darr pointed to the other chair. "Sit there," he said. He sank down to his knees and squatted on the floor, with his back against the door.

"She take you to the cleaners?" I asked.

"She got the house, the cars, the boat, the kids and the dog. I get to sleep out here, watch the turds float by my window mornings."

"Sounds rough," I said. "You don't have to live on a boat, though."

"Man I know told me you live on one of these boats you have to beat the pussy off with clubs."

I looked around the bleak little boat. The paint was peeling

174

everywhere and everything looked grey or green. The boat smelled of diesel fuel and sea water.

"Probably the guy selling you the boat," I said.

The Terminator gave a mucoid snort.

"Probably," said Darr. "Probably got tired of all that pussy, figured he'd let me have a shot at some of it."

"You better off," said the Terminator.

"So what do we do now," I asked, "aside from waiting for all that pussy to come barging through the door?"

Darr looked up at me from his crouch. Dark circles had formed underneath his eyes.

"I don't know," he said.

The Terminator made a gun with his fingers and pointed it at me.

"I say we go bang," he said.

"Then what?" said Darr.

"Then we party."

"Darr," I said, "you should be able to spot bad advice when you get it."

"You'd think," said Darr.

There was a scuffling sound from outside the boat. I could hear someone walking across the plank that led from the dock. The boat rocked gently as someone stepped onto the deck. There was a heavy rap on the boat door.

"Go see who it is," said Darr to the Terminator.

The Terminator shrugged his massive frame and hobbled off to the door.

"He's all right," said Darr. "Don't take him too seriously."

"I won't. Three hundred pound gorilla threatens to blow my head off, I figure he just wants attention."

I could hear the Terminator opening the door; there was an exchange of some sort and then someone shouted precisely: "Get out of my way, you crippled lummox."

It was Seybold Knesterman. He walked into the front room with a flourish, the Terminator limping in behind him. He was wearing a lightweight brown suit and a custom-made shirt with a high narrow collar. He looked at Darr and then he looked at me.

"I hope for everyone's sake, Mr. Asherfeld, that you are going to tell me that you are here of your own volition."

"Hell, no," I said, "these guys forced me to come. I told them I had a golf date, too."

Knesterman turned toward Darr, who had lowered his head at the hopelessness of it all.

"Have you utterly taken leave of your senses?"

The Terminator shuffled over to his seat and sank into it with a *woosh* of breath.

"Counselor, no speeches, all right?" Darr said. "How you know we were here?"

"How'd I know?" asked Knesterman, incredulous. "You told Cindi exactly *where* you were going and *who* you were going to see."

"Nice going," said the Terminator.

Darr nodded his head.

Knesterman turned toward me. "Mr. Asherfeld, I can only hope that you will find it in your heart not to press charges against my client."

I got up from my chair. A little wave lifted the houseboat gently; some of the boards creaked and then there was a plashing sound.

"We all came out here to see about the pussy, Knesterman." I looked around the dismal little room. "Darr told me the boat's supposed to be magical. Ten minutes after you get on board, they start pounding on the door." I looked at my watch. "We've been here more than a hour. I guess he was wrong."

Knesterman asked: "Can I offer you a lift back to the city?"

"No," I said. "I'll take a bus in." I walked back toward the front room. When I had reached the door I yelled back: "Thanks anyway."

176

Powwow

I didn't hear anything about anything for a week. That was fine with me. I took care of some things that needed to be taken care of. I got my laundry done; I had a haircut, and I read a book about the Kennedy assassination that explained how someone had secretly removed Kennedy's brains on the flight back from Texas. It sounded like a lot of work to me, but the book was very persuasive. I figured Kennedy's brains were sitting in a jar somewhere, irritated as hell and just dying to get out and tell the world what really happened.

On the Monday of the following week Hubert Dreyfus left a message on my machine. I thought that whatever it was he wanted to tell me, it might as well wait; but that afternoon someone rang my bell three times in a row. I pushed the downstairs buzzer. The guy who came bounding up the stairs was from a messenger service all the attorneys use.

"Like pushing doorbells, do you?" I said.

He was one of these young kids we get in San Francisco who think life as a messenger is wildly romantic. He was unwashed and absurd.

"Why waste time, you know what I mean?" he said. He handed me an envelope and a clipboard with a form to sign.

"Especially if you got so many important things to do, like delivering messages."

"You're right," said the kid. He took his clipboard and clattered down the stairs.

I opened the envelope before going back into the apartment. It was a summons all right: Dreyfus wanted to depose me as a witness.

I called him up right away and he said Hey and I said I got

your summons and he said sorry about that and I said let's get this over right away.

"Not a problem," he said. "Tomorrow at eight be good?"

I said terrific with what I thought was an explosive burst of sourness, but I was there in his office the next morning anyway.

"Hey," said Dreyfus, "you don't look so bushy-tailed this hour. You want some coffee, maybe a Danish?"

I didn't want coffee and I didn't want a Danish and I didn't want to be there.

I don't like depositions. You're always facing an aggressive young woman with bad skin and three names. I had hoped that Dreyfus himself would do the work, but he said: "Look, gotta run, but stick around afterwards and I'll fill you in."

I sat by myself in Dreyfus' office, looking up at the ceiling and out the window, feeling sleepy and irritated.

Someone knocked at the door; I said: "Come on in." I didn't say it with that special sparkle in my voice.

A short woman with broad shoulders and bad skin entered the office. She had the kind of hairdo that made her look as if she were wearing a German military helmet. She was carrying a boxy tape recorder in one hand and an enormous briefcase in the other. She swung the machine on the desk and dropped her briefcase to the floor. She began setting up the tape recorder immediately. She was as brisk and as efficient as a chain saw. "Shulamith Feigen-Bogen Smith," she said, almost as an afterthought. She might have been there to depose the windowsill.

"*Four* names?"

Shulamith Feigen-Bogen Smith stopped what she was doing and stood by the desk.

"You have a problem with that?"

"Me? No problem. Woman can never have too many names."

"I'm glad to hear it," she said. She didn't seem especially glad to hear anything.

"You have a problem working with a woman?"

178

"Hell," I said. "I wouldn't have a problem working with a Saint Bernard. Woman be a piece of cake."

Shulamith Feigen-Bogen Smith continued to look at me as if she were examining a specimen of sputum. She was trying to think of something to say.

"We going to get on with it," I finally said, "or do you want to stand there and accumulate grievances?"

I can be pretty terrific when the odds are a million to one in my favor.

Shulamith Feigen-Bogen Smith gave me a pursed lips look and resumed setting up the tape recorder.

When she had finished she sat down behind the desk and took out a yellow legal pad. She flipped through the first half dozen pages with satisfaction. She had a lot of questions to ask. Women with four names always do. I tried to estimate how long the deposition would take by guessing at the number of questions she had prepared. I thought it might last for a century.

I told her what I knew. There was no one left to protect and no point in protecting them.

I told her that LeRoy had hired me to collect a debt from Roger Ellerbee.

She wanted to know how the debt was incurred.

"No idea," I said.

"You have no idea?" she said suspiciously.

"No idea," I said.

I told her that LeRoy, Darr and Kong had all served together in Vietnam.

"This is something you *know?*" she asked.

I spread my hands apart, the palms upward. "It's what I've been told."

I told her that LeRoy had had a pretty compromising picture of Roger Ellerbee and a young woman.

"Compromising how?"

"Roger Ellerbee had exotic tastes," I said.

179

I told her that someone had sent a copy of that picture to the deputy assistant district attorney.

"Imbiss Deukmajian?"

I said it was.

I told her that LRB had missed filing for a variance.

I told her that Chico-Chico and the Gargoyle had worked me over.

"Worked you over? Did you report that to the police?"

"What for?"

"What for? Because these people assaulted you?"

I spread my hands apart as if to say there would be no point in that.

"Why? I mean why did these people just march into your apartment and beat you up?"

"Probably because Darr thought it might be a good idea to give me a warning."

"This is just conjecture on your part?"

I shrugged. I was under oath but not bound in deposition by the rules of evidence. "Just conjecture," I said.

I told her about Shmul Wasserstrom and I told her that Aztec owned the dummy corporation that owned the Palace.

I told her that I had spoken to Lauren Ellerbee and J. Madford Wunderman and Seybold Knesterman.

I told her about Darr and Doxie and Aztec.

I told her about Angelita and I told her about Kong.

I told her that Kong was delivering drugs to Aztec and I told her that I figured Kong was making drug money deliveries to The Toilet.

"You agreed to make a delivery for this person Kong knowing that it might have been drug money that you were handling?"

"Yes," I said, "yes, I did."

"The thought that you might be committing a crime obviously didn't deter you."

"Money has no memory, counselor."

"What did you do with the money?"

"I put it back where I found it," I said.

It went on like that for almost four hours. When I had finished telling her everything I had to tell, Shulamith Feigen-Bogen Smith rewound the tape spools and packed the tape recorder efficiently. She marched out from behind the desk and shook hands briskly with me.

At the door, she said: "Good-bye," and nodded her head curtly.

I said: "Charmed," as she was exiting, but I didn't say it loudly and I didn't say it quickly.

Hubert Dreyfus had said that he'd fill me in on the big picture; but when he came back he looked frazzled and distracted and said he had a fire somewhere and he'd be in touch.

It was the next morning before he was back in touch.

"Hey, sorry about yesterday," he said, "can you be over here today?"

I said that would be fine and Dreyfus said hey, great.

I got to the Federal Building a little before eleven. Dreyfus wasn't in his office when I called, but someone in shirtsleeves, with a row of red ballpoint pens lined up in his pocket, came downstairs and said: "You Asherfeld?"

"That's me," I said.

"Chief'll be tied up for couple minutes, asked me to take you up."

"Sure," I said, "don't want to be late for the Powwow."

Shirtsleeves looked at me blankly.

"Never mind," I said.

When I got to Dreyfus' office, I lit a cigarette and walked over to the window. Dreyfus came bounding into the room before I had finished; he was with a short, very stocky, baldish man dressed in a white shirt and one of those absurd fat paint-splotched ties that are suddenly coming into fashion, and somewhat soiled slacks that were cut to allow his stomach to swing over his belt. J. Madford Wunderman was with him, too. He was

181

wearing an impeccable double-breasted blue blazer, the kind with two rows of six gleaming gold buttons up the front.

"Asherfeld," said Dreyfus, "this here's Manny Edelweiss, he's head our accounting division."

I shook hands with Manny Edelweiss.

"And Wunderman you know, right?"

I said absolutely. Wunderman said hello in his deep church organ voice.

"So your deposition go all right?" Dreyfus asked. "Pretty swift little number, that Feigen-Bogen Smith. I bring her with me from New York. Manny here, too." Manny flushed with pleasure and nodded. It was tough for him to get the whole nod in because his shirt was too tight for his neck and he didn't have much neck to begin with.

"All the comforts of home," I said.

Dreyfus gave a chuckle. "Thought I'd fill you and Jack in on the Big Picture," he said. "Put you in the ballpark."

I said I loved seeing the Big Picture. I wanted to be in the ballpark.

Manny walked over to Dreyfus' desk and sat in his chair and arranged his papers on the top. He had the accountant's sense of tidiness. Every paper on the desktop had to be just so. Wunderman and I sat in front of the desk and Dreyfus roamed the room, chewing on a matchstick. Finally he came to rest by the window, his back toward us.

"First thing is we're going to RICO Aztec, shut them right down," he said.

"About time," I said.

"For sure," said Dreyfus. He turned from the window to address Wunderman. "You understand what that means?"

Wunderman shook his head slowly and said: "Not entirely, I'm afraid."

"We RICO a company we got reason to believe they're involved in racketeering or corrupt practices. We seize their assets, make it impossible for them to do business. Hell of a tool."

182

"Almost as good as the Star Chamber," I said.

"Come on, Asherfeld. We've got them coming and going," said Dreyfus. "Here, let me ask you, who you think owns The Toilet?"

"This is a toughie," I said. "Aztec?"

"You're on the money. So what they're doing they're using the place to take in drug money in cash. It's a natural. Place does a cash business, you got these dippy teenagers standing on line dying to hand over ten dollars. Who's to know that some of the net is coming from pharmaceuticals and not business."

"Sounds good to me," I said.

"Hear that, Manny, sounds good to him? Do we have a kidder here or what?" Dreyfus had relaxed. He was pretty jovial. J. Madford Wunderman shook his head carefully in a semicircular arc to indicate that he appreciated the remark. Manny gave a kind of choked fat man's chuckle.

"Let me ask you something, Dreyfus," I said. "How do you know The Toilet is taking in drug money?"

Dreyfus looked at me with his head cocked.

"It's coming straight off your deposition, Asherfeld," he said. "It's what you told Feigen-Bogen Smith. You even tried to make the delivery for the Kong. You tell her you're taking money right to The Toilet. Can't do better than that," said Dreyfus. "Now we're really coming to the good part. Manny, show them what's up."

J. Madford Wunderman and I got up and walked around so that we could look over Manny's shoulder.

Manny took one spread sheet from a pile and smoothed it with his hands.

"Here's the month-to-date postings over at Aztec. See where I put the tick." He pointed to a red check beside some of the figures. "That's the posting from The Toilet, regular as clockwork. See the dates. The posting goes to Aztec after the weekend. Anyone asks anything, all Aztec has to say is we had a hell of a show."

"You know what these clubs are like," said Dreyfus from the window. "A lot of dumb kids out there. Couple years my own kid'll be standing on line outside one of these clubs telling me he has to see some guy bite the head off a chicken or take a dump on stage."

Wunderman smiled slightly and said: "Kids." It was the first time his moustache moved. He turned to me. "You have any children, Asherfeld?"

"No."

"You don't know what you're missing," said Dreyfus.

I said: "You're right about that."

"That's half the laundry business," said Dreyfus. "The local talent misses it out here because basically they don't know squat about doing the wash. In Jersey we had three clubs doing no business but racking up big points. Remember, Manny?"

Manny looked up, his fat eyes smiling in recollection.

"What were they?" said Dreyfus. "The Troc over in Fort Lee and what else?"

Manny put the eraser of his accountant's pencil to his thick lips and said: "The DV8 over in Newark and Club Tango, I think it was Hoboken."

"That's right," said Dreyfus.

"What's the other half?"

"Half of what?" asked Dreyfus.

"The laundry business."

"Right," said Dreyfus. He was looking out the window, his back toward us now. "Problem is you got a cash cow like The Toilet you want you should bury the money so you don't get hit by the IRS."

"That's where LRB comes in," said Manny.

"Exactly," said Dreyfus. He turned and pointed dramatically to J. Madford Wunderman. "This you're not gonna like."

"I'm sure I won't," said Wunderman.

"Who does your books for you over there?" asked Manny.

Wunderman said: "We have a service for bookkeeping, but Roger is our financial officer."

Manny gave another of his snorts. "What Roger don't know about finances fill a telephone book." He looked over at J. Madford Wunderman and said: "No offense. I'm just telling it like it is."

Wunderman nodded sadly.

"What I got here," said Manny, smoothing out another photocopied ledger, "is your last three three-month ledgers. You see it goes June September, September December, December now."

J. Madford Wunderman bent over to look at the ledger sheets. "They look all right to me," he said dubiously.

"And what we got here," said Manny, "is the computer tape, records every posting from Aztec over to you."

He smoothed out a photocopy of a tape with a series of numbers.

"In December," said Manny, "your ledger shows a posting of one hundred thousand dollars. Supposed to go for operational expenses, payroll and all."

Wunderman nodded and said: "I still don't see the problem." His voice was so deep he might have been singing Amazing Grace.

Manny Edelweiss took a second ledger from the pile and put it next to the one he had already smoothed on the table. "This here's Aztec's ledger, same period. Let's take December to now. Your books show that Aztec posted one hundred thousand dollars to your account. That figure is high on account of you screwed up the variance and didn't get your ass into production. So basically Aztec is floating you, am I right?"

Wunderman began to say something and then just shook his head glumly.

"But here on the Aztec ledger, what've you got? You've got *two hundred thousand dollars*. See what I mean? It's called overposting. Done all the time back east. Now the reason we know it's

185

overposting and not some screwup is that we also got the computer tapes of the wire transfers."

"I'm not sure I'm following," said Wunderman. It didn't seem all that complicated to me.

"Your cash transfers they go by wire, first of the month, each wire hits, the transfers logged in on a computer tape. See over here, here's your December posting. Only one hundred thousand dollars. Aztec records the transaction as two hundred thousand dollars. The computer tells us that Aztec is overposting on its books."

"What's the point?" asked Wunderman.

"What's the point?" Dreyfus asked from the window, as if he simply couldn't believe such innocence. "Manny, tell him the point."

"Over three months, Aztec puts out three hundred thousand dollars. You think you've got three hundred thousand dollars. But on Aztec's books, three hundred thousand dollars looks like six hundred thousand dollars. Basically Aztec's gone and buried more than a quarter of a million dollars."

"The money comes in from The Toilet and then just disappears," said Dreyfus. "The IRS asks any questions, it's not Aztec's problem, it's *your* problem."

"You see the point now?" asked Dreyfus.

"Isn't that just a foolish risk to run?" asked Wunderman. "It seems like the sort of thing that would be easy to check."

"Only if you know what you're doing," said Dreyfus, "and out here no one knows what in the hell they're doing."

"See," said Manny Edelweiss, "standard audit's always on a company, it's never what do you call it? Comparative. To spot the overposting you need both sets of books and the computer tapes. Lucky for you we got all three."

"Lucky, lucky," I said. "How does hitting the Fatman fit in all this?"

"Not my department," said Dreyfus, "but I'll tell you what I think. First I figured it had to be Roger. He's in over his head on this variance thing, the Fatman is about to blow up his marriage, so he figures he's got nothing to lose, takes a whack and runs. Lot of guys do that. When Roger disappears, I figure the man's scared and he's hiding."

"What changed your mind?"

"Well, seeing how the police found the rifle that did LeRoy in the Kong's car helped a whole lot. But the more I think about it the more it seems to me that Roger is being set up. He's got the motive; in fact, he's got two motives—getting out from under this variance thing and making sure his little picture stays out of circulation. He's just the kind of patsy to walk into a setup."

"Setup by whom?"

"Darr and them sweet guys over there at Aztec. They make a lot of noise about the variance, they make sure that someone over the DA's office sees that nifty picture of Roger with some bimbo."

"How'd they get the picture?" I asked.

"No idea," said Dreyfus, "not my department."

"You know what I don't understand is why they did all this," said Wunderman ponderously.

"Shut down LRB before they go into production."

"For heaven's sake," said Wunderman, "why would they want to stop us from going into production?"

"On account of the fact that you were just a dummy corporation far as Aztec is concerned, a place to launder money. Go into production and Aztec is out big bucks. Fold up and Aztec just writes off the loss. You see it now?"

Dreyfus was amused as he delivered this speech. The innocence of the world afforded him pleasure.

"Now Aztec can't just say sorry and close up shop. They need to have LRB closed. Hitting LeRoy kills two birds with one stone.

"Getting rid of Roger's in their best interest. You got to remember Roger knew something was wrong with the books. He comes to us in December, tells us that he's smelling fish and it ain't Friday. Which we know Aztec knows on account of the fact that we tell Aztec in December that we got a problem with their books. Here's a way to settle the matter. Hit the Fatman, make it seem like Roger's handiwork. That way, when we look at the books over at LRB, we figure naturally that whatever dirt is coming out is coming out from their side."

"So you're saying that these people killed a man just to make Roger look bad," said Wunderman.

"Roger was pretty close to figuring out what was going on," said Dreyfus. "But as I say, we're out of it."

"Pretty clever," I said.

"Real clever," said Dreyfus.

"For a couple of dopes like Darr and Kong," I added.

"We learn one thing over in Jersey it's not to trust the dopiest-looking guys," said Dreyfus. Then he addressed Manny, who was putting away his papers. "Wouldn't you say that's true, Manny?"

"Absolutely. It's definitely true."

Dreyfus looked at his watch conspicuously and said: "Gotta run, guys."

"I know," I said, "there's a fire to put out."

Dreyfus smiled and said: "Manny'll take you downstairs." He shook hands with J. Madford Wunderman and shook hands with me: "Hey," he said, "you did okay on this one, Asherfeld. I knew you were lucky minute I set eyes on you."

I smiled back and said: "Luckier than all get out."

Manny took the two of us downstairs and saw us out of the building.

We walked together in silence toward O'Farrell. From time to time, J. Madford Wunderman shook his large head and allowed his sleekly shaved jowls to wobble and hawked into the open air and looked distressed and saddened and relieved all at once. He was getting ready to say something. He needed a lot of warm-up.

"I can't believe anyone would do a thing like that," he said as we stopped for a red light.

I walked next to him without saying anything.

"Me either," I finally said.

Loose Ends

Imbiss Deukmajian called me a few days later. He needed three secretaries to make the call. Each asked me to hold for the other. After clearing his throat wetly, Imbiss said: "I thought you might like to know that I've been sent a fax of your deposition, Asherfeld."

He meant his call to sound like an outstanding professional courtesy.

"I appreciate that, Imbiss."

Deukmajian gargled again. "I think you should know also that this office is considering criminal charges against James Darr."

"What for? You don't mind my asking, do you, Imbiss?"

"Not at all. This Minnewasser fellow, we've gotten a positive report from ballistics on the rifle he was carrying. It was definitely the weapon used to kill Lawrence Williams."

"So how does Darr figure in this?"

"I think you know very well, Asherfeld," he said, his voice peremptory. "The two of them served together in Vietnam. Minnewasser was a drug courier for Darr. This office thinks Darr arranged to have Williams assassinated. It's a case of contract murder."

"Does this office have any proof?"

"Of course," said Imbiss, a little too smoothly. "Changing the subject, I was very disturbed to learn that you were physically assaulted some weeks ago."

"I didn't think it was anything you'd loose sleep over."

"Regardless of what you *think*, Asherfeld, it's something that this office takes very seriously."

"Sure," I said.

"I'm hoping that you'll allow us to press charges on this matter."

"Why is that? I mean the outrage you're feeling excepted."

"I think that this person, Menendez, could be a very valuable resource."

He was talking about Chico-Chico.

"You mean you want to put pressure on Darr?"

"I can't say that Mr. Minnewasser has been very cooperative, especially since Mr. Knesterman entered the scene."

"Knesterman probably told Kong he had the right to remain silent," I said. "No telling what an unscrupulous attorney will do."

"Yes," said Imbiss Deukmajian gravely, "no telling."

He was pretty silky when he wanted to be.

"Can I count on your support then, Asherfeld?"

"I'll let you know," I said.

"When?"

"Twenty-four hours."

"Very well," said Deukmajian. "Very well."

I didn't much want to visit Chico-Chico in his office, where he might have the opportunity to show me how much he enjoyed a brisk indoor workout; I called the Palace from my apartment at a little past twelve.

I got a recording, of course, but at the end there was a number to call for further information. It must have been the number at the box office itself. I told whoever it was that answered the telephone that I wanted to speak to *Mr.* Menendez. I tried to make my voice sound heavy and tired and blunt.

"Unlisted," said No Name.

"This is the IRS," I said.

"Still unlisted."

"That's IRS as in Internal Revenue Service."

"Could be the President hisself wanting to give Chico the Medal of Honor, still unlisted."

"Do yourself a favor, pal," I said. "Give Mr. Menendez this number. Do it in the next thirty seconds. Tell him to call if he doesn't want to be spending the rest of his worthless Spic low life in tax audits. Tell him we're not big on waiting for return calls over here. You got that?"

I gave Mr. Charm my telephone number. Chico-Chico called within thirty seconds.

"Thees Mr. Menendez," he said politely.

"Chico," I said, "listen up. This isn't the IRS and it isn't your lucky day. I want you should meet me in front of the Palace in ten minutes. Be there. And be alone."

I hung up abruptly. I hadn't given myself much time. I clattered downstairs and got over to Mission via the Embarcadero in eight minutes. I parked in a U-Park lot on fourth, one of those deals where you have to fold a dollar bill five ways into a numbered slot. I walked the block up to the Palace and leaned against a parked car on Market. I was about a minute ahead of Chico-Chico. He came out of the theater with a scowl on his scowl.

"You," he said when he spotted me. "What you wan'?"

He looked surprised but he didn't look angry.

I put my arm around his shoulder and said: "Walk with me, Chico, don't give me any grief."

He must have been baffled by the business with the IRS; he didn't say anything and he allowed me to steer him away from the Palace.

"You like Folsom a lot, Chico?" I asked.

191

"What you wan' from me, greaseball?" he asked, but he asked it softly.

He was the kind of man who knew he was beaten even before he was beaten.

I took out a dollar bill from my pocket. I had taken five out for the parking lot and only slipped four into the slot. I stopped walking; I held the bill up so that Chico could see it. I rubbed the bill between my fingers.

"See how wide this is, Chico?"

"So what? What you getting at?"

"That's how far you have to go to do ten to fifteen years at Folsom for aggravated assault. You come out you're going to be one of those guys shuffling up Market asking for spare change. That's *if* you come out."

Chico-Chico didn't say anything for a moment. His eyes had a look of remote sadness. Nothing had worked out in his life. I could tell.

"I don't think you the kind of man do something like that," he said.

We had reached the corner of Fifth and Market. There was a place on the corner that sold cinnamon rolls and sweet breads; they thought they were very French. There were a few iron tables on the sidewalk underneath the torn awnings. We sat down at one of them.

"I'm not that kind of man, Chico, but what I'm doing I'm not doing because I want to be doing it."

"Why you doing it then, man?"

"Because my ass is more important to me than your ass. Give me some straight answers and I'll try to save both our asses."

"What you wanna know?"

"Did someone named Darr tell you to work me over?" I asked.

"Who that?"

"Darr," I said. "Should I spell it for you?"

"Some Jew? You talking about some Jew, man?" said Chico-

192

Chico irritably. "I don't work for no Jew, man. No one tol' me to work you over. I don' do that kind of work for other people."

"You just decided it was a swell night for a beating, that right? Got the Gargoyle and said: 'Hey, let's work over Asherfeld.' Give me a break, Chico. You're going to spend a long time in a rotten place if you're protecting someone."

"I'm not protecting no one. I got a business to protect," Chico-Chico said sullenly, "that's what I got to protect."

"I'm confused, Chico, how am I threatening your business. I just went over to your place talk to a few of the girls. Next thing I know you and the Gargoyle are doing the rumba on my spine. You've got to fill me in on this. Put me in the picture."

"They tol' me," he said, "them cows tol' me about the pitchers. You were going around flashing my pitchers."

"*Your* pictures?"

"I got a business on the side. I set up girls, do pitchers."

I didn't say anything for a long while. The sky above the tattered awning was gray and low and heavy with fog.

I got up from the table and looked down Market Street. The thing was supposed to look like a Parisian boulevard. It looked like a cesspool.

"It's a tough world," I said to Chico-Chico.

"You right there, man," he said. He was still sitting in his chair.

Talking Pictures

I took the photograph that LeRoy had sent me and put it on my desk and looked at it in the warm midmorning light.

I had gotten up late and I had nothing better to do.

It was not a photograph without evidence of professional skill, as such things go; it was a pretty embarrassing piece of work. It was meant to be.

I thought that LeRoy might have had his photography done in Oakland, but when I looked at the photograph closely, I could see that someone had stamped something in the upper right-hand corner of the photograph back; the top of the stamp was faded, but the bottom said SF.

There were four advertisements listed under the Erotic Photography heading in the 1989 San Francisco telephone directory. I had found the book at the bottom of my closet. Anatol Chumetz had evidently found something better to do than erotic photography. His telephone number was no longer in service and no new number was listed.

The second advertisement was a full-page display for a studio called The Foxy Lady. There was a picture of a plump middle-aged woman posed alluringly on a red couch, a margin of brimming flesh just visible at the top of her gartered black nylons. She was wearing a white corset with pink tassels and looked ready to purr.

The studio was on Chestnut, in the Marina. I called and got the Foxy Lady herself.

"It's something pretty special," I purred into the telephone.

"I specialize in special things." she purred right back.

I said I'd be by in a little bit. She purred: "Anytime, lover."

If we did any more purring, we would have been ready for Kitty Litter.

I drove over to Van Ness and cut across Green to Fillmore and found a parking spot at the corner of Chestnut and Steiner.

The Foxy Lady's studio was on the second floor of a building that had taken a pretty heavy hit in the earthquake; the facade was cracked and hadn't been repaired. I walked up, bypassing a tiny elevator that looked as if it badly needed its rest.

There were two tin doors on the second-floor landing. On one, there was a red sign with a picture of a fox in furry profile.

I knocked and the doorlatch clicked open.

"Come on in, lover," someone said.

I came on in. There was a little waiting room with red paint on the walls and a little red couch and a little red table with a few scattered brochures and a couple of disorganized peanut spotlights by the ceiling that no one had bothered to focus.

The foxy lady herself poked her foxy head through the bead curtains that separated the waiting room from whatever else there was and said: "Hold on a sec," and then rummaged noisily around in the back somewhere, and then pushed operatically through the curtains.

She was a fleshy woman of perhaps forty, dressed in red tights and a long purple sweater that came down considerably below her ample hips. She had frosted red hair and a broad Slavic face. She gave off a wenchy smell, despite her perfume.

She shook my hand and said, "So."

I said So right back.

"You called," she said.

"I called."

"Whose the lucky lady?"

"Actually, I had something else in mind. Something special."

"That's what you said," she remarked, remembering our conversation vaguely. "What's that, lover?"

"The lucky lady is kind of a business associate. I need someone to capture her at dramatic moments."

195

"Dramatic?"

"Dramatic as in with someone else who would die if they knew they were being photographed. Room is all set up. All you have to do is work your magic."

The Foxy Lady shook her hennaed head vigorously from side to side, as if she couldn't believe what she was hearing.

"Just what do you think I am?" she finally asked.

"I don't know," I said. "I was hoping a cheap pornographer."

The Foxy Lady lifted her broad nose into the air; her blue eyes filled with tears and her chin began to tremble.

"I'm sorry," I said, "that was uncalled for."

The Foxy Lady pointed toward the door. "Get out," she said.

"I guess this means we're not a couple anymore," I said.

"Not even close," said the Foxy Lady.

That left two other advertisements. I had ripped the page listing San Francisco's erotic photographers from the telephone book earlier in the morning and folded it into a small square. I walked back downstairs; when I got to the street I fished the square from my pocket and looked at the entries again.

Someone named Mr. Carl had taken out a little advertisement for a place called Black and Blue. I walked over to the pay phone in the middle of the block and called. I'll be back in just a jif, said an answering machine. The studio was in the Castro, by Market and Guerrero. I didn't hold out much hope for Mr. Carl, but I drove over there anyway.

Except for the photographs in the window, Black and Blue looked like any other photographic studio. There were a couple of travel posters on the wall by the right window, and a display of a few old-fashioned cameras with cards underneath them, explaining where they were from and which company had made them. The black-and-white enlargements mounted in the left window showed a variety of meaty young men posing in ripped shorts.

I walked in, sounding an urgent blatting buzzer as I opened

the door. Someone behind the counter was talking on the telephone. A cubby hole behind his head was filled with prints. "I can't be in two places at once," he said, with the air of a man explaining a logical impossibility to an uncaring audience. He had short neatly trimmed hair, and one of those little moustaches that make so many San Francisco gays resemble a cross between Adolph Menjou and Adolph Hitler. I noticed that he was wearing a Patek Philippe watch. He listened intently for a moment and then said: "No, all right, good-bye." He hung up the telephone with a flounce. "Some people," he said.

"Some people," I agreed. "Are you Mr. Carl?"

He looked at me straight in the face. He had suddenly acquired an expression of severe dignity.

"No," he said slowly. "I'm Bruce."

"I'm looking for Mr. Carl," I said.

"It's going to be hard to find him."

"Why's that?"

"Carl died two years ago this April."

"Were you partners?"

"Lovers."

"I'm sorry," I said.

"Me too."

"Do you know how many funerals I've been to this year alone?"

"No," I said, "I don't."

"Thirty. I've been to thirty funerals."

"Terrible," I said.

"You'll never know. This isn't a condolence call, is it?"

"No," I agreed, "it's not. I wanted to ask Mr. Carl a couple of questions."

"What kind of questions?"

"Whether he did any kind of speciality work, that sort of thing?"

Bruce wrinkled his nose and said: "Specialty work?"

"A man I know was in the insurance business, he needed pictures of people in compromising positions."

"Sunshine," Bruce said with a smile, "that was but definitely *not* Carl's line of work."

I arched my eyebrows. "You're sure?"

"Cross my heart and hope to die."

It wasn't exactly what I would have said had I been in his shoes, but it was good enough for me.

It was later than I thought it would be by the time I left Mr. Carl's studio; I bought myself a couple of pretzels at a place calling itself All Twisted. I washed that down afterwards with a can of diet Dr. Pepper.

The last name on my list was Horst Wesselman. He had taken out a one-line advertisement that said simply: Erotic Photographs in the European Style. I called from inside the B of A building on Market and Guerrero and got Horst himself. He told me to *ja ja* come on over he could see me right away. The address was in the sunless Sunset.

Wesselman had a storefront photography studio on Twelfth street, just off Moraga. There were a lot of very glossy black-and-whites in the window of women posed dramatically in chains or sitting tied up in chairs, and a couple of covers from the European edition of *Vogue*. I could see that the photographs and the covers were well done. They reminded me of pictures I had seen before. They were printed on heavy lustrous paper.

The door was closed and locked, but there was a plastic intercom beside the door and when I pushed the soiled concave button the door latch retreated with an obedient click.

I walked in and said "yo."

Someone said, *"ja,"* from the back room and then Wesselman came into the studio like a locomotive and shook hands with me. He had a big square head and wore a grape-black beard; he had a barrel chest and one of those thrusting central European stom-

198

achs that seem too *massive* to be made of fat. He had enormous hands and feet.

I told Wesselman he came highly recommended. He beamed enthusiastically. *"Nah, ja,"* he said. "I try."

I walked over to the window and made a show of looking at the magazine covers, which were set at an angle so I could see them from inside the store.

"Very impressive," I said.

Wesselman nodded. "Those I did with Helmut."

"Helmut?"

"Helmut Newton," he said. "I was in Hamburg his assistant for three years."

Now I knew why I had recognized the style.

"Big change from Hamburg to the Sunset," I said.

"Ja," said Wesselman, "big, big change."

"What happened?"

Wesselman smirked and then chuckled. He had trouble keeping things to himself. "Some people have no sense of humor. *Überhaupt nicht.*"

"Like the police?"

This didn't strike him as quite so amusing.

"Like the police," he said slowly.

I took LeRoy's photograph from its envelope and put it on the glass counter.

"Kind of an odd paper," I said. "Know what it is?"

Wesselman ran an enormous index finger over the surface of the photograph.

"Nah zo," he said sibilantly, "varigram."

I looked at Horst quizzically.

"You develop it with the filter. That way you shoot in the dark light."

I nodded. "Pretty big in Europe?"

Wesselman nodded again. "In fashion," he said. I pushed the photograph across the glass counter and toward Wesselman.

199

"Sort of thing that Helmut might use," I said. "Or his assistant."

"I don't have to talk with you," said Wesselman sulkily.

"It's a free country," I said.

I picked up the picture from the counter and returned it to its envelope. "You just stand there like a dummy. I'll go on home, write a few letters to the authorities about the little business you got going here."

"I have my green card," said Horst. "You don't frighten me."

"Who said anything about the *American* authorities?" I said. "The way I see things, lot of people in Hamburg be interested in knowing where good old Horst wound up. Especially the girl's parents."

That seemed to hit home. I thought it might.

Wesselman leaned back from the counter and took in a sharp breath.

"Are you threatening me?" he asked.

I said: "Yes."

Wesselman thought this over. *"Ja,* just so I know," he said.

"Now you know. Tell me about LeRoy."

"Nah, alzo," he said. *"Der Schvartz?"* Wesselman made a cocking motion with his hand and finger.

I nodded.

"Nothing," said Wesselman, "there's nothing to tell."

"Horst, baby," I said, "anyone ever let you know that covering up the truth is not your strong suit?"

Horst folded his enormous arms across his enormous chest. *"Ja,"* he said sadly, "all the time. I'm too good."

He meant good-natured.

"Tell you what," I said. "I'll tell you the story, you just sort of nod if I'm getting things right."

Wesselman nodded his heavy shaggy head.

"LeRoy would set up the contacts, give you a call. Am I right?"

Wesselman nodded carefully.

"You go out, do the shoot in some motel or apartment, make a print. The negative you keep on file, LeRoy, he gets a copy of the print. I imagine you must be pretty close with copies. Nothing ruins blackmail like overexposure." I looked up at Wesselman, who seemed fascinated by what I was saying, as if it all made sense to him for the first time. "Time to nod, Horst," I said. Wesselman nodded obligingly.

"Now LeRoy had one copy of this photograph and he gave that to me. And you kept the negatives right here. So what I want to know is how another photograph got into circulation?"

Wesselman shrugged his heavy shoulders and pointed to the color Xerox in the corner of the store. "Copies are easy," he said.

"That's true," I said, "but what's going around isn't a copy. It's printed on the same heavy paper as this. The way I see it, Horst, only the man with the negative could have made another varigram copy." I tapped the envelope with the photograph. "So how many copies did you make?"

"One only," said Wesselman. "That was absolute law. Never more than one copy. *Streng verboten.*"

"But there are two going around. That's pretty strange, Horst baby. Don't you think that's pretty strange? I'll bet some of LeRoy's friends'll think that's pretty strange, too. You know the kind of friends I'm talking about? Eleven-foot blacks with razor blades, love nothing more than come over here and carve your heart out."

Wesselman knew the kind of blacks I was talking about; he stood there, sulky and confused.

"Anybody working for you in the studio, Horst?" I said. "Someone might have made a copy without you knowing it?"

"*Ja, aber nein,*" he said decisively, "No one. It was *unmöglich.*"

"You're sure," I said.

Wesselman nodded his big shaggy head vigorously. "*Ja, ja,*" he said. "I'm sure. *Ganz sicher.*"

"Don't you worry about the girl's parents, Horst," I said. "They're probably laughing about the whole thing right now."

The Professor

I walked back to my car from Wesselman's studio and sat behind the wheel for a while. It was already late in the afternoon; the cold heavy fog that almost always covers the Sunset in the late afternoon had already covered the Sunset in the late afternoon. Russian immigrants wind up in this part of the city. There must be an agency somewhere that tells them that the Sunset looks like Odessa. There are Russian bakeries and delicatessen up and down the avenues. Most of the Russians can't wait to get out once they get a taste of the fog, but some people swear by the neighborhood. There are Irish families here who came early and who have never left the place; but then again there are Irish families who have never left Ireland. It's no great recommendation.

I sat for a while longer and then drove slowly down Twelfth Avenue and over to the drive in Golden Gate Park. I didn't know what I didn't know. It felt like the tickle before a sneeze. I wanted to see the ocean before going home. It was there all right, low, flat and oily, with the fog coming off its surface.

I drove up the ragged end of Highway 1, past what used to be Playland and past the Cliff House and past the corny little souvenir stand with its row of green telescopes; I finally took Geary back into the city.

There was a UPS package propped up against the door of my apartment—that and a batch of bills. The Chairman had signed for the package with an elegant Chinese character.

I had asked the Alumni office at Yale to send me back copies of their newsletter. The woman who answered the telephone with an arch New England accent had said: "I presume you are yourself a Yale graduate?"

"Me? No way," I said. "I'm strictly Harvey Mudd Junior College."

There was a pause on the line while the woman with an arch New England accent contemplated her options.

"Of course, I can always talk to the people at Harvard about Asherfeld Hall. They get stuff to me right away."

"Asherfeld Hall?"

"It's this building I want to endow," I said.

I slipped into my apartment without turning on the lights. I needed to feel the soft silky twilight around me. After feeling it for a few minutes, I dumped my jacket on the couch and turned on my desk lamp.

It took me an hour or so to get through the personals and announcements. Two members of the class of 1965 had died in a boating accident. A sophomore had rearranged his girlfriend's face with a brick. The campus chaplain had testified in his behalf. He felt that Yale had let the sophomore down. He was pretty eloquent. There were seven deaths in Vietnam. The usual marriages and divorces and happy announcements. A few odd postings—the campus clown to the Harvard Divinity School, a Rockefeller to the Peace Corps. I seemed to remember that the Rockefeller had been eaten by cannibals in the South Pacific. He had jumped out of his little dinghy on some awful island and bang! The next thing he knew he was being seasoned for kebobs.

No news from Roger Ellerbee.

I turned off the light and put my feet up on the desk. The fog was scudding by my living-room window. I thought of time passing and time past.

I took my dinner later that evening at a place in North Beach serving miniature pizzas. The little jobs were baked while you waited. The owner was a tall mournful Sikh who wore an elegant heavy turban.

I lifted my haunches onto the round backless counter seat.

"Kind of an odd line of work you're in," I said, as I watched him knead and slap the elastic ball of pizza dough.

203

"Oh no, sir," he said. "It is my calling."

"Your calling?"

I had never heard pizza making described as a calling before.

The turbaned Sikh lifted the satiny dough and slapped it on the marble counter for the last time. Then he flattened it with the heel of his hand and fluted the edges.

"It is the path the Goddess has chosen for me."

There was a picture on the wall of an Indian goddess. She had six arms and appeared to be waving them all simultaneously. She would have been a big help in the pizzeria.

The Sikh's pizzas were very transcendental. I could taste the influence of the Goddess. I had two of them, and then I had a cup of vile black coffee. The Goddess was strictly pizza; someone else handled beverages.

I was in the mood for spiritual instruction. The pizzas had set me up. Or maybe the Goddess with six arms was reminding me of my own calling.

In the early eighties, I had defended a drug dealer named Draino on two counts of possession. He was up for big time; I got him five at Lampoc. He was out in a brisk eighteen months. After his release from prison, he became dissatisfied with his way of life. He taught himself to read classical Chinese. He developed an interest in mystical literature. He asked probing personal questions of heroin addicts and drug dealers. One day, a dealer not much interested in the spiritual life beat Draino to a pulp with a heavy metal flashlight. "Teach him to mess with my mind," he said indignantly to the police when questioned. The beating persuaded Draino that he was meant for higher things. He purchased The Metaphysical Light Bookstore on Grant from the one-legged World War Two veteran who had owned the place for years.

I ambled up Broadway and then crossed over to Grant. North Beach gets a lot less fog than the Sunset, but the stuff seemed to be everywhere that night, slithering up the streets and crawling into the alleys.

Draino's store was in the middle of the block. The street used to be full of junky little stores and dark gloomy bars. There had been a place that sold Panama hats and another place that sold military medals. Now it was starting to go upscale. There was already a store selling cookies on the block and a store processing film in an hour. The northwest corner had been taken over by someone selling fancy leather goods for lesbians. It was pretty depressing. It was only a matter of time before the dark gloomy bars would disappear. The man selling military medals had moved on years ago. I had watched him pack up his medals. He was planning on moving to Beaverton, Oregon. He had a married sister there. He held up a large medal, with ruby-colored glass surrounding a cluster of ivory *fleurs des lys*. An inscription on the bottom was in a language I could not read. "It's Hungarian," he said sadly, "from the Great War." I held the beautiful heavy thing in my hand. "I don't suppose there'll be much call for this up in Beaverton," he said.

I didn't suppose there would be.

I walked up the block, past the leather goods store, and the cookie store, and the store processing film in less than an hour.

There was a wooden bookcase in front of Draino's place; it was filled with old magazines and decaying clothbacked books. The store window had a magical symbol inscribed on one of its dirty glass panels. It was supposed to represent the eye of God. I pushed open the door and walked in and smelled the deep, papery, damp cardboard smell of the place.

Draino was sitting in the highback chair he always sat in; it stood on a brick platform in the center of the store, next to an old-fashioned potbellied stove that was never lit and that always stank of cinders. He had a beautifully sculpted oval face, with a large strong nose and very white teeth that looked somewhat too large for his mouth. He wore his thinning steel-gray hair combed straight back over the metal plate that the doctors had put in his skull after his beating; it was fastened in the back into a small pony tail. He dressed always in black boots and pants and a black

205

jacket over a white shirt, which he buttoned all the way up. He was stoop-shouldered and he had spidery white hairless hands.

He looked up from his book.

"Asherfeld," he said, without surprise and without pleasure. "Peace and love."

I said peace and love.

I sat down in the worn leather chair in front of the stove.

"What're you reading?"

Draino held up the book so that I could see the cover. It was called *The Thousand Faces of Krishna*.

"You'd think one would be enough," I said.

Draino looked at me sadly. "It's all the same," he said. "The One is the Many, the Many is the One."

"Sure," I said, "I forgot."

Draino placed his opened book face down on his knees and looked at me with an expression of peacefulness. "It doesn't matter," he said.

"Glad to hear that," I said. "I wouldn't want my Yin to be out of line with my Yang."

Draino allowed a little air to burst explosively from his pursed lips.

"No, really," I said. "I worry a lot about my spiritual quest. Whether I've cleared enough space for my healing."

"Leave yourself a *lot* of room," said Draino.

"You think it's that bad? Probably all that red meat I eat."

I got up and walked over to the wooden bookcases; there wasn't a book on the rack that looked less than fifty years old. Most of the volumes had peeling cloth spines.

"Spiritually speaking," I said, "would it make sense to bury a lot of loose change in the receipts of a rock club?"

"I'm out of it, Asher," Draino said, "honest to God I'm out of it."

I turned and looked at Draino in his chair. "I know you're out of it, Draino," I said. "I want you to think of yourself as an elder

206

statesman. I mean you've got an obligation to drug dealers not yet born, right?"

Draino closed *The Thousand Faces of Krishna* and placed it gently on the little wooden table next to his chair; he drew his arms across his chest.

"Whatever you say, Asherfeld, whatever you say."

He had had a kind of thrilling energy about him in the old days. He offered the illusion of purpose. Now there was no defiance left. He had dried out in ten years. He thought of it as growth.

"I'm guessing that this is money you don't want to declare."

"Good guess."

Draino patted the side of his sleek head and pulled on his nose with the tips of two fingers.

"Club's doing ten thousand a week business, suddenly starts doing fifty thousand? You're asking is that a good idea?"

"I'm asking is it a way of doing business?"

"It's a little like hydroponics," said Draino thoughtfully. "All the heat on growing pot, guy figures he'll grow the stuff indoors. Six months later the DEA is on his doorstep, a copy of his electricity bill in their hands, wanting to know how come his monthly bill is two hundred times higher than it used to be."

I nodded to show my appreciation. "This is wonderful, Draino," I said, "better than KQED."

KQED was San Francisco's educational station. It featured programs in which a Japanese-Canadian scientist would expatiate solemnly on the lives of the grubworm.

Draino gave a kind of cackle and shifted his lean frame in his chair.

"Of course, you still have to lose the money once you launder it."

"That's very metaphysical, Draino. I put my money into this club. Then it disappears. How am I ahead?"

"Asherfeld, if your money disappeared, what be the point of laundering it?"

"That was my question."

"Asherfeld, a question the answer to which you already know it isn't a question."

He had a point.

"What do you think of overposting?"

Draino looked thoughtful and professorial. "You mean double-entry bookkeeping, one set of numbers for me, one set for them?"

"That's what I mean."

"It's a system," said Draino. "Sometimes it works. Thing is, there's one problem with overposting, though."

"What's that?"

"Pretty easy to spot. All you have to do is compare the books."

"There's something else I need to know. Tell me about the Buddhist?"

"I can't discuss personalities with you, Asher, you know that."

"Why not?"

"It's a matter of principle."

I walked over to the highbacked chair and leaned over and grasped the arms so that my face was a few inches from Draino's face.

"Draino, just because you've read more than two books, don't tell me you've suddenly got principles. Tell me anything, but don't tell me that."

Draino slumped into his chair and made a vague motion with his hands. It wasn't hard to intimidate him anymore.

"I don't know much about him. He was after my time. Ran a modest operation from someplace in the country. Mainly very good grass, cocaine."

"Another spiritual type. Tell me anything more about him?"

"Honest to God, Asher, I can't."

I walked over and began looking at the books on the other bookcase, the ones I hadn't inspected.

"You're right there, Draino," I said. "I don't expect you to cut your throat for me." I took a volume from the shelf. It was entitled *The Dark Night of the Soul and Other Mystic Writings.* I said: "What you expect to get from reading all this."

Draino looked down at the book in his lap. "Peace," he said. "Getting it?"

He thought about the answer for a long time.

"No," he finally said.

Phat Farm

The Buddhist? I really had no idea. I checked the Yellow Pages and the only thing I could come up with was the Vedanta Institute, a store specializing in Buddhist literature, and a vegetarian restaurant on Mission called Buddha Works. I called the Vedanta Institute and was told by someone speaking clipped Indian-accented English, that He could only enter into an Exchange with Serious Scholars, which I presume, he added, You are Not. When I asked whether the Buddhist meant anything to her, the woman at Buddha Works wanted to know if this was some kind of a television thing, you know, like Wheel of Fortune, and was there a prize for the right answer? The number for the store specializing in Buddhist literature had been changed. The new number was not available.

I was about to forget about the Buddhist when I remembered Bhat Phat. He had had a strong following in the Bay Area. In the early 80s he had founded The Church of the Inward Eye and opened a kind of retreat in Sonoma County. He preached that happiness is a matter of getting loose and getting laid. He called himself The Dancing Buddhist and gave interviews in which he would giggle insanely. He claimed to be one of a group of select Enlightened; the others included Harry Truman, Albert Einstein, and Marcus Welby. He said he could fly if he wished. He bought a good many expensive cars and drove them whimsically into trees. Many people sold their houses and contributed the proceeds to the Church.

An attorney I knew named Throckmorton called me up and said: "Honest to God, Asher, I think the crazy bitch is up there with these lunatics." I made a trip to the retreat and found his wife living with ten or so other women in a harem. "Go home?" she asked with utter astonishment. "To *him?*"

I set off a little after two; a few wisps of fog were still trailing over the Bay; but Marin was blazing in extravagant sunlight. I had nothing better to do, and nothing better in mind.

I drove for an hour or so with my left elbow resting on the car's window frame, steering with the wrist of my right hand.

A little past Petaluma, I turned off on 91 going west. There's a lot of tack by the freeway: Subaru showrooms with pennants floating in the breeze, and lots displaying great sturdy tractors, and used car lots with corny names, and video outlets, and places promising all you can eat of Mom's cooking; a few miles away you get rural California again, all dwarfed oak trees, and those golden hills, their sides folded up like elephant hides, and that fantastic hard clear light that makes every other kind of light seem pale and washed out.

I followed 91 until I came to a two-lane road that wandered back into the hills; I knew the way. I drove slowly past a couple of ruined apple orchards, and past a herd of dappled cows, solemnly munching their cud and swishing their tails in the sun, and past a small pond with a windmill standing by it, its rotors barely beating.

Further on, the road split again. A white wooden sign pointed left toward Garberville; I went right. Another sign said: NOT A THROUGH ROAD.

I turned off the air-conditioning and rolled down my window.

The smell of summer came into the car—warm earth, cut grass, here and there something sharp and sweet, wild strawberries or sage. Of all the things in my life, only the smell of the earth hasn't changed at all.

After a few miles, the road narrowed and came to an end in a scruffy little clearing just large enough to turn a car around. A footpath wandered off from the clearing, through a meadow, up a little hill and over a rise. I trudged through the meadow in the hot bright sun, walking slowly. Going up the little hill, the path was shaded by trees. I could smell the last of the winter's moisture in the cool earth. There was a wooden railing at the steeper parts. I liked the feeling of the old wood in my hand. The path came out of the woods by an enormous field of California grass. Someone had built a wishing well just where the path emptied onto the meadow. It was made of gray stone and was shaded by the last of the trees. A few pennies and a couple of dimes gleamed in the water. There was a sign mounted on a board beside the well. It said: *Come in Silence: Leave in Peace.* It was written by hand in very black India ink.

I stopped and looked up. A red-tailed hawk was almost directly overhead, circling in the warm air, aloof.

Up ahead was a beautiful old-fashioned California farm house. It was nestled between two oaks, the kind that must have been there for centuries. There were open fields all around and a green-and-gold hill rising up behind the house. I could hear the dry leaves rustle and I could feel the dry heat rise up cleanly from the ground.

I trudged through the grass till it gave way to a little path and walked up the path to the porch of the beautiful old house. A porch swing was swaying slightly in the still, warm air. I could hear bees buzzing far away, a low murmur.

I rapped on the screen door several times. A slight breeze, an undulation in the air, set a delicate pentatonic wind chime to tinkling.

211

I rapped on the screen door again and listened to the rapping disappear in the silence.

After a while, someone said "coming" in a rich somewhat theatrical baritone.

Nothing happened. I rapped again. The voice said "coming" again, without any irritation.

I turned and sat down on the porch steps, my back against a weathered gray wooden post.

I heard someone shuffling toward the door, but I didn't get up.

Someone said: "Such a fire you got going you couldn't wait a minute?"

I got to my feet. "Louie Epstein," said the Someone, holding the screen door open with his shoulder, his hand extended.

"Asherfeld," I said. He took my hand in his and pumped it very solemnly, all the while looking directly into my eyes.

He was a man in late middle age, with a large square head, white hair, combed neatly in a part, alert blue eyes behind octagonal wireless spectacles. He had a wide thin mouth. He was wearing a loose-fitting knit polo shirt and white shorts and sandals. He had a gold chain with an onyx pendant around his neck, the chain wandering in and out of his chest hairs. He carried his head so that it seemed thrust forward.

"I would welcome you to this house," he said, "but we're closed."

"Since when?"

Louie Epstein shrugged his shoulders. "Long time," he said. "Sit, be comfortable. You wouldn't mind a beer?"

I said I wouldn't mind a beer at all.

I sat back down on the wooden porch and Louie Epstein went into the house and then came out with two beer bottles. He handed one to me and sat on the creaking wooden porch swing, hunched forward, an elbow on his knees.

"You're not from the real-estate agency?" he asked.

I took a swallow from the bottle and let the cool beer roll over my throat. I said I wasn't from the agency and I didn't want to buy the land.

Louie Epstein said: "Beautiful. I love you," and sat back comfortably on the porch swing.

"Nice piece of property, though," I said, sweeping the landscape with the beer bottle.

"It goes back almost two hundred acres over the hill," said Epstein. "There's nothing like it left. Sometimes you close your eyes and you can see the land the way it was when it was made."

I closed my eyes and tried to see things the way they were when the land was made. It was hard going.

"This used to be a kind of Buddhist retreat, didn't it?"

"A retreat, a spiritual center, a place of growth and love. The house was full of people. Beautiful young women used to dance in the meadows, their hair drying in the sun. I want to thank you for letting me remember that."

"Do a lot of drugs back then?"

"Of course," said Louie Epstein. "Drugs, food, love, friendship. What more does a man need?"

It even sounded good to me.

"So where's the Buddhist now?" I asked.

"So where's the wind?" Louie Epstein answered.

"What happened?"

Louie Epstein took a swallow from the brown beer bottle and sat up. "What happened? What always happens. Shit happens."

"Just like that?"

"Just like that. I was a young man I used to think shit happens someone makes it happen. Now I know. Shit just happens."

"So that's it, shit happens?" I said. I was getting into it.

Louie Epstein smiled grandly, showing me his gold molars. "What? You want more? You want to know *why* shit happens. When you stop asking why shit happens you'll know why shit happens."

"You learned this from the Buddhist?"

"The Buddhist, the Swami, Werner, The Training. They all taught me the same thing."

"Which is that shit happens?"

"It's a very beautiful experience when finally you get people to see that shit happens."

I took a long swallow and finished up the bottle of beer. It must have been a little past three in the afternoon. I felt warm and drowsy. Louie Epstein sat back in the porch swing and began to rock gently.

After a while, I got up heavily. "I'll be off now," I said.

Louie Epstein looked up at me from the porch swing. "Listen, when was the last time you thanked your wife for allowing you to love her?"

"I can't begin to remember," I said.

"Good," said Louie Epstein. "That was an honest answer. I want to thank you for coming," he added in his rich throaty baritone.

I walked back through the California meadow and over to the wishing well. When I entered the copse of trees I looked back. Louie Epstein had disappeared. He was probably thanking the cows in the field for mooing.

Worm Turns

On Saturday afternoon, Lauren Ellerbee called me; she sounded alert and assured and adult. She addressed me as *Mr.* Asherfeld; she wanted to know if I could come down to Atherton; she said there were a few things that we needed to discuss. Maddy will be here, too, she added. Maddy? She meant J. Madford Wunderman. That was a terrific inducement.

I thought of asking Darr to come with me and then I thought again. He'd probably ask the Olympic wrestling team to come with him.

I called Doxie instead. She answered her telephone right away.

"You busy this afternoon?" I asked. I figured I'd be lucky to hear of a free hour somewhere in the next century.

"No," she said. "I'm not busy at all."

She listened to what I had to say without comment. She didn't seem especially excited by my plans. She wouldn't have been excited by tachycardia.

"Well, I don't know," she said dubiously, after I explained things.

"It'll be terrific," I said, "better than the Stairmaster."

"Well, I don't know," she said again.

I picked Doxie up from the front of her apartment later that afternoon. She lived on Russian Hill in an apartment facing the cable car tracks. I could see from the street that the place had beautiful bay windows; but the noise from the cable cars would have been enough to drive me nuts. The things clatter up and down the hills until two in the morning. Tourists in short pants are always hanging from the damn wooden platforms, looking cold and dumb and miserable.

The late afternoon sky was clear as we drove through the city streets, but the freeway was crowded, even though it was Saturday and the sky over the peninsula was brown and heavy hanging. It was the kind of afternoon in which everyone was travelling to someplace they didn't much want to go in order to be with people they didn't much want to see.

Me too.

Doxie sat with her knees pressed together. She was nervous and sulky and on edge.

We got to Atherton at a little past four; I parked underneath

215

the great elms on Montecito. Bobo's red Trans Am was in the driveway and Lauren Ellerbee's Jaguar was parked on the street behind it.

Someone had left the heavy iron gate slightly ajar; I pushed it open and felt the mass of the gate swivel on its hinge. Iron is an unyielding metal. Doxie followed me into the yard.

Lauren Ellerbee met us at the end of the slate walkway. She was dressed in a creamy flowing skirt and an angora sweater with a scooped neck. The scooped neck was a mistake. The skin on her throat and chest had been roughened by the sun. Her hair was tied back in a chignon. Her lips were pale pink. Her blue eyes were absolutely silent.

"Thank you for coming," she said gravely as she took my hand.

"I brought a friend," I said.

Lauren Ellerbee allowed herself a faint suave serene smile.

Then she turned toward Doxie and said: "It is *so* nice to see you again, Doxie."

Doxie smiled her own ragged smile and said: "I hope you don't mind, Mrs. Ellerbee."

"Not at all, Doxie," said Lauren efficiently. "Maddy's in the back. This won't take long. I promise."

We walked back through the stately cool foyer into Roger's study.

Wunderman was standing by the huge globe, spinning it idly with his fingertips. He turned when we came into the room and said, "Asherfeld," with as much heartiness as was compatible with not disturbing his moustache.

"That's me," I said.

"Jack, you know Doxie," said Lauren Ellerbee. "For some reason, Mr. Asherfeld thought it might be important for her to be here."

"Of course, of course," boomed Wunderman. Then he said: "Sit down, sit down."

I sat at the end of the leather sofa and Doxie sat primly in the middle.

Lauren Ellerbee said: "Can I get you two a drink? Something to eat. Anything at all?"

"I'm fine," I said.

Doxie said, "Maybe a Calistoga?"

Wunderman sat down at Roger's desk and arranged his feet comfortably on the desk top.

Lauren Ellerbee disappeared from the room and reappeared with a Calistoga in a tall glass.

Doxie drank it down gratefully and wiped her lips with the back of her wrist. It was her first charming gesture. It was her only charming gesture. Lauren Ellerbee noticed it and smiled as she sat down on the opposite end of the leather sofa from me, her feet tucked demurely underneath her flowing creamy skirt. I could see the outline of her thigh through the fine wool. Under the cool indoor light, her face had regained its loveliness, that way she had of projecting her beauty into the ambient atmosphere. She liked having Doxie in the room. It made her feel secure. I could tell.

"You've heard from Roger," I said. I leaned forward on the couch to say it so that I could speak around Doxie.

Lauren Ellerbee flushed just slightly and said: "He called me yesterday. He's coming home."

"I thought he might."

"It's all very complicated. Mr. Asherfeld, and some of it is very, very private."

"Sure," I said.

"None of us are very happy with what happened," said Wunderman, his voice deep and husky, "but at least we understand what's been going on."

I said: "That's great."

I could feel Lauren Ellerbee shift uncomfortably on the couch. She said: "Please, no sarcasm, not now."

I leaned back into the couch. Doxie sat with her knees pressed together, her wrists folded over her thighs. She kept the tall glass clutched in her hand.

Wunderman went on: "We've been taken to the cleaners, but it could have been worse."

"Much worse," said Lauren Ellerbee decisively.

"Much, much worse," I said.

Wunderman coughed sententiously. He was coming to the kiss off. "A lot of doors opened up wouldn't have opened up if it hadn't been for you." He meant it as a compliment. He was almost ready to rub his hands together, like an undertaker. "Lauren and I both think you should be compensated for your time and trouble. I know Roger's going to agree."

Wunderman withdrew a check from underneath the blotter on Roger's desk and said: "We'd like you to have this."

I held up my hand. "Wunderman, you don't owe me a thing. I don't work for you. I've never worked for you."

Lauren Ellerbee said sharply: "Don't be a fool, Aaron, don't be a fool all of your life. That's a check for ten thousand dollars. Take it and let's end all of this."

"Ten thousand dollars is a lot of money," I said.

"It certainly is," said Lauren Ellerbee.

"But it's not enough money," I said brightly.

Lauren Ellerbee started to say something and stopped; Wunderman just stared at me.

"Enough money for what?" said Doxie. "Would you mind explaining what you're talking about?"

"Sure, Doxie," I said. "I'll explain what I'm talking about. Wunderman is asking me to tiptoe out of here. The funny thing is that generally I *am* the kind of guy who likes to sneak across lawns in the middle of the night with his shoes in his hands. Not this time, though. Not for ten thousand dollars."

"Are you trying to shake me down?" asked Wunderman. "Is that what this is all about?"

"Jack," said Lauren Ellerbee.

"You know better than that, Wunderman," I said. "I'm not

interested in your money. Now Lawrence William's estate—
that's another matter. I don't suppose you've settled your accounts with his attorney? Probably not, what with the polo
season about to start and your moustache starting to droop."

Wunderman lifted his hand to his face and smoothed down his
moustache with the tips of his fingers. He had no idea he was
doing it.

"Near as I can tell, you still owe the estate a quarter of a
million dollars. My fee'll come out of that. I get ten percent. Now
that's a lot of money."

Wunderman started to wind himself up to say something.
"You're not seriously suggesting that after all this we should pay
off that . . . that person's *estate?*" He was almost sputtering.
Lauren Ellerbee had turned her head, showing me her shapely
ears, and the tensed tendons in her neck.

"Sure, that's just what I'm suggesting."

"But *why*, Aaron," asked Lauren Ellerbee explosively, her
head swivelling. "I mean that man was doing nothing more than
asking for a bribe. It was unconscionable."

I got up from the sofa and walked over to the enormous globe
and spun it with my fingertips; the thing revolved from east to
west. I watched the blue oceans slip past my fingers and then the
multicolored continents. California rose up underneath my right
hand and passed sedately over the hump of the globe, and sank
back out of sight. It was night in San Francisco by the mahogany
panels behind the globe, but the dawn was coming up like
thunder, out of China in the east.

"LeRoy wasn't asking for a bribe. He was a lot of things, but
he wasn't stupid. That's one thing. Here's another thing. You
didn't need LeRoy to fix a variance and if you did it wouldn't
have cost two hundred and fifty thousand dollars. You probably
could have gotten your variance by writing a letter of apology to
the city attorney. The request was in disclosure when Aztec did
site selection."

I looked at Doxie for confirmation. "That right, Doxie?"

Doxie nodded rapidly. She was looking at the floor.

"Attagirl," I said.

I turned from the slowly spinning globe and I put my hands behind my back.

"What are you getting at?" said Doxie. "I think I have a right to know." She looked up from the floor.

"Doxie, please," said Lauren Ellerbee. Her voice held a high bat squeak of uncontrolled emotion.

"No, really, Mrs. Ellerbee," said Doxie. "I did the site selection with Roger. I'm involved."

"I'm with you, Doxie," I said.

Lauren Ellerbee threw her hands up in the air in exasperation. "Oh you'd be with anyone if you thought it would irritate someone."

"What was Mr. Williams supposed to do that was worth all that money?" Doxie asked. She was getting her courage up. My heart went out to her; ugly women have it hard.

"He was supposed to act as if he wanted a bribe."

"This is insane," said Lauren Ellerbee. "Are you saying that we agreed to pay this preposterous person two hundred and fifty thousand dollars to go around like a presumptuous buffoon and *pretend* he was asking us for a bribe?"

"Sure, that's just what I'm saying."

"Are you going to explain yourself?" said Wunderman. He was speaking as much to Doxie as to me.

"LeRoy was kind of a Marxist hoodlum," I said. "Berkeley is full of them. Sixties draft dodgers, rabble-rousers, people who think Nicaragua is a terrific place for a winter vacation, still have pictures of *Ché* on their walls."

"Oh please," said Lauren Ellerbee. "You're not going to give us your philosophy of life, Aaron."

I didn't pay any attention to her.

"LeRoy and Darr served together in Vietnam," I said. "It wasn't the sort of thing LeRoy wanted the world to know. He probably buried his Purple Hearts out in a cabbage field somewhere. But it's the reason he was a silent partner in Aztec. I learned that from LeRoy's attorney. Amazing how many confidences an attorney will violate."

"So?" said Wunderman. "So what?"

"So a connection between LeRoy and Aztec. So a connection between LeRoy and whatever was dirty at Aztec. Nothing obvious so that everyone would know about it and nothing so obscure that I'd never find it."

"I don't understand," said Doxie.

"You're certainly not the only one," snapped Lauren Ellerbee.

"It's kind of a Zen thing, Doxie, you get it all of a sudden."

"It's late and we're all very tired. This hasn't been easy for any of us," said Lauren Ellerbee. "And you're speaking in riddles."

"It's like the sound of one hand clapping," I added.

Wunderman threw his hands up into the air with a mincing ineffective gesture. "I knew this was a mistake, Lauren," he said.

"You haven't even heard the best part," I said.

"I can see there's not going to be any stopping you, Aaron," said Lauren Ellerbee archly. "You might as well get it off your chest."

I turned from the globe and walked over to one of the Peale prints. It depicted an enormous chestnut stallion standing beside a dwarfish groom.

"The official version of events is that Aztec was taking in drug money through The Toilet and laundering it through LRB."

"What do you mean 'official' version. That's exactly what happened, Asherfeld," said Wunderman, banging his heavy fist on the top of Roger's desk.

"No, I don't think so," I said. "It was meant to look that way, but that's not what happened at all."

"What did happen?" said Doxie in a small quiet voice. She had leaned forward on the couch so that her forearms were on her knees.

"Beats me," I said. "Detection's not in my line. But why would someone launder something that they didn't have?"

Wunderman shifted his torso in his seat to look at me.

"Well?" he said, glowering.

"No reason at all," I said. "It *is* like Zen."

"What on earth does *that* have to do with anything," asked Lauren Ellerbee.

"I don't think there was any drug money coming into Aztec. Drug money has to come from somewhere. Aztec's source was someone hasn't been in operation for years. The Buddhist banged up his last Rolls-Royce years ago. He's probably not even in this country anymore."

"Do you know this for a fact?" said Doxie.

I shook my head. "Fact, theory, what difference does it make. A fact is a small theory. A theory is a big fact. It sounds good to me."

Lauren Ellerbee snorted on the sofa.

Wunderman said: "And you went and told this man Dreyfus that one of Aztec's clubs was being used for drug laundering. I heard you."

"You're right. That's what I said on deposition. I *assumed* that Kong was delivering drug money. I *assumed* The Toilet was taking it in. Well, I was wrong."

"Just like that?" said Lauren Ellerbee bitterly. "You say one thing under oath and now you say something else."

"Just like that," I said. "It's the kind of mistake that's pretty easy to make. Darr *did* have an ivory nose. So did everyone else at Aztec. Doxie told me. A couple of years ago, they probably *were* laundering money through The Toilet. A couple of years ago, Ronald Reagan was President of the United States. He's not now. Aztec's not laundering money now. But accuse a drunk of being drunk and everyone will swear they smell whiskey on his breath. It doesn't matter if he hasn't had a drink. You counted on that."

"What else did we count on in this ridiculous theory of

222

yours?" asked Lauren Ellerbee. She had flung up her hands as she asked the question.

"Lots of things. You counted on Dreyfus to be cocky and confident. Roger made a point of setting him up in December. The main thing, you counted on Dreyfus and his people looking at the books and coming to the conclusion that Aztec was over-posting its accounts."

"That you can't pull, Asherfeld," said Wunderman. "I saw the books with my own eyes."

"So did I," I said. "But if Aztec wasn't taking *in* any drug money, they'd have no reason to overpost their accounts. What I saw wasn't overposting by Aztec. It was *underposting* by LRB. I think you had someone doctor the computer tapes. Probably that little twerp of yours, Finklestein. Hell, he'd do it for a subscription to *Penthouse.*"

"To what end, Mr. Asherfeld?" said Doxie.

"To get the SEC to RICO Aztec. Roger and Wunderman figured that funny books and the general smell of drug money would be enough. They were almost right. The story was close enough to the truth to be almost true. That's generally enough for people like Dreyfus."

"That doesn't make any sense," said Lauren Ellerbee, from the end of the couch. "Why should Maddy and Roger go through this elaborate conspiracy in order to destroy their own investment bank?"

She had crossed her arms across her chest and pressed her back into the sofa back. She turned to face Doxie. "It just doesn't make any sense, does it, Doxie? I mean it is utterly preposterous, isn't it?"

Doxie said: "I don't know, Mrs. Ellerbee."

"Sure it does. It makes lots and lots of sense," I said. "All that money coming in every month from Aztec. You've been skim-ming it. You've got a hot little item here, that mouse of yours. Why go into production with it when you can sell it again, this time to the Japanese? Roger wasn't hiding in Los Angeles or doing anything of the sort. He was *negotiating*. It's what he's been doing for weeks. It's a wonderful scheme. Everybody thought he was frightened. Not so. Good old Roger was taking very prominent meetings with Japanese investors. That's because good old Roger knew that LRB is going to be up for grabs. The idea all along was to take the money and run. That's why you let the variance slide. All that you needed to do was eliminate Aztec."

I shrugged my shoulders.

Lauren Ellerbee said: "Like everyone else, you think you're smarter than you are, Aaron."

Wunderman pressed his back against Roger's leather chair and straighted his legs in front of him.

"I see I've got your attention," I said.

"Oh, don't be flippant," said Lauren Ellerbee, lifting her arm and letting it fall heavily on the sofa bolster.

"What are you going to do with this theory?" Wunderman asked.

"Me? Don't be silly. I'm not going to do anything. Besides you're all going to punish yourselves."

"Just how are we going to do this?"

"You'll see, it'll be easy. Pretty soon you'll start accusing one another. I figure the two of you'll be at each other's throats before I'm out the door." I pointed with my finger toward Wunderman and Lauren Ellerbee. Doxie will tell the people at Aztec what happened, someone'll file a civil suit, you'll be spending your time giving depositions and arranging court dates. You'll start to wake up in the middle of the night. You'll hire attorneys who meet you in their offices and tell you that their fees start at eight hundred dollars an hour and *yes* the clock is running *now*. All that money you were going to spend on the Riviera or in Brazil or wherever will be going to people like Seybold Knesterman. There'll be bits about you on the news at eleven. Hey, you'll get to watch your legal talent on the tube saying things like 'We Resent this Outrageous Accusation' or 'My Client has Nothing to Hide' or 'We Welcome the Opportunity to Present our Case in Court.' Afterward, your lawyer will take you aside and say 'Maybe we Should Settle' and you'll do a quick calculation and you'll say 'Not on My Life' and the lawyer will say something like 'I was Hoping You'd Say that, Maddy' and sort of punch you on the shoulder to show you what a tough guy you are and then tell you that he can't even *file* the motion without another fifty thousand. You'll see."

I stopped talking. J. Madford Wunderman's face was mottled and red. Lauren Ellerbee had tears in her eyes. "It's all so hateful," she said.

"You're right about that," I said.

I didn't say anything else. After a while, I got up and walked out of the house. Doxie came out a minute later. "I know," I said, "you don't feel too good about yourself.

Doxie looked me in the eye.

"I feel just fine about myself, Mr. Asherfeld," she said.

A Clean Sweep

I had hoped that Lauren Ellerbee wouldn't call and that she wouldn't come by my apartment; but she called on Sunday morning and she came by my apartment a little after eleven o'clock.

She was dressed in a white pleated skirt and a white turtleneck sweater; she was wearing very fashionable burgundy boots that came up to the middle of her shapely calves; her hair was washed and set and fell around her face in ringlets.

She said, "Hello, Aaron," at the door; her smile was strained.

225

I never knew what she meant by what she did. I didn't think she was glad to see me.

She walked over to the living-room window and looked out at the bay. The morning was absolutely clear.

"It's so beautiful," she said vaguely. She crossed her arms over her chest. I could see her frail shoulder blades rise and fall. She said: "I didn't want you to think it was the money. I don't know why, but I didn't want you to think that."

She turned from the waist and looked at me with her cool, level stare. I crossed the living room and sat at my desk chair facing her.

"I never thought it was *only* the money," I said.

Lauren Ellerbee sniffed softly and turned her torso back to face the bay.

"You probably want to know everything," she said. "You're that sort of person. You have to know what's under the bed and in the closet. You're not even curious. You just want to know things."

I spread my hands apart in the air above my lap. I was the only one in the room who could see the gesture.

"How very different we are," she said to the window. "I know everything I want to know. I just want to forget things."

I didn't say anything.

"I suppose you're all boyish eagerness to tell me how you figured everything out."

"It didn't take much figuring, Lauren," I said. "You set up everything so that sooner or later I'd see what you wanted me to see."

"Did I?" she asked bleakly. "Is that what I did?"

"*You* sent me the picture of Roger and Angelita. Not LeRoy. *He* had no reason to blackmail Roger. He was horrified when he realized I had a copy of the photograph. He wanted to tell me about it that night he was murdered."

"I needed you to get involved."

"Once I figured that out, you knew it would only be a matter of time before I tracked down Wesselman."

"You're very predictable, Aaron. You may not think so, but you are."

"And once I knew where the pictures came from, I'd be bound to figure out who gave them to you. It was Bobo, wasn't it? He was working as Wesselman's assistant."

"It was just an accident. Like everything else in life."

"Bobo told you about Roger and Angelita. You've known all along."

"All along," said Lauren Ellerbee.

"Roger has no idea?"

"He has no idea. He thinks he's very discreet."

"He's your son, not Roger's," I said.

"I didn't think you'd find that out," she said, still watching the water. I could see that the curve above her hips was thickening. She was still lovely, still frail, but time was closing in on her.

"It's hard to keep things secret. Roger wasn't married when Bobo was born. I checked the Yale yearbook."

"So very clever," said Lauren Ellerbee. "You are so very clever."

"Some things are hard to hide."

"He loves me," said Lauren Ellerbee.

"Roger?"

She turned from the window, the pure cold light from the bay framing her lovely face, lighting her blonde hair from the back.

"My son loves me," she said.

"I guess," I said softly. "He was willing to commit murder for you."

Lauren Ellerbee turned to face the window and the water again. She held herself again and shuddered.

"They couldn't even do that right, those two."

"Roger and Wunderman?"

Lauren Ellerbee shook her head; she had the look women get when they are contemplating the boundless stupidity of men.

"They thought that all they'd have to do would be to make a lot of noise about the variance and someone somewhere would come and rescue them."

"You knew they needed a brisk bubbling murder to get people like Dreyfus and Deukmajian involved."

Lauren Ellerbee shrugged her shoulders, hunching them toward her neck and keeping them hunched for a moment.

"A brisk bubbling murder? Is that what you think it was?"

"Nobody cares about things like drugs anymore," I said. "Not really. No one commits a crime because of a variance. Dreyfus and Deukmajian wouldn't have bothered with Aztec just because they were laundering drugs."

"They needed something dramatic," said Lauren Ellerbee. "I gave it to them."

"You put the rifle in Kong's car. You framed Darr and Kong and everyone at Aztec and made it look as if *they* were framing Roger."

"Me. Bobo. It doesn't make any difference. The picture gave Roger an apparent motive. That was the key. It all follows. You just have to take all the steps to the end."

"And they say that women are illogical."

"The they saying that are never women," said Lauren Ellerbee. She turned her face from the window again. She allowed a smile to play across her face and then turned back to face the window and the bay beyond.

"But that's not all, is it?" I said.

"No, of course not, Aaron. That's not all."

I said: "It's Roger's rifle that the police found in Kong's car."

The silence in the room was cold and complete.

Lauren Ellerbee nodded, her back still toward me. "It's his rifle, and it has his fingerprints all over it."

"You got everyone, didn't you?"

"Everyone," she said.

I went over the list. "LeRoy is dead, Angelita gets to spend every penny she ever made rescuing Kong, Darr is ruined,

Wunderman is going to spend his life huddled with attorneys, and Roger is going to be charged with murder."

I leaned very far back in my chair so that the hinges squeaked.

"A clean sweep," I said.

"Almost," said Lauren Ellerbee.

"Except for you and Bobo, of course. No one gets the two of you."

Lauren Ellerbee turned and looked at me with contempt. "You still don't understand, do you?"

"I guess not."

"You're going to tell the police about Bobo."

"Me?" I said. "I'm out of it."

"No you're not," she said. "You're not that kind of man. It's like trying to unsee something you've seen. You won't be able to do it. In the end, you'll tell the police everything. They'll do terrible things to Bobo. I know that. That will be *my* punishment."

She was right. I knew it as soon as she said it. I leaned back in my chair.

"A clean sweep," she said, shaking her head. "You have such a gift for vulgar phrases. They thought it was a wonderful joke, ruining my life. They were all in on it. All those buddies."

Neither of us said anything. Neither of us wanted to.

"I used to believe in such simple things," she said after a while.

"Me too."

"Now we know better," she said.

"I guess we do."

Lauren Ellerbee crossed the living room and opened the apartment door and closed it gently behind herself.

I could hear her footsteps going down the two flights of stairs; I could hear them tripping faintly over the hall toward the front door; I could hear the front door open, and then I couldn't hear anything at all.

* * *

I called Imbiss Deukmajian that afternoon; he must have prepped his secretaries to expect my call: They put me through right away.

I said what I had to say: "I'm not going to press charges against Menendez."

Deukmajian cleared his throat and coughed sententiously.

"Why not, Asherfeld? This is a very serious matter."

"It was all a mistake," I said.

"Good heavens," said Deukmajian, "that is *not* what you said on deposition."

"I changed my mind," I said. "It happens. It's a free country."

"Are you going to explain yourself or should I just assume you've taken leave of your senses?"

"You can assume anything you want," I said.

I hung up and for a long time after that I watched the gray fog move over the cold waters of the bay.